THE GOLDEN DAYS

THE GOLDEN DAYS

Elisabeth McNeill

This first world edition published in Great Britain 2001 by
SEVERN HOUSE PUBLISHERS LTD of
9–15 High Street, Sutton, Surrey SM1 1DF.
This first world edition published in the USA 2001 by
SEVERN HOUSE PUBLISHERS INC of
595 Madison Avenue, New York, NY 10022.

British Library Cataloguing in Publication Data

McNeill, Elisabeth
   The golden days
   1. Woman journalists – I
   2. Journalists – India – B
   3. Bombay (India) – Fict
   I. Title
   823.9′14 [F]

ISBN 0–7278–5719–3

Typeset by Palimpsest Book Production Limited,
Polmont, Stirlingshire, Scotland.
Printed and bound in Great Britain by
MPG Books Ltd, Bodmin, Cornwall.

The Golden Days

*C*aught *in London's Sloane Avenue in nose-to-tail traffic,
Dee Carmichael found herself staring from the driving
seat of her car into the foyer of a characterless block of
flats. A doorman in an ill-fitting uniform and silver-trimmed
peaked cap was standing in the hall staring back at her.
His dejected expression became angrily disconcerted when
he saw her smiling.*

*She wished she could tell him, 'I'm not laughing at you. It's
nothing personal!' The man made her smile only because he
reminded her of Ronnie who, strangely enough, used to boast
that he lived in a service flat in this very avenue.*

*Of course the man in the foyer wasn't him and it was all
so long ago that Ronnie would now be much older than the
scowling doorman.*

*She was still smiling when the traffic unsnarled itself and
the cars in front moved on. Thinking about Ronnie cheered
her up and eased her rush-hour frustration. He'd been a fake
and a liar of monumental proportions, but remembering him
brought a rush of other memories of the golden days.*

One

Bombay, 1965

The magicians made their appearance to the sound of a drum that at first sounded like distant thunder but soon grew to be an insistent thudding in the ears. Two men and the drummer walked out of the jungle and bowed to Ben and Dee Carmichael, who were picnicking on a Sunday morning in October with their two little girls, Annie and Kate, beside Lake Tulsi, fifteen miles from Bombay city.

Ben looked at the men and groaned. 'I might have guessed!' It seemed that wherever he went in India, even to the most remote parts, some mendicant turned up with a hand out asking for baksheesh.

'Just give them some money and they'll go away,' said Dee resignedly. Like her husband she accepted that there was no such thing as solitude in India.

However, the tallest and oldest of the three strangers understood what she said and looked haughtily at her as he replied in English, 'We are not beggars, memsahib. We are magic men and we will give you a show you will never forget.'

When she looked back at him she felt a strange shiver of apprehension. His pale golden eyes were outlined in black like a rapacious hawk and his direct stare, as well as the dignified way he spoke, awed her. He was wearing a white dhoti and shirt topped by a battered brown felt hat like the sort worn by race-goers to National Hunt meetings at home. Behind him stood a younger man with a disfiguring mark of white pigmentation halfway across his face. The third

2

member of the party was the drummer, a lanky youth in a dhoti and overshirt, who rhythmically thudded his knuckles against the taut skin of a gourd tabla drum hanging over his shoulder. His insistent drumming seemed to say, '*Watch* us, *watch* us, *watch* us.'

'We don't want a magic show,' said Ben shortly, but Dee, who was mesmerised by the three men, put a hand on his arm.

'Let them do their tricks,' she said, surprising Ben, for usually she ran away in primitive terror from mendicants and especially from fortune tellers. 'The children might like to see the magic,' she added, as if in explanation.

On her lap she was holding three-year-old Katie, while Annie, aged five, sprawled sleepily on a rug under the shade of trees by the lake where they'd all been swimming.

'It'll only be the usual juggling rubbish,' said Ben, pulling on his shirt to show it was almost time to leave.

'Let's see it anyway,' she insisted and turned to the waiting men to ask half jokingly, 'I don't suppose you can do the Indian rope trick?'

The leader stared back at her. 'We can, but that trick is expensive,' he said.

'How expensive?' she asked.

'Two hundred rupees,' he replied.

Ben exclaimed in warning, 'Get a grip of yourself, Dee!' Two hundred rupees was a month's wages for most Indian office workers.

'I'd pay two hundred rupees to see the Indian rope trick,' she said quietly to him.

He made a scoffing noise. 'There's no such thing. It's just a story. Nobody's ever seen it.'

'We can show you the Indian rope trick,' said the leader of the magic men, 'but not today because the boy who does it is sick.'

'I told you so,' said Ben triumphantly to his wife, who looked crestfallen. In her extensive reading of old books in Bombay's Asiatic Library she had come across two first-hand descriptions of the Indian rope trick that sounded believable and she longed to see it done. However, like Ben, common sense told her that the writers of the accounts she'd read had probably been deluded.

Seeing her about to lose her enthusiasm for their show, the leader of the men raised his voice and said insistently, 'We are real magicians and we *can* do the Indian rope trick. If you come back next week we'll do it, but if you let us perform for you now, I promise you will not be disappointed.' The drumming reverberated in the background as he spoke.

'How much will you charge us?' asked Ben, whose interest was also being engaged.

'We leave that to you. When you have seen our show, pay what you think is a fair price.'

Ben looked at his watch and said good-naturedly, 'All right, but we can only stay here for another half-hour before we start for home. Put on your show!'

They sat in the shade of a banyan tree with the sleepy children sprawling at their feet while the trio of magicians did simple conjuring tricks, taking chickens out of the children's ears and producing long streams of coloured handkerchiefs from thin air. None of these tricks were very spectacular or unusual, and when their audience began to show signs of boredom, the oldest man suddenly pointed at an uneaten mango in the picnic basket and said to Dee, 'Do you want that mango, memsahib?'

She looked at him in surprise, wondering if he were hungry, and said, 'No.'

'Please eat it,' he told her.

'Why?' she asked.

'I want the stone,' he explained. Behind him the drumbeat speeded up as if in anticipation.

Dee lifted the yellow fruit and cut into it with a table knife so that she could strip off the peel. It had a strong paraffin-like smell and the sticky, orange-coloured juice ran down her forearm when she bit into it. The taste was succulent but she was not hungry and strands of flesh still clung to the stone when she handed it over.

The chief magician held it up in front of her eyes and said in theatrical tones, 'Is this is your mango?'

'Yes,' she agreed. Of course it was. He'd seen her eat it. The drum was still being beaten but was hardly audible now, like a muffled heartbeat.

'Now watch,' he said and made a few passes in the air with the dripping stone while the second man produced an earthenware flowerpot out of a canvas bag he'd been carrying and scooped handfuls of sandy soil out of the bank where they were sitting. Through his fingers he sifted the earth into the pot and then showed it to Dee.

'Make sure there's nothing in the pot except earth,' the leader told her, so she stuck a finger in the soil. Apart from a few small bits of gravel there was nothing else there. She handed it back and watched as her mango stone was stuck end-on into the pot and more earth sifted over it till only the pointed end of the stone was showing.

Once again the pot was handed over for inspection. Once again it was passed back with nothing strange found in it.

The leader made a few hand waves over it, muttering as he did so, 'Watch, watch.' Obediently Dee fixed her eyes on the pot. Out of his pocket he brought a white handkerchief which he ceremoniously draped over the top of the pot so that its ends touched the ground all round it.

The shrouded pot was then placed between the Carmichaels and the magic men, who all sat down cross-legged on the ground. None of them could touch it without standing up.

The drum beat quickened again as the second member of the troupe took a bamboo flute out of the fold in his dhoti, closed his eyes and began to play a weird, haunting tune. The notes of the flute and the beat of the drum seemed to rise and fall, over and over again, up and down, swaying and twisting like snakes. Dee turned her head to look at Ben and saw that he was staring fixedly at the shrouded pot.

When he saw her attention wandering the chief magician

hissed again, 'Watch, watch,' and, feeling slightly giddy, she again fixed her eyes on the pot. What seemed like an age passed till suddenly, slowly, very slowly, the handkerchief began rising upwards.

She blinked and looked more intently. It *was* slowly rising, as if something beneath it was prodding it upwards. When the drum and flute music was at its fastest, the rise was most marked. When it died away the rising almost stopped. When it paused, there was no movement from the handkerchief.

She stared in fascination. The music became more frantic and up the handkerchief kept on rising till the centre of it was three inches off the top of the pot. Then with a swift wave of his hands the magician whipped it away.

Ben and Dee leaned forward together and saw that where there had only been the chewed end of a mango seed, a green seedling with a few folded leaves at the top of it was spiking out of the earth. The mango seed had started to grow!

'Touch it,' said the magician to Dee who leaned forward and gently touched the tip of the shoot with her fingertips. The stem felt soft and sappy, undeniably alive and growing.

The flute and drum music stopped and she was jolted into awareness. 'It's real all right. Touch it, Ben,' she whispered in disbelief.

The three Indians were staring at her. Ben looked as astonished as she felt when, like her, he put out a hand to touch the sapling and rubbed its leaves. 'It's real,' he agreed.

'Yes. It is magic,' said the leader of the band with satisfaction in his voice when he saw how confused the two of them looked.

'How did you do it?' Ben asked.

'By magic,' was the reply. There was no way they would ever get another explanation.

Ben looked at his watch and said to Dee, 'It's time to go. How much should I give them?'

She shook her head dreamily and said, 'I don't know.' Her eyes were still fixed on the pot with the healthy-looking green shoot sprouting out of it. *If I'd planted that seed in the garden it would take a year before it grew as much as it has grown in half an hour*, she was thinking.

Normally street jugglers or acrobats were paid a few annas but Ben was so impressed that he handed over two twenty-rupee notes from his back pocket. The chief magician accepted the money calmly as if it was only what he expected.

When the men picked up their trappings to go, their leader said to Dee, 'If you come back here next week, we will do the Indian rope trick for you, memsahib.' Then they all made folded hand gestures of farewell and noiselessly melted away into the thicket of bushes that lined the clearing. Behind them they left only a heap of scattered earth but no mango seed and no sapling.

Ben and Dee swiftly gathered up the remains of their picnic and carried their sleeping children to the car. Neither of them spoke while they were driving away down the track that led to the main road. When they were finally on the tarmac, she turned and asked him, 'Did we really see that?'

'Yes, I think so.'

'What did you see?' she persisted.

'I saw a little mango tree start to grow out of the stone you put in their pot,' he told her.

'But that isn't possible, is it?' she asked.

'It must have been a trick,' said Ben.

'I wonder how they did it,' she said in wonderment. Her head felt woolly, as if she was recovering from the flu or a bad hangover.

'God knows how they did it,' said Ben, 'but I can tell you one thing. I'm not coming back to see their rope trick.'

Many times in the weeks that followed Dee remembered the magic mango tree and tried to work out how the trick had been pulled on them. For it *was* a trick, it had to have been. It was only later that she began to wonder if the magic had been worked on her and Ben and not on the mango stone.

Two

'Psst, psst, memsahib, memsahib!'
Babu was leaning over Dee's side of the bed with a slip of paper in his hand. He was trying to wake her without disturbing Ben who was, of course, the most important member of the household as far as Babu was concerned.

Dee opened her eyes and stared blearily into her bearer's anxious, pock-marked face.

'London telegram, memsahib,' he whispered.

She groaned. When was the *Sun* news desk going to realise that cables fired off after an evening in the pub would be delivered to her at half-past three in the morning? Not that the news desk would have cared. Stringers deserved little consideration, especially a stringer in an un-newsworthy place like Bombay. She should count herself lucky they remembered about her at all.

'Leave it on the bedside table,' she whispered and turned over to go back to sleep. Time and time again she'd tried to reassure Babu that it was not necessary to alert her the moment a message came from London but he always refused to wait till morning. She suspected that he relished the cloak-and-dagger aspect of her work and enjoyed his part in it. *Babu Parwar, Fleet Street runner . . .*

By a stroke of luck, when she had returned to Bombay in 1961, Dee had managed to get herself accredited as Bombay stringer for the *Daily Herald* before it was reborn as the *Sun*. She was only paid for the stories that they used and was far from overworked because not much happened in Bombay that was considered to be sufficiently interesting for *Sun* readers.

8

The only guideline given to her by the Foreign Editor, a bluff fellow with red, mottled cheeks and a snappily cut pin-striped suit, was, 'Just remember, if three million Indians die in a flood, I don't want to hear about it unless there's one Englishman among them.'

This cynical criterion often came back into her mind when she burned to awaken *Sun* readers' consciences to some terrible happening in the Indian sub-continent, but she knew she would be wasting her time.

In spite of the pay being erratic and not over-generous, stringers had definite advantages because they were given an official press card that ensured entry to political meetings – should they want to attend any – and were also able to have a telephone installed in the flat. Telephones were about as rare as dinosaurs in Bombay. To have one made Dee the envy of all her friends and acquaintances who communicated with each other by notes carried round the town by servants. Even some offices conducted their business that way.

When she woke again at seven o'clock after Babu's early morning interruption, she found a butter-coloured cable form tucked under her glass of freshly squeezed orange juice.

INTERVIEW ASAP RONALD C WESTON BRITISH NATIONAL ARRESTED BOMBAY AIRPORT SMUGGL-ING GOLD 6 OCTOBER 1965

Today's the seventh, she thought. *Ronald C. Weston will be in a city jail by now*. She turned to Ben and said, 'This is interesting. An Englishman's just been picked up for gold smuggling.'

Her husband always started his day with black coffee and a cigarette, which he was lighting as she spoke. 'Poor sod,' he said, drawing on his first Lucky Strike of the day. 'I wouldn't fancy doing time out here.'

Neither of them gave a moment's speculation to the possibility that the information in the cable might be a mistake. Gold, which was avidly sought after by Indians, especially during the wedding season when it was given to daughters as dowries, was smuggled into Bombay in huge quantities from the Gulf or from Europe where it could be bought much more cheaply than in India.

'They want me to interview him,' she said.

'Good, that'll be a nice story for you,' said Ben.

She frowned. 'The trouble is I haven't the time to track him down. I'm playing in a bridge tournament today.' She'd only recently taken up the game and was obsessed by it.

Good-natured Ben got the message. 'On my way to the office I'll look in on Tommy and find out where your man is, if you like,' he offered.

Tommy was a friend, an officer in the Bombay Police. Because Ben was captain of the Gymkhana rugby team, he was on cordial terms with the police whose team frequently played – and beat – the Gym's. The benefits of his rugby links included being waved through traffic jams by whistle-blowing points policemen, especially the handsome giant who controlled the city's busiest junction at Flora Fountain and also played prop forward in the police first fifteen. Anglo-Indian Inspector Tommy Morrison, the police team manager, was an invaluable source of information for Dee when she was pursuing her press stories.

Before she left for her bridge competition later in the morning, the telephone rang and an amused-sounding Ben said over a crackling line, 'I saw your smuggler in Byculla jail. Tommy said he won't let any other journalists see him before you get there.'

'What's the smuggler like?' asked Dee. She'd never knowingly met a smuggler before, apart from the bootleggers who sold them bottles of gin or whisky in prohibition-plagued Bombay.

Ben laughed. 'He's a chancer. I pulled his leg a bit and told him I was from the *Daily Express*. He offered to sell me his exclusive story for five hundred pounds!'

'He's got no chance of getting any money out of the *Sun*,' said Dee.

It was fortunate that her bridge game was not good that day. She and her partner were eliminated from the competition very quickly and, running from the Malabar Hill flat where she'd been playing, she jumped into her waiting car and told the driver to take her to Byculla.

Since Ben's elevation to the position of India-based managing director of a London engineering company, which he had joined after their first departure from India in 1960, the Carmichaels' financial and social position had greatly improved compared to their hard-pressed early married days. Nowadays Ben enjoyed a large salary and they had two Ambassador cars and two drivers at their disposal.

Ben's chauffeur was Akbar, a dignified old Mohammedan who proudly boasted that he had once driven Mohammed Ali Jinnah, the founder of Pakistan. He made it very clear that Ben as passenger could never live up to that great man's prestige.

Dee was allocated the second driver, Jadhav, a young, plump, paan-chewing Maharastrian, who was actually a better driver than Akbar but whose liking for chatter and gossip annoyed Ben.

Jadhav and Dee got on very well together most of the time. Having a chauffeur was not entirely a benefit as far as she was concerned, however, because it meant that she could no longer roam Bombay at will as she had done in the old grey Studebaker which had been sold to pay for the delivery of Annie, the Carmichaels' first daughter. Sometimes Dee spotted the old car still trundling around the Bombay streets and was filled with longing for it and her old penurious freedom.

Jadhav not only would never allow her behind the wheel of his precious Ambassador, he also tried to control where she went. He thought she should not frequent low-class areas like her beloved 'Thieves' Bazaar' or Crawford Market, and even had his favourites among her friends, sulking if he was told to take her to some house or flat in an unfashionable district.

As well as enjoying the use of chauffeured cars, it was no longer considered suitable for a director like Ben to live deep in the countryside. He was told to rent a superior flat in the city, which would not only be his family's home but could be used to accommodate – and impress – company visitors.

By a stroke of luck the Carmichaels managed to find a house that in terms of desirability competed well with their beloved Gulmohurs, the rural bungalow where they had spent the first years of their marriage, and which they thought could never be matched by any other house.

Their new home was tucked away off busy Walkeshwar Road, which linked Chowpatti beach with Malabar Hill. Their flat was part of a Corbusier-style building which had just been built by a rich Indian industrialist who occupied the top floors and wanted tenants for the bottom two floors which he found himself owning almost by mistake. His architect had hit problems while building the house, which was originally intended to perch alone on the top of an outcrop of land overlooking the sea. When work began, it was discovered that the site was part of an old Portuguese fort and the rocky headland contained an extra two layers of deep dungeons that nobody had known were there. Cleverly, the architect turned the dungeons into another flat with the Indian client's home perching on top of it.

The owner of the building was understandably very particular about who would live beside him in this showpiece house but fortunately he and his sweet-faced wife took to Ben, whose fluency in Hindi impressed them. The delighted Carmichaels became the first tenants of one of the most original and beautiful homes in the city.

It was entered by a flight of stairs leading down from a narrow little lane that twisted round the visible walls of the old fort. The front door opened into a long drawing room with two windows overlooking the sea. Behind it were the kitchens and servants' quarters. On the floor below that were three bedrooms with three bathrooms and an enormous store room that must once have been a Portuguese dungeon and which the servants said was haunted.

Outside the bedroom windows, at sea level, was a long narrow garden sheltering behind a sea wall. Anyone sitting in the garden could see right across the stretch of Back Bay to Colaba Point and its lighthouse, beyond which rose the blue misty outline of mainland India. During the monsoon, wind and sea spray battered with magnificent ferocity against the bedroom windows and made the banana trees and coconut palms that Dee planted in the garden bend and sway like dancers.

The floors and stairs of their flat were made of mottled grey marble and every room was air-conditioned, so the Carmichael family were living in unparalleled luxury. Not only was their accommodation ideal, but they had also been able to gather together a houseful of loyal servants.

Their bearer, Babu, a snub-nosed, pock-marked elf of a fellow, was the son of one of the Gymkhana club waiters. At the time he presented himself at Walkeshwar Road in search of work, another bearer hired by Dee had left after only two days because he said the house was haunted. He claimed to have seen headless men wandering the corridor late at night.

Asked if he was worried about ghosts, Babu only gave his gap-toothed grin and said he didn't mind them, in fact they interested him and he'd met one already in the lift of the Victoria Hospital where he had been working as a porter. His most endearing quality was his sense of humour and constant cheerfulness – nothing ever depressed him – and he would stay with the Carmichaels till they left India for good.

The second boy, Prakash, was also to be with them till their departure. A poor Brahmin boy from Kerala, he was extremely intelligent and artistic. The sand sculptures he made for the children on trips to Marvi and Mud Island showed that he had inherited the artistry of the sculptors who'd adorned South India's temples. Dee was particularly fond of Prakash, who also had a gift for arranging flowers and was skilled at completing her jigsaw puzzles – especially the difficult ones, on which he worked when she was out.

He shared her love of gardening too and could always tell if a sickly plant was going to survive, no matter how dead it looked, by stroking its stem and lowering his head so he could listen to it. He showed her how to encourage reluctant growers by gently stroking the stems or leaves. It never failed and she used his methods in her various gardens for the rest of her life.

The other two servants in the Walkeshwar Road house were Christians – old Alex, the Goan cook, and Mary, a Mangalorean ayah, whose tendency for petty peculation was kept within manageable limits by Babu. These people made up a very happy menage.

In their house by the sea, the Carmichaels were enjoying their golden days.

Three

It was with a certain amount of deliberate provocation that Dee told her driver, 'Take me to Byculla, Jadhav,' as she jumped into the back seat after leaving the bridge game.

He stopped chewing and eyed her disapprovingly in the rear-view mirror. Though he was not impolite or rude he never called her 'memsahib' in the unctuous way of some servants and she admired him for his independence.

'Byculla?' he asked and she could see him wondering what she wanted there, for it was a very insalubrious district.

'Yes, Byculla Police Station,' she said firmly and sat back.

Jadhav shrugged as he switched on the ignition. The police station was not too bad. At least she wasn't going to visit someone in a broken-down block of flats.

The police station and its adjoining courthouse had been built by the British about the time of the Mutiny as a District Officer's house, from where he would dispense justice. The lime-washed stone walls were thick, and facing the street was a wooden verandah with fraying coconut chicks hanging down outside to keep the interior cool. The house was surrounded by a square of hard-baked earth that had once been a garden.

Tommy Morrison, grey-faced, grey-haired and tired-looking, came out of his office when Dee walked in and greeted her in a friendly way.

'Have you still got the gold smuggler here?' she asked as they shook hands.

Tommy nodded and said, 'Yes. Ben said you'd be in to speak to him. No one else has been yet.'

'What'll happen to him?' she said.

Tommy shrugged. 'He'll be up before the magistrate on Monday morning and the case'll be deferred for a while, I expect. If he's any sense he'll plead guilty. There were twenty gold bars in the pockets of the waistcoat under his jacket when they pulled him in.'

'Twenty!' exclaimed Dee. It was October and the post-monsoon heat was still oppressive, for the cold weather had not yet started. A waistcoat loaded down with all that gold would have been smotheringly hot to wear.

Tommy laughed. 'The men who brought him in said he could hardly walk. He looked like a tortoise waddling off the plane. God knows how he thought he'd ever get past Customs.'

'He sounds like an amateur,' Dee said and Tommy shot her a shrewd look.

'Or a fall guy,' he agreed.

The cells were at the back of the station where the smell of DDT and Jeyes Fluid was throat-catching. Dee followed a blue-clad constable along a narrow passage to the last cell where a European man in a baggy brown suit sat on a wooden bench with his head in his hands. Around him, in the same cell, sprawled a collection of local malefactors – illicit street traders and pickpockets, a shifty Goan with a pencil-thin moustache, a couple of young boys, a muttering madman with bloodshot eyes, and a fat Gujerati in a white dhoti who jumped up and started shouting the moment he spotted a visitor.

'Wisitor for Weston!' shouted the constable and the European raised his head in eager anticipation. When he saw Dee his face visibly fell.

'A woman!' he groaned. 'What do you want?'

'I'm Dee Carmichael, of the *Sun* in London. I've come in to see if there's anything I can do for you,' she said, brandishing her press accreditation pass as she spoke.

The pass cut no ice with Weston, a seedy-looking, skinny character of indeterminate age, which could have been anything between thirty-five and fifty. His crumpled suit was flashily cut but made of cheap material and his nylon shirt was so soaked with sweat that it was clinging to his chest. He wore no tie – presumably it had been taken away from him in case he tried to hang himself – and his shirt collar was unbuttoned.

He glared at her through crafty little eyes like a ferret and the look in them reminded her of the seedy men she'd seen hanging around racing stables trying to pick up information.

She could read his mind. *He's desperate for a smoke*, she thought.

Though she did not smoke herself, she always carried a packet of Camels or Lucky Strikes in her handbag because they were often useful in breaking the ice. When she offered Weston the open packet, instead of picking out only one, he took the full pack and stuck it in his pocket.

'Thanks, love,' he said in a patronising way. His accent was South London and his attitude aggressive, but his hand shook when he held a burning match to his cigarette.

'You've had a bit of bad luck, haven't you?' she said. That approach usually worked.

He drew on the cigarette and agreed. 'You can say that again! But you're a bit late, darling. The *Express* man was here this morning and I've promised him an exclusive.'

So Ben had played his part well. Dee hid her amusement. She opened her blue eyes widely as she gave a naïve-sounding gasp and said, 'Gosh! That's a pity. But I didn't know the *Express* has anyone out here.'

'Oh yes,' said Weston, 'a real Fleet Street type, a tough guy.' The inference was that she was only an amateur playing at being a reporter.

'He probably wouldn't mind you telling me the details. A bit more publicity at home won't do your case any harm, and there must be people wondering what's happened to you,' she said.

This suggestion obviously took root because he considered it for a moment before saying, 'I've promised him an exclusive. He's going to pay for it.'

'Really? How much?'

'Six hundred quid,' he said. *You liar*, she thought.

'That's a lot of money,' she said innocently. Her secret weapon as a reporter had always been acting the dumb female and she loved the game of deception. The first editor she'd worked for used to send her on difficult stories because she could persuade witnesses and policemen into talking to her when they wouldn't talk to male reporters.

The trick worked with Weston too. He grinned. 'Yeah, six hundred. But the *Express* is a big-time paper, isn't it? Your rag wouldn't be able to match that.'

She shook her head. 'I'm afraid not. I was thinking more in the way of a packet of cigarettes than money. But is your story worth so much?'

The cigarette had calmed him down and he said cockily, 'You can bet your life it is. I've got the lowdown on the gold-smuggling racket.' He was obviously relishing his five minutes of fame.

'Six hundred pounds' worth?' she asked.

'Yeah, but it won't come to that. When my people at home hear about me being in here, they'll get me out,' he said confidently.

'In that case I hope they read the *Express*. You wouldn't want them to miss it,' said Dee. The irony went over his head.

Before she left she wrote her phone number on a torn-out page of her spiral notebook, and handed it to him. 'If the *Express* man lets you down, give me a ring,' she said. She was sure she'd hear from him after he'd had time to cool his heels with his unsavoury cell companions.

In the main police office, Tommy showed her Weston's charge sheet and she noted down his address in Sloane Avenue, London, as well as his profession, which was stated as 'company director'. She put her finger on the words and looked at Tommy, who only raised his eyebrows and grinned.

Weston had given his age as twenty-nine, which sounded

equally unlikely. His full name, she was amused to see, was Ronald Colman Weston. 'His mother must have been a film fan,' she said.

She left the police station with enough information for her first dispatch and feeling cheerful. One man's bad luck was another woman's lucky break. *This gold-smuggling story has great potential*, she thought. *It could run and run, especially if he talks.*

From Byculla, Jadhav drove her to the Central Post Office where Sami, the cable clerk, presided in solitude over a long room full of battered desks and broken-down typewriters. The only decoration was a large, luridly coloured picture of the monkey god Hanuman that hung precariously from high up on the end wall. The frame was festooned with bits of tarnished tinsel and withering marigold flowers and there was a strong smell of joss sticks.

Sami was a great stickler for rules and one of them was that all stories to be sent by cable had to be typed on official paper under his eye. He acted as censor as well as cable clerk.

Dee would have preferred to write out her bulletins at home on her own portable machine because not one of the Post Office typewriters was in serviceable condition. Some couldn't make margins; others didn't type particular letters or the letter cap-tops were missing, so they punctured her fingertips when she typed. Some shredded the copy paper, while others had ribbons so tattered they looked as if they'd been chewed through by worms.

It was useless to argue with Sami though. Either she used the office typewriters or her cables were not sent. It was so difficult to produce a readable script on those awful machines that she never bothered to translate her stories into cable-ese and cost her newspaper hundreds of pounds in extra charges, which had probably contributed to the *Herald*'s collapse not long after she joined it.

Rushing into the cable office with the gold-smuggling story already forming in her head, she headed for the only typewriter that was almost workable – it could produce every letter except 'e' – and settled down to hammer out her first bulletin about Ronald C. Weston using the information given to her by Tommy.

As she typed, Sami leaned over the back of her chair and breathed garlic down her neck. Not much happened in his office and he was always eager for diversion.

'Arrey!' he exclaimed, reading the words that appeared on the paper. 'An Englishman smuggling gold. How much?'

'Tw-nty slabs the siz- of bars of Cadbury's milk chocolat-,' she typed without replying.

'What is that worth?' asked Sami.

'Mark-t valu- in Bombay about 135,000 rup--s, approximat-ly t-n thousand pounds,' she typed.

'Arrey!' said Sami again, very impressed.

Dee pulled the paper from the carriage, inked in all the missing 'e's, and handed it to him for transmission. Quite how he did that she never knew, especially since telephone links with the rest of the world were notoriously unreliable, but all her dispatches from Sami's ramshackle office reached their destination in astonishingly quick time. He probably used Morse code and, like Babu, revelled in his association with distant Fleet Street.

When she left the office she waved to him and said, 'I'll be back soon. This is going to be a big story, I hope.'

The trouble was, she didn't realise how big.

Four

It was half-past eleven and the chatter of female voices in the main office of the Bombay *Tatler* had been gaining in volume for the last hour.

They sound like a cageful of parrots, thought Lorna Wesley as she sat with one long brown leg slung idly over the arm of her revolving chair and slowly filed her nails.

Twitter, twitter, chirp, chirp, rasp, rasp. On the other side of her office door the voices rose in volume and she frowned as she wondered what they were talking about. Whatever it was, she knew it wouldn't be work.

Work was the last thing these girls came here to do. They used the office as a place to gossip, to arrange assignations with each other's brothers or cousins, to backbite or slander their friends and relations. Lorna's chattering female workforce did not need money, which was just as well because her father only paid them a meagre pittance, but they clamoured for the jobs he had on offer because they enjoyed the prestige of going around Bombay describing themselves as journalists with the *Tatler*.

The Shirins and Sorayas, the Miriams and Mayas who Jack Wesley employed flitted from party to party in beautiful silk saris with golden bracelets jangling on their arms, ostentatiously carrying reporters' notebooks in which they chronicled the doings of Bombay's high society. They loved saying, 'I'm with the *Tatler*!' because that gave them power. In their high-class circles it was social death not to be mentioned in the *Tatler*'s columns as being among the guests at the biggest parties and weddings of the year. If your name was not there, it would be assumed that you were dropped, and once dropped from one social list, there was a danger of being dropped from them all. That would be as bad a fate as being turned out naked into the jungle.

Lorna put down her nail file and yawned. On the desk in front of her sat an old Remington typewriter with a sheet of foolscap on its roller. The edge of the paper was gently wafting up and down under the draught caused by an overhead fan. She leaned forward and read the words she'd typed.

There was tremendous excitement at the Willingdon last week when Mr and Mrs Ramesh Officer held a reception for over 1,000 people to celebrate the wedding of their daughter Anita to Homi, only son of import/export millionaire Adi Walabhai and his beautiful wife Myra.

Pulling the paper out of the machine, she marked it up for the printer so that it could be printed in bold type to head up six pages of black and white photographs of the most important people among Bombay's Parsee community. Thank God for the Officer-Walabhai wedding! It would take up most of the editorial pages and ensure good sales. Everybody who attended the event would be avid to find out if their picture was shown, and people who hadn't been invited would buy the *Tatler* to criticise those who had.

'Oh God, what am I doing?' Lorna suddenly groaned aloud and put her hands into her blonde hair, ruffling it up till she looked like an unruly child. 'What am I doing writing a lot of rubbish about society weddings?' she said to an oil painting of a stern-looking old man in a high, stiff collar that hung on the wall facing her.

He stared glassily back with no sympathy in his eyes. 'Don't talk nonsense, girl,' he seemed to be saying. 'Get on with your work and think yourself lucky that I had enough sense to start a magazine that would keep you and your father and his father before him in comfort.'

The old man in the strangling collar was Lorna's great-grandfather Edmund Wilberforce Wesley, founder of the Bombay *Tatler* and patriarch of the Wesley family, feared and hated by both her father and grandfather but dead long before she herself was born. She had never known him and did not regret this. His portrait was bad enough.

Beneath the picture stood another of old Edmund's legacies: three large, glass-topped cabinets in which was displayed his collection of butterflies. They glistened like jewels, pathetically lovely, still glowing in myriad colours, some of them more than ninety years old, pinned heartlessly down with their Latin names and the date of their capture written in fading ink beside them. Some of them were as big as soup plates but others were tiny, like scraps of coloured cloth that must have looked magical flitting through the air before they were netted.

Edmund and his son Edward, Lorna's grandfather, had been ferocious butterfly collectors, travelling all over India and Burma in pursuit of their quarry. Neither Lorna nor her father had any interest in lepidoptera, however. In fact the pathetic state of the specimens in the glass cases repelled her in spite of the beauty of their wings. Sometimes she felt that both her father and herself were old Edmund's victims too, pinned down like the butterflies in the *Tatler* office and unable to get away.

When Lorna had come back to India from England to take over the family magazine she had suggested to her father that the butterfly collection be thrown out or given away because they depressed her, but Jack was horrified at the idea. 'Oh no, my dear. It's the most comprehensive collection of Indian butterflies in existence. It was my father's and grandfather's life's work and it's very valuable,' he protested. She could not explain to him that they made her feel like a prisoner, held by the responsibility of her inheritance.

When Jack and Ella Wesley had reconciled themselves to having only one child, it was taken for granted that she would follow the path destined for a son. In her turn she would take over the Bombay *Tatler*, the family's only asset and the source of their wealth.

After eight years at boarding school in England and then going to Switzerland for a year to be 'finished', Lorna was sent to spend two years in London learning the journalism business. She was clever at school with a strong bent towards the sciences and maths, so strong that she would have liked to study medicine, but that had never been considered by her parents. The editor's chair was waiting for her because her father, who in his turn had been hustled into it, was itching to vacate it.

Through a business contact, he fixed his daughter up with a job in *Woman's Own* where she learned how to set out pages and correct other people's copy. Living alone in a tiny service flat in Dolphin Square delighted the girl who had never known freedom before, so, when the summons came to return home, she went reluctantly. If Jack, who she loved, had not written that his health was bad and his heart was giving him trouble, she might have refused to go back but she had a strong sense of filial duty and knew there was no one else to share the burden with her.

Back in Bombay she discovered that Jack's heart trouble was largely imaginary, but she could not get away again because, almost immediately, her father stopped going to work every day and retired to a life of inactivity. His only effort after that was directed towards finding someone to buy his magazine because he was not insensitive and knew what a burden he had placed on his daughter.

'If you keep it running for a while, I'll sell up as soon as I can and split the money with you,' he promised.

He'd watched the rapid increase in Indianisation of Bombay businesses and put the word around that his property was up for sale. For a long time the *Tatler* had been solidly profitable, so one or two prospective buyers had nibbled at the bait but so far their offers had not been of sufficient magnitude to tempt him. Anyway, they usually backed out when they found out that the property was no longer as valuable an asset as it once had been. The *Tatler* was a relic of the Raj and the new India had a different set of values. Time was not on Wesley's side. If he did not find a buyer soon, he would have nothing much to sell.

He knew how much money he wanted for his magazine and put up a front of rich insouciance as if he was prepared to sit tight till someone met his price. In the meantime his daughter kept the *Tatler* running.

'Once it's sold,' her father told her, 'you can go anywhere you want.'

He and his wife Ella, Lorna's mother, planned to go to Portugal, but Lorna had no idea where she would go if and when the magazine was sold. She spent her days debating the question. Should she go to America? London? Switzerland? One thing was certain, she was not going to live with her parents. She loved her father with a sort of exasperated affection but there was little understanding between her and her mother.

In her youth Ella had been a great beauty, a Danish girl with long legs and brilliant yellow hair. She had met Jack when he was on holiday in Paris but her looks quickly faded under the glaring Indian sun and as she grew brown and wrinkled her daughter began to flourish, becoming taller, fairer and even more lovely than her mother had been. This was a bitter pill for Ella to swallow and it seemed to Lorna that her mother was only really happy when there were at least six thousand miles between them. Having the lovely girl in Bombay was a constant reminder of what Ella had lost and exchanges between them were conducted with strained politeness.

Lorna's dissatisfaction with life in India would not have been so bad if her work was more demanding, but there was no intellectual stimulus in it. Every issue of the *Tatler* was much the same as the one before it. The magazine only came out once a month, and covered the same round of social events each time. It also carried ineptly written criticisms of American films showing in Bombay, and a few book reviews, but never of anything stimulating or highbrow. There was also a crossword, a horoscope page, a bridge column and a cookery article, which was a farce really for the women who read the magazine rarely set foot in a kitchen, and when they did it was only to give orders. These last four regular articles were bought from an agency and all Lorna had to do was paste them up and stick them on the page. Once she ran the same crossword for two consecutive months but there had not been one complaint from any reader, and that deeply depressed her.

On the day she sat in the office filing her nails her life was to change, though there was no clue that something tremendous was about to happen.

She'd been back in India for two years and was desperately bored. 'What am I doing here?' she asked her great grandfather's portrait again in an agony of frustration. When there was no reply, she stood up and put both hands palm down on top of a butterfly cabinet. 'I hate you,' she was saying to Edmund Wilberforce Wesley when she heard a change in the sounds coming from the outside office. A note of almost hysterical excitement could be detected in the female voices.

Suddenly the glass door into her office opened and Bubbles Bulabhai, a lanky girl with a stiffly lacquered beehive hairdo like a black helmet, peeped round it to say, 'There's a man outside to see you, Lorna!'

'Who is it?' Lorna asked.

'I don't know, but he's English . . . and gorgeous,' said Bubbles breathlessly as she stepped aside to give Lorna a view into the front office.

And there he stood – a handsome, dashing man, just what she needed to brighten her life. Surprisingly she recognised him though she did not know his name. She'd seen him four days ago, walking along the sand at Juhu beach where she had been exercising her mother's two boxer dogs. The man had been behind her and one of the dogs, Barney, a stupid but good-natured animal who'd been swimming, had plunged out of the sea and rushed

26

up to him, put two paws on his shoulders and licked his face.

The stranger didn't shout out or flinch as some people would have done for he seemed to know that Barney was without aggression and only meant well. Lorna had run up and hauled the dog away, apologising as she did so, and the man had laughed. 'I'm used to dogs,' he said. There were two dirty wet paw marks on the shoulders of his white shirt and she apologised about that too.

She'd been struck by him then but had no idea who he was and there had been no expectation of ever seeing him again. Yet here he was, in her office!

Apparently unconscious of the curious eyes of the staff, who all stopped work to stare, he walked towards Lorna and said, 'Hi, I'm glad I've found you at last. I was wondering if you'd like to come out for lunch with me.'

She was completely cool, and gave no sign that she was in any way surprised by this unexpected invitation. 'What a good idea,' she said and walked back into her sanctum to fetch her handbag. In a funny way it was as if she'd known this was going to happen and was playing a pre-ordained part.

After running a comb through her tousled hair, she coolly went back to join him and they walked without speaking into the street.

It felt so familiar and so easy, she was sure that they'd met like this before in some previous life because she believed in things like that.

He was as cool as she was, putting a hand gently on her elbow to usher her across the crowded street and saying, 'My name is Rawley Fitzgerald. Where would you like to go? The Taj?'

She shook her head emphatically. 'I don't think so. I don't like those Europeanised places. Do you eat Chinese food?'

'Yes, I do,' he said. She noticed his hazel-coloured eyes had flecks of gold dotted around the iris, and there were deep laughter wrinkles at the corners.

'Then I know a place down by the docks. It serves real Chinese food. Let's go there,' she told him.

'Should we take a taxi?' he asked, still keeping a hand on her arm.

She was surprised by the way her skin tingled beneath his touch, but her voice was cool as she said, 'It's too far to walk in this heat. But I don't take taxis, I prefer to use gharries. There's one that waits for me on the corner over there. I always use him.'

She gestured to where an old, black hansom cab was drawn up with its hood down, in a patch of shade. When he saw her, Hussein, the driver, sat up straight on the box and flicked his reins so that the somnolent horse could be alerted to the fact that there was work to be done. It was a tall, ebony-coloured animal, over seventeen hands high, showing signs both of age and distinguished breeding. Shaking its head like a palsied old man it turned slowly in the shafts before nosing out into the honking traffic.

The man with Lorna laughed. 'I've never ridden in one of those,' he said.

She was already climbing up into the wide, leather-covered seat that had a half-eaten bale of hay tucked away under it, and turned to tell him, 'I never ride in anything else if I can help it. My mother says you get fleas off the seats but they don't bite me. I must be immune.'

Hussein, the cab driver, turned in his seat and asked her, 'Where to, Missy Lorna?' She gave him instructions and then sat back as they set off at a fast trot in the direction of the sea.

'So you're Lorna? I only knew your surname – Miss Wesley. Does it matter that we've never been introduced?' he asked.

'Well, it is a bit unusual, I expect,' she said. In fact it seemed perfectly normal to be going out to lunch with this man whose name she'd only just been told and whom she did not know. 'How do you spell your first name?' she asked.

28

'R-A-W-L-E-Y,' he said, then stuck out a hand to shake hers and laughed as he added, 'Hello, L-O-R-N-A.'

She laughed back and asked, 'How did you find me?'

He answered gravely, 'When your dog jumped on me I was bowled over – and not by the dog. I asked the old woman at the hotel that owns that bit of beach who you were and she said your name was Miss Wesley. Then another friend of mine said that a man called Wesley owned a magazine in Bombay and I went from clue to clue till I found a Burmese journalist who knows you. He told me where you could be found so, because it was lunchtime, I thought I'd invite you out.'

She frowned. 'The Burmese journalist must be a fellow called Ernest who works for a news agency across the street. He sometimes comes into my office for a chat.'

'Yes, his name was Ernest,' he said. 'He's a great source of information.'

She laughed again. 'It's nice to be going out for lunch, but shouldn't it be me taking you since my dog ruined your shirt?'

'It doesn't matter. I've plenty of shirts and I like dogs,' he said, looking forward at the pricked ears of the trotting horse. He nodded towards it and added, 'That's a nice animal too. Entire and with a touch of class about it.'

'It probably used to be a racehorse,' she told him. 'Most of the gharry horses are retired racehorses and a lot of them are stallions. They're shipped in from Europe and Australia. Poor things, some of them don't last long because the drivers work them to death and they're usually old and broken down when they get here. Hussein looks after his well, though. That's why I always use him.'

Her companion frowned. 'Like all Irishmen I love horses and hate to see them being ill treated. I wonder if I've backed this poor old thing on some racecourse or other. I used to go racing a lot.'

She leaned forward and spoke in Hindi to the driver who answered her over his shoulder with a torrent of words. After listening for a bit she told the man by her side, 'He's had this horse for three years. It raced in Ireland and won some races before it came here but he doesn't know what it was called then. His name for it is Jehangir. It behaves well if it's well treated but can be a devil if not. He bought it from another gharry driver who was afraid of it because it bit him and drew blood from his shoulder.'

Rawley Fitzgerald seemed pleased by this story. 'I'm glad it's got the guts to stand up for itself. That's because it's Irish. We don't like being pushed around.'

'You're very proud of being Irish, aren't you?' she said, though he had no detectable accent that she could hear.

'From deepest Cork,' he told her and this time he did have an Irish accent.

'I've never been to Ireland. Do you go back often?' she asked.

'Not a lot, not for years. We still have a family house there but it's falling down and needs a lot of money spent on it. My brother and I haven't the cash to do it up yet but one day we'll go back and repair the roof before it falls in completely.'

'Is your brother in India too?' she asked.

'Not at the moment, though he's been here in the past. He lives in France now.'

'What does he do?' she asked. She had no qualms about asking questions that might seem impertinent.

He laughed. 'He's an adventurer like me, a loose cannon.'

She said, 'You sound like another pair of Irish brothers who came to India – the Wellesleys.'

This pleased him and he caught her reference immediately.'You mean the Duke of Wellington and his brother? Funnily enough, somewhere way back we're related to them through the female line. My brother and I have both got his big nose. See.'

He turned his face to the front and sat still so she could study his profile. He did indeed have a prominent, high-bridged nose. 'It's big, but it's a very aristocratic nose,' she laughingly told him. 'I presume that you're not in the army like the Iron Duke. What do you do for a living?'

'I'm a pilot,' he said.

This was a disappointment to her because airline pilots were notorious philanderers. 'Which airline?' she asked.

His answer was, 'None. I have my own plane.'

If the Wellesley brothers were reborn, she thought, *they'd have their own planes too.*

The restaurant she took him to was in an alley near the docks and the tables were divided off from each other by flapping cotton curtains patterned with little flowers. In spite of the nursery prettiness of the curtains, it had an air of intrigue, as if it was a place to go to and not be seen.

The proprietor knew Lorna and solemnly showed her to a small table tucked away in a corner. Then he laid before her a large, greasy sheet of paper closely printed with Chinese ideograms but she waved it away for she knew the menu off by heart. 'I'll have my usual, please,' she said before turning and asking her companion, 'What sort of Chinese food do you like?'

He stared at the incomprehensible menu and shrugged. 'Just get me what you're having. Surprise me.'

She reeled off a list of numbers to the hovering man who backed off with a solemn nod.

'Is it possible to have a drink here?' Rawley asked.

'Sorry. Nothing stronger than lemonade!' she told him.

'Oh well,' he said. 'We'll just have to get drunk on each other.'

And that was exactly what happened. When she went back to her office at half-past three, Lorna Wesley was hopelessly, head over heels in love, something that she had been sure would never happen to her.

31

Five

O n Monday morning Ronald Weston was the last person
to be brought up before the magistrate in Byculla Police
Court. Dee had been sitting in the public benches for an hour
listening to a parade of pathetic cases but she did not mind
because she enjoyed the dramas being enacted before her. It
was interesting to watch the people both in the dock and out
of it, though today the audience was sparse.

In spite of the heat outside, the shadowy courtroom, with
its ceiling fans, massively thick walls and high vaulted
ceiling, was remarkably cool. This was a testimony to the
ability of early British residents in Bombay to construct
buildings that provided a more effective refuge from the
blistering glare outside than concrete constructions. Modern architects, even Indian ones, couldn't match the old
colonial ones for comfortably adapting designs to the local
climate.

When he finally appeared, Weston looked even shiftier
and shabbier than the first time she'd seen him. His suit was
crushed and rumpled and his shirt dirty, but he was clean
shaven and had made an attempt at combing his hair over
an incipient bald spot. It was even more difficult today to
guess how old he really was.

From his stance in the dock he stared around the public
benches as if in search of help or sympathy and perceptibly
brightened when he saw Dee. Asked by the magistrate how he
pleaded to a charge of illegally importing twenty kilos of gold,
he surprised everyone by saying quickly, 'Not guilty, sir.' The
magistrate, a grey-haired Goan, shrugged before announcing

32

that the case would be deferred for a week. Justice did not move swiftly in Bombay.

As soon as the judge's decision was announced, two policemen hurried the accused man away and Dee stood up to leave. Before she reached the courtroom door, however, an official hurried up and said that Mr Weston would like to speak to her.

'Is he allowed visitors?' she asked.

'Oh yes,' said the official cheerfully.

Weston was in a room at the back of the court, sitting behind a plastic-topped table with a chair opposite. A blank-faced police constable in blue leaned against the wall and appeared to be paying no attention at all.

When she sat down, Weston asked, 'You're the only journalist here today, aren't you?'

'I don't know . . . I expect the Bombay papers will be represented, but I don't know the people who work for them. What's happened to your friend from the *Express*?' she enquired wickedly.

'Call me Ronnie,' he said, lowering his voice as he leaned towards her. His manner was friendly and he was trying to be matey so she guessed a weekend in the cells with his assorted companions had either mellowed – or scared – him. 'I want you to do something for me.'

'What exactly?' she asked suspiciously.

He reached into his pocket and put a small piece of paper on the table. 'Do you have a telephone?' he asked.

'Yes,' she said.

'Then I want you to call this phone number in London and say that Ronnie's in jail and needs help,' he whispered.

'I don't know if I can do that. I live here and don't want to get into trouble with the authorities,' she demurred in a louder voice so the policeman could hear.

'Why should that get you into trouble? You're only passing on a message. My people promised they'd see I was all right before I left London. That was part of the deal. They've got to get me out of this,' he said urgently.

'I don't think that's going to be so easy. You were caught with all that gold on you. You couldn't have slipped it into your pocket by mistake,' she told him.

He rolled his eyes like a scared horse as he said, 'The policemen here have been telling me I could get five years. Five years in this hell-hole! It'd kill me. You can't imagine what it's like! They promised they'd see me all right and I want them to start right away.'

You should have thought about that before you got into this, she thought, but what she said was, 'Why did you plead not guilty? If you'd pleaded guilty you might have got a shorter sentence.'

He looked at her as if she were half-witted. 'If I plead guilty, they'll sentence me now. I'd be into the paddy wagon and away and there'd be no way my friends could get me out. If I can hold it off till they can organise things, it'll be better. I'm playing for time,' he told her.

'You must have powerful friends if they can influence the Indian authorities from London,' she said.

'I do. Will you phone that number for me?' He laid a yellowed finger on the paper lying between them and she bent forward to look at it. It was a Chelsea number, she noted.

'Just say Ronnie needs help,' he told her again.

She paused and thought a bit before she asked, 'What sort of person will I be phoning?'

'They're very respectable, a young couple, about your own age. They've got a baby and keep the pram in their front hall,' he told her without a trace of a smile.

She could not hide her disbelief as she looked at him but he nodded earnestly. 'On my word, they do. They're perfectly ordinary people. You'd never guess how they make their money.'

She found it hard not to laugh but she could see that he was completely in earnest and her journalistic antennae quivered. Gold smugglers with a pram in the hall! *I've got to phone them, it'll make a great story,* she thought.

'OK,' she said and lifted the piece of paper off the table.

The policeman at the wall never blinked but she had a pretty good idea he knew what was happening.

Before returning home, she went to the cable office and sent off a message about Weston's case being postponed. She said nothing about the request for a phone call. That and the pram would be saved for a bigger piece.

International telephone calls had to be pre-booked and when she called from her home phone to the exchange and gave the Chelsea number, she was told to be ready to make the call at ten a.m. next morning. That night she told Ben what she'd done and he blanched.

'For God's sake! You shouldn't get mixed up in a business like that! I'm going to phone Tommy and ask his advice,' he said.

Tommy did not sound too worried. 'I don't deal with smuggling cases,' he said. 'But I'll pass the information on and check on it. When's Dee meant to be making the call?'

'Ten o'clock tomorrow,' said Ben.

'Tell her to go ahead. Somebody'll listen in,' said Tommy.

Dee was thrilled. There was nothing she liked better than being on the edge of an intrigue and, buoyed up with excitement, she stayed awake half the night speculating about the telephone call.

Normally even booked calls were late coming through but this one was right on time and the line was suspiciously clear. Almost certainly someone was listening in. As the number rang out Dee crossed her fingers hoping the person she wanted to speak to would be at home. After the fourth ring a male voice said sharply, 'Yes?'

'Who am I speaking to?' she asked, but the man on the other end of the line was too clever to be taken in by that.

'To whom do you want to speak?' he said coldly. His accent was like cut glass.

'I'm ringing at the request of Ronnie Weston. He asked me to tell you that he's in trouble in Bombay and needs help. He's been arrested and is in prison,' she said.

The answer came as quick as a flash. 'I don't know what you're talking about,' said the man at the other end and without another word, rang off. Disappointed, Dee looked down into the phone receiver as if she expected it to come up with more. But all she got was the dialling tone. The people with the pram, as she now thought of them, were obviously used to receiving clandestine telephone calls and knew exactly how to deal with them.

Feeling very flat she went to the cable office and sent off a message telling the story of being asked to make the phone call and giving the news desk the telephone number of the people with the pram. If they wanted to investigate from that end, they were welcome to the job, she thought. By now she was beginning to wonder if Weston was a fantasist who'd given her the telephone number of his barber or his bank manager.

Six

The next time Dee was back in the Byculla courtroom, both public and press benches were packed. A line of seats at one side of the magistrate's bench was full of local newspapermen, and though she knew none of them, she could tell that they were journalists for the breed is international and can be picked out anywhere.

She slipped into a bench at the back and took out *The Times of India* to pass the time by doing the crossword, but before she could start her attention was caught by a man sitting alone in the middle of the front bench. It seemed as if he were so important no one else dared sit near him.

Moved by curiosity, she got up and went to a seat nearer to the front, immediately behind the solitary man. He was as imposing as a Roman senator, olive-skinned, grey-haired and dressed in flowing black robes. She recognised him as Oliver Grace, the city's most distinguished advocate. Till then she had not known of his presence and thought it strange to come across him again so soon as she'd seen him for the first time only a few weeks ago at a reception given for a visiting politician from Delhi. She'd received an invitation as a representative of the foreign press and someone there had told her that Mr Grace was one of India's most prestigious and respected barristers who had achieved his eminence in spite of being Anglo-Indian. That proved how clever he was because Anglo-Indians in post-Independence India had to be better than the best of their Indian contemporaries to achieve any fame or success.

It was chastening to realise that there were whole societies and communities in the city which were closed to her, and into which she could only stumble accidentally. Until she started working as a stringer she had only been familiar with the young expatriate society to which Ben and his rugby friends belonged. Beyond that she made only fleeting or indirect contact with people from the many ranks, classes and gradations of Indian society, ranging from maharajahs to paupers, and even less frequently with Anglo-Indian society which was neither European nor Indian. Apart from Tommy, most of the Eurasians that she knew were the beautiful, hopeful girls who were picked up by Ben's bachelor friends.

All of those different worlds were self-sufficient and it was possible to live one's entire life in Bombay without ever encroaching into another society's circle. Each had their own clubs and places of recreation, special places where they did their shopping, took their ease or worshipped. Yet, for all of them Bombay was *their* city; they knew it and felt at home in it. As a result, each set had a different Bombay, a teasing cheat of a city that presented a different face to them all. In London there was a more homogenous communal interest, a coming and going between the communities and classes. There the different sectors knew about each other's existence, even if only by repute, but the same situation did not prevail in Bombay.

The life Dee had known in the country, living in Chembur beside the peasant people from the buffalo camp, was completely different to the life she led in the city. She'd moved from a simple village world into another much more sophisticated, for her neighbours in Walkeshwar Road were refined Indians, rich, university educated and well travelled. They would have been as strange to the buffalo farmers of Chembur as Dee.

Every now and again, contacts made through her newspaper work showed tantalising glimpses of other Indias and these encounters made her feel as she did when she looked across the strait that cut Bombay off from the mainland to the dim outlines of the western ghats on the distant horizon.

She longed to go over there, to step out of her own world into a different one, but the mountains stayed forever just out of range, misty blue, unreachable and fascinating. She knew that even if she drove towards them, there would always be another tantalising line on the horizon.

Oliver Grace was part of the unknown Bombay. He was a prestigious barrister, only hired for the biggest cases by people with the deepest pockets, and her mind teemed with questions that could never be asked. Where and in what situation did he live? How had he reached the top of his profession? Where was he born, what sort of struggle had he faced in order to make his mark? What was his story?

She took her seat behind him and settled down to wait, wondering why the eminent Mr Grace, in his stiffly starched white neckcloth, was spending his morning in a humble magistrate's court. Surely his normal milieu was much higher up the legal ladder?

The day's business dragged along. One petty case followed another but through them all he sat as still as a statue, staring ahead. When Ronnie Weston's name was called, however, he suddenly stood up clutching the edges of his gown and an awed hush spread round the chattering courtroom. The men in the press bench were leaning forward expectantly, pencils at the ready, and Dee sat forward too.

'Your honour,' said Grace to the man on the bench, 'my client wishes to explain how he came to be arrested. He is not a smuggler. He is only guilty of attempting to help a friend by delivering what he thought was an innocent package on his friend's behalf. My client has led a blameless life till now and his feeble health makes it unlikely that he would be able to withstand incarceration in this climate. I ask you to discharge him.'

The words rolled out with such mesmerising force that even the magistrate looked impressed.

'Does your client intend to plead not guilty again, Mr Grace?' he asked.

'Indeed he does. Not guilty,' repeated Oliver in a most theatrical manner.

Pull the other one, thought Dee in disbelief. *How can he be not guilty with twenty gold bars stuck in his waistcoat? He couldn't have been carrying all that by mistake.*

'If he persists in pleading not guilty the case will have to be contested,' said the magistrate. 'So I'll postpone it till the court sitting next month.'

Satisfied, Oliver Grace bowed and sat down, but after a quick glance at Ronnie he shot back up to his feet again to say, 'Can my client be granted bail so he can move out of the police cells and stay in more suitable and comfortable accommodation? As I have said, he is not in the best of health.' Ronnie, in the dock, seemed to shrivel and slump in corroboration of this and the magistrate looked at him with something approaching sympathy, perhaps because the great Oliver Grace was pleading on his behalf.

'All right. I'll grant bail but he'll have to live under house arrest in the Ritz Hotel, providing he has the money to pay for it,' he said.

'Oh yes, he has the money,' said Oliver Grace. 'Thank you, your honour.'

In the confused bustle of an emptying courtroom, Dee hurried to follow on Grace's heels as they were leaving the court. In the hall, she boldly introduced herself, saying she was covering Ronald Weston's case for a London newspaper. 'He's very lucky to have you representing him,' she added.

Oliver Grace smiled pleasantly and said, 'I suppose he is.'

'How did he manage to engage you?' she asked, wondering how Weston had found Bombay's best pleader.

The great man beamed down at her and said, 'It's all a little strange really. I'm still surprised about it myself.'

She could see he was prepared to be friendly so she pressed on with, 'Really? Why?'

'Well, I was in my chambers yesterday afternoon when two Englishmen were shown in without an appointment. I didn't know them, but they were perfectly civil. One laid a big envelope on my desk and said, "That's for you so you can take care of Ronnie Weston."'

'What was in it?' asked Dee.

'It was full of money – wads of bank notes. I pushed it back at them and said I wasn't prepared to take part in anything underhand or illegal. But they said it was perfectly above board. They told me the money is to be used to look after Weston, to keep him comfortable, and, if he does go to prison, to make sure he's well treated there. I was very surprised, to put it mildly, but they seemed perfectly reasonable men,' said Grace.

And some of the money will pay your fee, thought Dee, but did not say that. Instead she asked, 'Surely your clients don't usually come to you like that?'

He smiled. 'You're right. But that's not the oddest part of the story. I can understand they needed someone to act for him – they couldn't hand him a wad of money when he's in prison, could they? – but I was really surprised when they told me that they'd flown in from London and were going back on the next plane. Such a journey to hand over cash! He must be important to them.'

She looked at him, wide-eyed, her mind racing. *Why are you telling me this?* was her first thought. *Are you as innocently bluff as you appear?*

She doubted if he could be as genuinely amazed as he seemed, for in a career like his, he must have come across a lot of very strange things. *Are you covering something up and leading me along a false trail? Why?* she wondered as she smiled innocently into his eyes and exclaimed in surprise at what he was saying.

She was well aware how people use the press. But there was no rule that said manipulation and pretence could not work the other way as well. Something piratical and renegade in her nature made her relish that aspect of her work and she wondered if all journalists felt the same.

She gave no trace of this to the great Mr Grace. Instead

she asked, 'Were the men who came to see you English?'
The pram man had been very English.

'Oh yes, English without a doubt,' he said.

They were walking out of the courthouse as they talked and by now were on the front steps. She wondered if her phone call to Chelsea had prompted the mysterious Englishmen's flight and considered telling Grace about that but decided against doing so. If the visitors from England did exist, she wanted to know what *sort* of Englishmen they were – what class of society they came from; what they looked like; what they were wearing. Oliver Grace was sharp enough to have made those observations for himself and draw his own conclusions but he was obviously not prepared to share them with her.

When his car drew up, he quickly gathered up his black gown and a chauffeur in a white uniform jumped out of the driving seat to run round and hold the back door open for him. With a benign smile and a wave of the hand like a departing god, he climbed into the car.

'Good luck with your newspaper article,' he said with a tinge of amusement in his voice.

She had just enough time for one question. 'Did they leave you a lot of money?' she asked as the door closed.

'More than enough,' said Oliver Grace grandly.

Curiouser and curiouser, she thought as Jadhav was driving her to the Central Post Office. She felt as she'd done when watching the magic men do their baffling trick. Had she really seen what she thought she'd seen? Could she believe what Grace told her? Were the things going on around her all that she imagined them to be? Was she being used as a pawn in some arcane game?

If two mystery men really had come on a round trip from London with an envelope full of money, was it as a result of her phone call? If it was, how did they know to go to Oliver Grace, Bombay's most prestigious and most expensive barrister? Insignificant-looking Ronnie Weston, who huddled like a badly dressed dormouse in the dock, didn't seem sufficiently important to give rise to such unusual, and expensive, events.

Her cable to the news desk took longer to write this time. In it she described the gold smuggler's lucky break after two mystery men had turned up in Bombay with a bundle of cash to hire a top-rank barrister for him. As a result he was exchanging the rigours of his police cell for the luxuries of first-class house arrest. 'The case continues next week, and in the meantime Ronald Weston is relaxing in air-conditioned luxury at the Ritz Hotel,' were the last words of her piece.

After she handed the cable form to Sami, she felt tired but jubilant. Just as she'd hoped, the drama was building up. It wasn't finished yet, but niggling little doubts kept troubling her as she was being driven home. By putting what Oliver Grace had told her into the story, was she only doing what he'd intended her to do? Was she providing him with an unlikely explanation for his intervention in the smuggling case?

The heat of midday made her feel giddy and she closed her eyes. *Don't worry about it*, she told herself, *he can't sue you. You didn't tell any lies, and you haven't made anything up. You wrote down what exactly what he said and what you saw happen . . . but perhaps it is all an illusion . . . like the little mango tree.*

Seven

B reach Candy swimming pool, a place of resort for
expatriates, retained the atmosphere and prejudices of
pre-Independence India. In spite of a growing feeling among
newer members that the policy was ill-judged and unfair,
the pool would not admit Indians and even the richest and
grandest of them were turned back at the gate purely because
of the colour of their skin.

Because of this Dee always felt uncomfortable when she
went through the guarded gate, but she excused herself for
going there with the thought that it was the only place where
her children could swim in safety for there was no other
bathing pool nearby and the sea was very polluted. Anyway,
she reflected, the bathing-pool colour bar could not last much
longer. India was changing fast.

The vast outdoor pool was built in the shape of the Indian
sub-continent as it had been in the days of the British Raj,
before it was arbitrarily cut in half by a bureaucrat's ruler.
Tucked away by the foot of it was a smaller pool representing
Ceylon, which was reserved for the use of children. In the
late afternoons, when the fierce heat was abating and people
began to re-emerge after their midday sleep, Dee's children
loved to go to play in Breach Candy's baby pool while their
mother sat in a sun chair by the water's edge keeping an eye
on them.

On the afternoon of the day she had watched Oliver Grace
appearing for Ronnie Weston, she took the children to the
pool as usual. While they were happily playing, she put on
her sunglasses and lay back on a sun chair. Ideas ran wildly

through her head but one predominated and drove out all the others . . . what was the true connection between Oliver Grace and Weston?

If two men really had flown in from London on his behalf, could the unprepossessing Ronnie be a big fish in the smuggling world? Was Grace in on the racket or was he fronting for someone else in Bombay? Surely not. He made a fortune defending people who were stupid enough to break the law, and wasn't likely to want to join them. Yet if Weston had succeeded in passing through Customs with his contraband, to whom was he to hand it over and where was that handover to take place? The London end of the operation was only half of the business. The other end was here, in Bombay. Would Ronnie ever tell?

She mulled over all those ideas and daydreamed about getting an exclusive scoop on international smuggling. In her imagination she saw a story with her byline on the front page.

GOLD SMUGGLING EXCLUSIVE
By our Bombay correspondent

"Wow!"

Was the shout that ran through her head at that moment imaginary, or had it come from the children's pool? Dee shot out of her seat when she realised that she really had heard a yell. It drove out all speculation out of her head.

The baby pool's shallow but small children can drown in only a few inches of water, she was thinking as she ran to the pool edge. Oh, thank God, her two darlings were safe and happily splashing each other. The yells which had so frightened her were coming from a small American child wearing an enormous pair of sunglasses. He was lying on his back in the water, kicking up his heels in frustration for some reason or other, and there did not seem to be any adult in charge of him.

She waded in to put him on his feet, and adjusted his

glasses. As she was lying back in her chair again, a dark shadow fell across her face, blotting out the sun. She looked up as a tall man with a towel draped over his shoulders stumbled over her sticking-out legs.

He looked down to apologise and she gasped in amazement. It took a few seconds before she fully assimilated her astonishment at the fact that she knew him and was seeing him there. He was walking away by the time she had sat up straight and was calling after him, 'Algy! I can't believe it's you.'

He stopped dead and turned slowly, his shoulders tightening as if in apprehension, while he stared back at her, screwing up his eyes against the glare of the dying sun.

'Is it really you, Algy? Algy Byron?' she asked, standing up and laughing with pleasure at this unexpected meeting with an old friend. She'd always liked him.

He still looked stiff, very much in defensive mode. 'Yeah, Adam Byron. That's me,' he said stiffly, emphasising the 'Adam'. It was obvious that he no longer used or relished the jokey name of Algy, which his Edinburgh newspaper friends had coined for him because his byline was 'A.L.G. Byron'. He'd been very proud of that impressive-looking name.

'Don't you recognise me?' she asked, grinning broadly in pleasure and surprise. 'It's Dee.' She didn't give her married name for he wouldn't know her as Mrs Carmichael. She'd married after he left Edinburgh.

Suddenly he mellowed. His hostility disappeared and he grinned broadly as he said, 'Hey! The last time I saw you was in Scotland.' She laughed, genuinely delighted to see one of her old friends from the wild days that seemed so long ago, in the distant past.

He walked back to her deckchair and sat down on the grass by her side as he said, 'Clever of you to spot me. How did you recognise me? I wouldn't have known you behind those black glasses.'

'How could I forget you? I owe the fact I ever became a reporter to you,' she teased him.

That was true. When they first met, Algy was working on a newspaper which rivalled the one that had taken on Dee for a fortnight's trial. It had been a miserable time for her. The chief reporter, who did not like women, never sent her out on a story; the sub-editors condemned any copy she wrote as being too 'fancy' because they were prejudiced against people with university degrees; the editor, a terrifying ex-Fleet Street man, raised his eyebrows in an eloquent gesture of dismissal whenever his glance rested on her.

Desperately anxious to make the grade, she hung around the office, answering the phones and getting in the way, but knew without a doubt that on the second Friday evening she would be fired. Disappointment burned in her heart because she could not bear the idea that she'd be turned down as unsuitable for the only job that she had ever wanted.

On what she thought was her last morning, she was the first reporter into the office, where a flustered-looking news editor stood at the desk with a telephone clamped to his ear.

'Get yourself down to the bottom of Leith Walk. There's a big fire,' he barked at her.

She ran all the way and reached the scene to find Algy there already. Even in his twenties he had had a wide, wry mouth and a prematurely aged, long, melancholy face that reminded her of the Hollywood actor and songwriter Hoagy Carmichael. Obviously he was infected with as bad a case of journalism mania as she was herself, because he was wearing a slouch hat at a rakish angle with his press card stuck in the ribbon. The rest of his outfit was a long, pale-coloured raincoat with shoulder flaps, epaulettes and a knotted belt, the uniform of a newshound as seen in the film *Front Page*. It was exactly the sort of raincoat that Dee herself longed to own, and was to buy from her first wage packet.

They stood together at the back of a melancholy group of neighbours and policemen staring up at a tall, five-storey block of tenement flats. Thick black smoke was billowing out of the window of a top flat and there was a throat-catching smell of burning wood. Two fire engines and an ambulance were already in attendance and another came clanging up as they watched.

Dee whispered to Algy, 'What's happened? Has anyone been hurt?'

He looked at her with a sort of eloquent pity as if he knew she did not have a clue what to do. 'Wait here. I know one of the bobbies; I'll go and ask him,' he said and sauntered over to the posse of policemen. She watched as he quizzed them for a while, and then disappeared into the building next door to the fire.

After about ten minutes he came back and said excitedly to her, 'A man's been killed. They've taken him to the Royal Infirmary but he's dead. Set himself alight in bed. Drunk, I guess. I spoke to his wife and she's given me all the details, his name, his age and what he did for a living.' A fire in which there had been a fatality was obviously a bonus as far as he was concerned, and Dee caught his enthusiasm. In journalism you hardened up fast or not at all.

Not only did he pass all his information on to her, he also gave her one of the two photographs of the dead man that he'd managed to prise out of the not-too-grieving widow. These showed a grinning man in sailor's uniform standing arm in arm with a hopeful-looking bride in white.

It was only later, when she became used to the cut-throat activities of newspaper reporters, that Dee realised how generous Algy had been to take such pity on her. He hadn't had to tell her anything and she could never have found out the details on her own.

When she got back to the office with all her information, the editor looked at the photograph, stared hard at her, burst out laughing and said, 'Hey, I was going to fire you tonight but I'll keep you on after all because you're obviously bloody lucky.' That was the start of her career; her initiation into the heartless world of journalism.

Now at Breach Candy swimming pool twelve years later she'd met him again. She couldn't believe it. 'Do you remember the fire in Leith Walk? The one where the man was killed and you got those two sad photographs from his wife?' she asked.

He laughed and said, 'Yes, I do. Gosh, we were green and brash then, weren't we?'

'*I* was very green,' she agreed. 'And I'd never have made the grade if it hadn't been for you telling me what to do.' She still felt green but tried to hide that from him, because it was obvious that greenness was no longer part of this hard-eyed man's make-up.

'What are you doing in Bombay of all places?' she asked. The last time she'd seen him he was heading for Fleet Street.

'I've come to reorganise a branch of a news agency here. I flew in last week from Hong Kong. The guy running the office wasn't sending in anything worthwhile so I've come to sort it out,' he told her in an important tone. He was still acting the big-time newsman.

She was impressed. 'Is it Reuters, or PA?' she asked, for they were the only news agencies she knew.

He shook his head. 'No, it's American. WWN – World Wide News. Bigger than PA. But what are you doing here? Are you still in the business?'

'I got married to a man who works here,' she said, pointing proudly at the little girls in the pool, 'and these are my daughters.' He was not much interested in children, however, and only looked vaguely at them.

'Is your husband a press man?' he asked.

'No, he's an engineer.'

'So you're out of the business?'

'Not entirely. I was signed up as Bombay stringer for the *Daily Herald* before it became the *Sun*,' she said tentatively, because she was very conscious that being a stringer was small beer compared to running a news agency.

He grinned and seemed pleased. 'Still got printing ink in your blood, then?'

'Yes, it's hard to give it up. I've been on a story today in fact,' she told him, happy to engage in the sort of professional conversation that she used to enjoy so much and still missed.

'A good one?' he asked. She could almost see his ears prick up. Remembering how he'd made things easy for her long ago, she was glad to share it with him.

'Yes, I think so. It's about a gold smuggler who was picked up in Santa Cruz last week.'

He nodded dismissively. 'Oh, that one. Weston. I saw it. Ernest, the chap in my office, went to check it out but it's just a run-of-the-mill smuggling story. These guys get picked up all the time. Don't waste your time on it.'

Her spirits slumped. If smuggling was so everyday in Bombay, it was unlikely that her story would run for long. She didn't say anything about the mystery men from London or about Oliver Grace representing Weston and excused this lapse by telling herself Algy would think she was making a mountain out of a molehill or had lost her touch. In fact she was hoarding that information and felt guilty about it.

'It's time I was taking the children home,' she said, standing up and rummaging in her bag for a card to give him. 'Where are you staying?' she asked.

He said, 'I move around but at the moment I'm staying at the Capri.' This surprised her because the Capri was one of Bombay's shabbier boarding houses, where the food was poor and the accommodation basic. Surely a man heading an important news agency would live in a better place than that?

'Come to dinner with us – any night. Just ring and say when. Here's my address and phone number,' she said, handing him the card. She didn't really know if he would turn up because one of his characteristics in the past was being very unreliable and difficult to pin down.

He was to surprise her, however. Two days later, at about five o'clock, the phone rang and it was him on the other end of the line. 'I'm sick of the Capri food. Does that invitation to dinner still stand?' he asked.

'Of course. When would you like to come?' she said.

'What about tonight?' was his reply and promptly at half-past seven he was on their doorstep. Ben and he took to each other and if Algy was impressed by the air-conditioned luxury of their flat, he didn't show it.

After dinner, the three of them sat out in the garden while the men shared a bottle of duty-free whisky which Algy had brought with him. As she listened and watched her old friend, it struck Dee that he'd become the sort of person he was always pretending to be when he was young. Now he was a hard-boiled newspaperman who had seen it all. He'd been everywhere, all over the trouble spots of the Far East, and had lived for some time in Singapore, Hong Kong, Australia and New Zealand.

She remembered how their Edinburgh colleagues had scoffed at him for playing the big-time reporter but, while they were all still back home, wearing sports coats and flannels and writing the same old stories, he was wandering the world.

He seemed to think it unsurprising that he'd been married three times though he was still only thirty-four or five. Each marriage had ended in strife and divorce, he said, but none of that seemed to worry him. His wives had passed like ships in the night. He even had difficulty remembering their names. If he had children, he did not mention them.

The solitary, rootless life he was living made her think of the wandering friars of the Middle Ages, or the fervent priests who went out into the heathen world to spread their gospel and save souls.

He did not want to talk much about journalistic matters, apart from saying that his news agency specialised in investigative features. Run-of-the-mill news stories, like the one about Ronnie Weston, did not concern him much. It was midnight before he went away but, before he left, he invited Dee to call in at his Churchgate Street office one morning to be introduced to his backsliding assistant, a Burmese called Ernest. 'He knows more about what goes on in Bombay than anybody you'll ever meet. He might be helpful to you in the future if you want leads on a story,' he said.

His hostess was left with a sense of unreality, as if she'd imagined his visit. 'Did we have a man called Algy to dinner here last night?' she half-laughingly asked Ben while they were having breakfast next morning.

'Yes, he was a good chap. My hangover tells me I liked him,' was her husband's reply. So she was reassured that Algy's sudden appearance out of the blue had not been another mirage.

Eight

O ne of the problems of being a stringer for a London daily was the near-impossibility of reading stories that had been sent off with high hopes. Dee's desire to see her work in print was not an ego trip, but a critical exercise.

I could have said that differently or *I didn't stress that point enough* often came into Dee's mind when she read her own articles. Also it was important to find out whether her work ever actually appeared in the newspaper. If it didn't – why? What was wrong with it? Sometimes, when she could not open the newspaper and find her own piece, she felt like a castaway on a desert island sending off messages in bottles.

The Ronnie Weston story took such a strong hold of her mind that she was avid to find out how many of the stories about him that she'd cabled home had actually gone into print. But it was impossible to find recent copies of the *Sun*. Friends at home sometimes sent her a copy of the newspaper if they saw her byline but they used sea mail, which took nearly three months to reach her. By the time she read the story, she'd forgotten ever writing it.

One morning she telephoned the British High Commission office in the Fort to say she was searching out old copies of a British newspaper and wondered if any member of the expatriate staff took the *Sun*. There was a pregnant pause before the man at the other end of the telephone replied, 'The *Sun*? I'm afraid not. Several members of staff have subscriptions to *The Times* and I'd probably be able to find you an old copy of that if you don't mind the crossword puzzle being finished.'

53

The Times, with or without its crossword, was not what she was looking for, she told him, and she sat with her chin on her fist for some time puzzling out how to get her hands on a *Sun*. Then she remembered that the British Council maintained a reading room in Bombay where English periodicals could be consulted.

A quick flip through the telephone book informed her that the reading room was on Marine Drive, so she was driven by an approving Jadhav to the address which turned out to be an elegant 1930s block of flats overlooking the sea. In the foyer an address board told her that the British Council library was on the second floor.

When she pushed open its unlocked door, she was disappointed to find herself in a depressing-looking room furnished in Ministry of Works style with dusty net curtains and Parker Knoll chairs upholstered in a peculiarly nasty shade of orange hessian. Laid out on low coffee tables were well-thumbed British magazines and newspapers, presumably chosen to give an idealised picture of English life because they included titles like *Popular Mechanics*, *The Lady*, *Woman's Realm*, *Country Life* and *Gardening World*. Official government pamphlets and publications were lined up in pale-coloured bookshelves suspended from the walls by black iron brackets.

The only other occupant of the reading room was a lanky Indian youth in horn-rimmed glasses. He was immersed in *Punch*. From the corner of her eye, as she searched through the publications on offer, she watched him turn over page after page. Solemn and unsmiling, he carefully perused each cartoon without breaking into a smile. In fact, the more he read, the more the magazine seemed to depress him and she longed to ask why he was reading it, but did not dare.

The only newspapers she could find were highbrow ones – yellowing copies of *The Times*, the *Daily Telegraph* and the *Manchester Guardian*, all at least six weeks old. Sorting through them desperately for a second time, she found a month-old copy of the *Yorkshire Post* but not a sign of the *Sun*.

Picking up her handbag, she was about to leave when a door at the end of the room opened and a burly man came bustling in. He was a big, bearded fellow in his late forties, dressed in an open-necked, pale blue bush shirt and baggy khaki shorts. On his enormous feet were flip-flop sandals made of bright yellow plastic.

'Hello, hello, hello!' he cried ebulliently, sticking out his hand in greeting. 'Come in to see our reading room, have you? I'm Brian Meredith, the British Council man in residence. Pleased to meet you. We don't get many Brits in here, I'm sorry to say. I don't think they know we exist actually.'

She told him her name and said, 'I came in to see if you have any copies of the *Sun* on display.'

He wrinkled his brow. 'The *Sun*? It's not the sort of thing we take really. Are you a regular reader?' At least he wasn't *openly* condescending, she thought.

'I wish I could be. I'm their stringer out here and I'd like to see my work in print sometimes,' she explained.

'A journalist!' he boomed as if he'd come up with a gold brick in a lucky dip. 'Well, well. It's good to meet you. What sort of stories do you send your newspaper from here? Do you follow Indian politics?'

'Not a lot. I interviewed Krishna Menon when he was standing for election in Bandra and he invited me to lunch. In fact it was a scoop because I was the only journalist he'd speak to,' she said.

She'd been proud of that story. Though British and American journalists had besieged him for an interview, Menon, a hate object to the Western press because he was thought to be a rabid Communist, refused to speak to any of them. He only relented towards Dee because of the *Herald*'s left-wing stance and because, when he was a trainee barrister in London, he'd read the serialised works of Dickens in the newspaper.

Brian Meredith was impressed by the mention of Menon. 'A strange man,' he mused.

'But charming,' she told him, 'and he hasn't turned out to be a big red bogey after all, has he?'

Meredith guffawed. 'Fair enough. In the reading room we prefer to show a more establishment picture of England than the *Sun*, though.'

Dee bristled. It always annoyed her when people used the word 'England' when they meant 'Britain', and she was also annoyed at the slur on her newspaper.

'That's a pity. A lot of people at home read other papers than *The Times* and the *Telegraph*. I don't suppose you display the *Mirror* or the *Sunday Pictorial* either, and where do you stand on the *News of the World*?' she snapped.

He did not take offence, only grinned at her. 'You're angry at me because you write for the *Sun*, aren't you? Never mind, I won't hold it against you!' he teased in a jocular tone.

Imagine sending such a dopey man to spread British culture abroad, she thought, staring critically at him and noticing with distaste that thick brown chest hair was peeping out of the open neck of his shirt and that his fingernails were none too clean. It was, however, obvious that he wanted to make it up to her for being so dismissive of the paper she represented, because he went on in a conciliatory tone, 'As well as interviewing Krishna Menon, what other sort of things do you write?'

'News reports mainly, but it has to be a big story before they use it. Sometimes they send me cables about things they want followed up,' she told him. 'When I was hired the Foreign Editor informed me that he didn't want stories about famines and floods even if thousands of Indians were killed, but if there was one English person among the casualties, he wanted to hear about that.'

A little devil in her had goaded her on to tell that story to Meredith to see how he'd react but he only looked back at her blandly and said, 'He was quite specific, wasn't he? What sort of story are you working on at the moment?'

'About all the gold that's being smuggled into Bombay right now,' she said. It sounded bigger than it actually was but she wanted him to realise that the *Sun* could deal with as big themes as *The Times*.

This time he did react. His eyes shone and he said enthusiastically, 'How interesting! It can't be easy to find out about that, though. How will you go about researching it?'

'There's an Englishman on bail right now who was picked up for trying to smuggle gold through Santa Cruz. With any luck I'll find out something from him,' she said, sounding more confident than she felt.

'Do take care,' he warned earnestly. 'Getting involved with that sort of person can be dangerous.'

He's a typical man, she thought. Because she was a woman he had to warn her off. If it had been another man who was trying to find out about gold smuggling, he wouldn't have told him to take care. He'd have clapped him on the back and said, 'Good luck!'

She waved a hand at the displayed magazines and the Indian student who was still absorbed in *Punch*. 'Should I stick to the sort of story that readers of *The Lady* or *Amateur Gardening* might enjoy?' she asked.

He gave a good-natured laugh and said, '*Touché!* I'm sure you can look after yourself. It's been very interesting to meet you; I'll try to bring in some copies of the *Sun* for you on my next delivery from home. My consignments are sent out by air so they should be more up to date than anything sent by ordinary mail.'

He isn't so bad after all, she thought, and smiled her thanks.

'Do you have an office in the city?' he asked, but she shook her head.

'No. I'm only a stringer. I work from home, in Walkeshwar Road.'

'Which road is that?' he asked. 'I've been here over a year but I find the road names hard to remember, especially the Indian ones.'

'It's out there.' Dee gestured with her arm. 'It's the road that leads up to Malabar Hill from Chowpatti Beach.'

Meredith nodded and asked, 'Have you lived there long?'

'About four years but before that I was two years in an out-of-town village called Chembur,' she said.

'A long-time resident, an old hand,' he said pleasantly. 'You'd be a great help to my wife Phoebe who's very anxious to know more about the real India. Could you come to dinner? I've some very good claret that came out in the last diplomatic bag. Bring your husband too . . .' He'd obviously spotted her wedding ring.

'Thank you, that would be very nice. My husband's partial to claret and it's impossible to get any out here,' she said.

'Is your husband a journalist?' he asked.

'No, he's a mechanical engineer, the head of a company out here.'

'How interesting,' he said enthusiastically, 'Say "yes" to dinner and then I'll know you've forgiven me for not appreciating your newspaper. Can you come on Saturday night?'

He was so boyishly apologetic that she did say 'yes', and an appointment was made. 'Seven thirty for eight,' he said. 'I've got some promotional films that have just come out. Perhaps you'd like to see them.'

'That would be very nice,' she said. 'But where do you live?'

'Here,' he said, spreading his arms wide. 'This is our flat. We live on the premises.'

When she told Ben that they'd been invited to dinner to see British government films he looked horrified. In the past she had dragged him to see every cartoon show that ever appeared in the Bombay cinemas and they were both satiated with Mickey Mouse and Mr Magoo.

'There won't be any cartoons, will there?' he asked.

'No, I don't think so. They'll probably be travel films about the beauties of Britain,' she assured him but he still groaned.

'I hate home movies even more than cartoons.'

She thought she'd sweeten the pill. 'You'll enjoy it because the host said he was going to serve a good claret.'

'I haven't tasted claret since the last time we were on leave, and that was two years ago,' said Ben. 'I'd even sit through another Donald Duck movie for that.'

Nine

Before she met Rawley Fitzgerald, Lorna Wesley had thought that love was an illusion. When she was at school and her friends spent hours talking about their love for some marvellous boy or other, she told them they were deluding themselves.

Love, she believed, was only a biological scam to make men and women mate and procreate. Human beings were as much at the mercy of their basic urges as rabbits, and they were misleading themselves if they thought that love could last forever – or even for a few years. It was all a huge confidence trick played on them by nature.

Her cynical theories were backed up by observation of her parents and their married friends who were all either totally indifferent to each other or lived in a state of sustained hatred. Her parents, Jack and Ella, seemed to be so deadened by domesticity that they had stopped feeling anything at all. He dulled his sensibilities with whisky and she took solace in gin and her bridge games, which began at ten o'clock in the morning and went on till late afternoon.

They only tolerated each other's company when darkness was falling. Then they sat together on the verandah of their old bungalow on Colaba Point, watching the sun sink down over the sea. Every night Jack kept up a monologue about the changing colours of the sky, wondering if he would be able to see the 'green flash' that was meant to appear just as the sun sank below the horizon. He never saw it, but that did not stop him looking.

Nightly his wife talked about the bridge games that had

filled her afternoon. Her voice droned on, saying things like, 'I had four aces but no kings and my stupid partner bid six no trumps. No wonder we went down.'

Occasionally Jack changed the theme by fulminating against some politician or other whose doings he read about in *The Times of India*. Both he and Ella would be talking at once but neither of them would be listening to the other. To their daughter it sounded as if two long-playing records were running at the same time, each one churning out a different tune.

When she agreed to come back from Europe, she stipulated that she must be allowed to lead an independent life. A separate apartment in the bungalow was turned over to her and days could go by without her ever seeing her parents. In fact she deliberately avoided their company, especially in the evenings when, fuddled as they were with gin and whisky, their bickering conversation was impossible to follow. It was hard for her to believe that once they had been swept away by romance.

Then Lorna, the arch cynic, surprised herself by falling in love.

And how deeply in love she fell! Of course, when a non-believer is converted, they are always the most fervent.

It hit her like a hammer blow, as unexpected as a lightning strike. Sitting in the Chinese restaurant, sharing spiced pork, crab meat and noodles with Rawley Fitzgerald, she looked at him and knew, *This is the man for me. This is the man I want to spend my life with. No matter what happens, I must have him.*

Lorna was not a virgin: a handsome Swiss ski instructor at her finishing school had obligingly relieved her of her virginity when she was eighteen. She'd been glad to be rid of it, but quite dispassionate about the man. She felt as if he'd opened a gate and allowed her into the adult world. She'd grown up. She was not promiscuous, however; when she lived in London, she had only gone to bed with one man.

Because she was such an eye-catching girl, she'd had a

succession of suitors. They sent her flowers, took her to dinner and the theatre and asked her to marry them but only one, the son of a rich Swiss industrialist, met with any success. He pursued her doggedly so, because he was handsome and tantalisingly roguish, she slept with him, but without being emotionally involved. Marrying him would have been a shrewd move because it would have meant that she did not need to go back to Bombay and could look forward to a life of rich idleness, but something warned her against it. He still wrote to her frequently, pleading with her to return to Europe and marry him, but she always refused.

Then it happened. Struck down as if by an axe blow, she fell for the Irishman like a ton weight being dropped from a high building. When she returned to the office after their first lunch together, she could hardly hear what was being said to her by the curious girls who had never known her to take such a long lunch break before. Her whole body throbbed as if the blood was flowing faster in her veins, or as if she'd been enchanted.

She locked the office door and lay down flat on the floor in a yoga position with her eyes closed, trying to achieve tranquillity, but without success. *Rawley Fitzgerald, Rawley Fitzgerald*, was all she could think about, as if his name was written in letters of gold inside her head.

That night she hardly slept, but by breakfast time, she had talked herself into a more collected frame of mind. *Be adult!* she told herself.

Walking into her office at nine o'clock next morning, she looked and acted like her old self, but halfway through her work she threw down the pencil with which she was marking a proof and gave up to despair. He hadn't telephoned; he hadn't come into the office. When they parted yesterday he'd said nothing about future meetings, but she'd been confident they would see each other again soon. Now she was having doubts.

She stayed in the office during the three-hour lunch break, again lying on the floor attempting to empty her mind, but not succeeding. By five o'clock she was on the verge of tears. Lorna, who always got everything she wanted, found it difficult to believe she was not going to get Rawley Fitzgerald.

The city rush hour was at its maniacal peak when she walked out into the street at six o'clock. Taxis, motor cars, lorries and sweating coolies dragging laden barrows filled the roadway. She pushed her way through crowds of hurrying people to reach the corner when her gharry usually waited. It was there. She could see it through a veil of tears that dimmed her sight.

Hussein lifted his whip to acknowledge he'd seen her and she hurried to reach him. *I'll go to the Gateway of India and watch the sun setting over the sea*, she thought. She could not face going home to listen to her parents' pointless chatter.

Her right foot was on the metal step of the carriage when a figure sat up from the seat where it had been lying and a hand reached out to pull her in. 'It's late. You work hard, don't you?' said a teasing voice with a rising Irish note in it.

She shook her head for it felt as if a battery of brilliant firecrackers had exploded around her. 'What do you mean?' she managed to ask.

'I mean I've been sitting here in your favourite carriage for hours. I even went to sleep. But now you're here, where are we going?' He was still holding her hand and she did not draw it away.

'I thought I'd watch the sunset from the Gateway,' she told him.

'I've a better idea than that. Let's hire a dhow and sail out into it,' was his suggestion.

The dhow they hired had two enormous eyes painted on its prow and they had it all to themselves, with only a silent and indifferent man at the tiller. They sat side by side on a rough plank across its breadth, and above them the single sail swelled in the evening breeze. As they headed for the silken stretch of open sea, the whole boat creaked and groaned as if it was alive and complaining about having to work so hard for its living.

The dying light streaked the still surface of the water with a kaleidoscope of colour, red, orange, pink and mauve, and Lorna felt she was sailing into a magic world. *If I was to die now, I'd go in a state of blissful happiness*, she thought.

In the middle of the harbour the temperature dropped slightly and Rawley put his arm round Lorna because her thin cotton dress was sleeveless. 'Are you cold?' he asked.

She shook her head, for she couldn't speak. He took off his jacket and draped it around her. 'Share it with me,' she managed to say and they sat pressed close together with the jacket pulled tight between them. Then he kissed her and her whole body felt as if it was melting and merging with the colours of the sky.

Both of them were awed and silent when the dhow tied up at the foot of the flight of stone steps leading up to the huge stone arch that the British had built to mark the entrance to India. It was from that spot too that their departing army had taken the last Imperial farewell.

Lorna and Rawley walked up to street level hand in hand, oblivious to the clamouring beggars that swarmed round them, all chanting for baksheesh. Rawley stopped suddenly and said, 'We can go somewhere for dinner but then I'll have to leave you because I've something I must do. I don't want to, but it's work. I'll be back in three days though.'

Work? At this time of night? she wondered, and then realised she had no idea what he did for a living. He'd told her he had a plane but they'd never discussed the matter beyond that.

'What sort of work exactly?' she asked.

'I hire out my plane and I've a charter for tonight,' he said.

'You go flying in the dark?' she asked.

'Yes, if it's not too far. Some people are always in a hurry. They hire me to take them to places that bigger planes can't land. Tonight I'm flying out at midnight to Bangalore.'

'But that won't take three days surely?' she asked.

'No, it won't, but tomorrow I take the same client up north somewhere – Darjeeling or Mussoorie, I think, but I won't know exactly till I get my final briefing. Now you've quizzed me, let's go to eat and then I'll take a taxi to the airstrip,' was his reply.

They went back to the same Chinese restaurant and held hands over the table. When it was time to part, she said to him, 'Take care of yourself. I've only just found you and I don't want to lose you.'

He laughed. 'I'm a survivor. You can bet I'm not going to take any risks now. I think you're going to be stuck with me for a long time.' Then he kissed her again and when they went back into the street to look for taxis and go their separate ways she felt as if she were completely drunk.

During the next two days she discovered that a spin-off effect of her infatuation was a greater tolerance towards her parents. She even spared the time to smile at them and listen to what was uppermost in their minds without snapping their heads off.

Jack was the first to comment on the change in her. 'Did you notice that Lorna's being very pleasant these days?' he asked his wife who was playing patience beside him.

'Is she? Perhaps she is. She helped me with the crossword puzzle this evening,' replied Ella abstractedly. She then added, 'I hope she's not coming down with anything. This is the fever season after all. But even if she is sick, she won't tell me. She'll take herself off to one of those Ayurvedic quacks that she believes in.'

'I suppose they're as good as any other kind of doctor,' said Jack, refilling his whisky glass. 'But have a word with her, my dear. Suggest she tries those Vitamin B injections that everybody's having. Or if she's hard up, tell her I'll give her more money.'

'She doesn't need money,' said Ella. 'She never spends anything. I think she must be ill. I hope she isn't pregnant.'

Jack sat bolt upright, shocked out of his usual languor.

'Pregnant? Who by? She hasn't got a man in her life, has she?'

'Not that I know of, but you know what she's like. She tells us nothing. It could be some Indian that she's met somewhere. It could be *anybody*!' said Ella, putting a red nine on a black ten.

'My God,' said Lorna's father and downed his whisky in one swallow. 'Let's hope she doesn't do anything rash until the sale of the magazine goes through.'

It never occurred to either of them that their daughter was sick with love.

Ten

The desire to help his friends was one of the predominant elements in Adam Byron's nature.

It was that quality which made him share his information with Dee on the first day they met. He went through life fixing things up for people, even though some of the recipients of his attention either had no idea that they were being sorted out, or were resentful at being taken in hand.

Even if the objects of his interference proved to be ungrateful, he couldn't stop himself. He liked linking people up, pushing them into situations that he thought would be to their advantage. When he speculated about what he might have done had he not been a journalist, he thought he'd have made a good vicar, dispensing advice and benevolence to his parishioners.

On a steamy October morning he sat in his shirtsleeves in the office of his news agency, World Wide News – or WWN, as it was referred to in the journalistic world. His assistant Ernest Nilsen, a craggy, impassive Eurasian who looked like a Red Indian chief though he was descended from a Swedish seaman and a beautiful Burmese girl, was at the back of the room, passing lines of ticker tape through his hands and tut-tutting in irritation.

'Anything interesting?' Algy asked.

'No, just a lot of rubbish put out by those political gasbags in Delhi,' said Ernest. When he was only half intoxicated – for he was never entirely sober – he was a brilliant newspaperman with a nose for a story and the gift of encapsulating complicated events in readable prose. He was a real wordspinner; one of the best Algy had ever worked with. Unfortunately he'd drink anything and in prohibition-blighted Bombay he knew the whereabouts of every illicit drinking den. Some of the places he patronised sold alcohol that could strip paint off wood, and the customers frequently ended up dead or blinded. Not Ernest though. *If he still has a liver it must look like a piece of dried leather*, Algy thought.

As well as being an alcoholic, Ernest took drugs. Cannabis, heroin or opium were all welcome to him, but his drug of choice was cocaine.

Strangely there was one vice of which he disapproved and that was cigarette smoking. He hated it when Algy lit up a cigarette in the office. 'Don't you know those things are bad for you,' he'd say in his sing-song voice.

Algy only laughed. 'That's rich coming from you,' was his usual response.

After work Ernest went on drinking sprees, which usually ended with him staggering back to the office to sleep in an armchair. He had no fixed home, no woman in his life, no children, no ties of any kind.

Most nights he invited Algy to join him and the invitations were occasionally accepted but, although Algy showed no disapproval of his colleague's way of life, he didn't copy it. One or two beers were the most he'd take when out with Ernest, and offers of drugs were always firmly refused. For a newspaperman he was remarkably abstemious, almost puritanical, though he was not censorious about other people's vices.

If Algy thought that Ernest's private life was a mystery, Ernest thought the same about Algy. For a man so curious about other people, Algy was remarkably secretive. He liked to move his lodgings frequently and did not tell colleagues where he was living. Any personal mail he received went to a post office box number and was never seen at the news office. Personal questions were stonewalled or answered abruptly. Yes, he'd been married three times; no, he wasn't married any longer, was the most he'd say.

Urged on by curiosity, Ernest contacted the agency's Hong Kong branch to ask about his superior's past record. He was told that Byron had been working there for about eighteen months but that he'd been moved on to India by a higher authority. No one at his old place of work knew any more about him than Ernest did.

A selection of Bombay newspapers and magazines were spread out on Algy's desk and the ticker-tape machine chattered away, spewing out strips of paper covered with printed words. He and Ernest were combing the local papers in an effort to find something to send out in their nightly bulletin.

Lifting up a copy of the Bombay *Tatler* from the pile in front of him, he said, 'What's this? It looks like something from the 1930s.'

'It is a bit old-fashioned,' Ernest agreed. 'The man who owns it is a lazy fellow who can't be bothered to change it. He's trying to sell it and I heard that some Bombay businessmen are thinking of making an offer.'

'Friends of yours, are they?' asked Algy.

Ernest shook his head vehemently. 'Definitely not. They're a bunch of Sindhis and I don't like Sindhis. You know what they say about Sindhis, don't you?'

Algy sighed. 'I don't, but you're going to tell me, aren't you?'

'They say that if you meet a snake and a Sindhi in the road, kill the Sindhi first.' Ernest laughed uproariously, wiping his streaming eyes. Such extreme emotion showed he'd already been mainlining heroin that day.

'How do you know about the offer on the *Tatler*?' asked Algy.

'I've lived here for thirty years. I know all kinds of people,' said Ernest. His vast local knowledge was his greatest strength. The agency chiefs could get fed up with his drinking and doping, but they couldn't cover India without him. Algy might have been sent out to spy on him, and read him the riot act, but he wasn't going to fire him. It was always possible to hire a young hopeful to write copy but nobody else could provide Ernest's background knowledge, or his savvy.

With a critical look on his face Algy was turning over the pages of the magazine. 'It could certainly do with some readable copy. Do you think the Sindhis will get it?' he asked.

'Probably. They're crafty, they're playing a waiting game. Jack Wesley, the man who owns it, is asking a big price but he'll have to come down eventually. He's not getting any younger and he wants to get out of India so the Sindhis are tempting him with foreign currency and gold bars,' Ernest told him.

'What sort of man is Wesley?' Algy asked curiously.

'A bit of a relic. An English gentleman, left over from the Raj, not a bad fellow though,' was the reply.

'Does he edit this rag?'

'No; his daughter's the editor but she's only keeping the thing ticking over till they get their money. She didn't want to come back here when she left school, but she's an only child and so she had to,' said Ernest.

Algy looked back at the magazine. 'The layout's good and there's plenty of ads so it must be making some money. It's the copy that's poor. What's her staff like?'

'Jack Wesley won't pay decent wages so he only gets society girls filling in their time till they're married. Advertisers stay faithful because old-fashioned, rich Indian families read the *Tatler*, but that market's shrinking,' Ernest told him.

'Sounds like the daughter's got a job on her hands,' said Algy.

'She has and she knows it. She's a nice girl, and very good-looking. I like her. You should meet her. You might make a match of it,' said Ernest jokingly.

Algy didn't laugh. 'Don't try matchmaking with me. I've been married too many times already and I'll never try it again. I'm like you; I travel light and stick to local tarts . . . This magazine interests me, though, because I can see what could be done with it. I know a woman here who used to work with me back home. Her stuff would spark this thing up a lot.'

'If she's a professional she probably won't work for the money Wesley pays. Look, the *Tatler* office is just across the road, in that big block with the clock on the front. Sometimes I drop in to tip Lorna Wesley off about a local story. She needs all the help she can get,' said Ernest, more seriously.

'Don't tell me you're sorry for her,' said Algy.

'Yes, I am,' was the reply, 'She tries hard for her father's sake but one of these days the Sindhis are going to pick the *Tatler* up for next to nothing. The more moribund it gets, the better they're pleased.'

'Pity,' said Algy, closing the magazine. 'Could you fix it up for my friend Dee Carmichael to see her? It might be to the advantage of both of them. Dee's doing some stringer work for a London newspaper but that's all news and she's really best at features. I don't think she'll be too worried about the money.'

Later that morning he telephoned Dee at home and said to her, 'I've been thinking. Have you tried selling features to local magazines?'

'Which magazines have you in mind?' she asked, 'They're all either full of syndicated stuff or are too specialised for me, full of political comment and things like that.'

'I was thinking about the Bombay *Tatler*. It needs some decent material and you've got plenty of time. You should keep your hand in. My assistant Ernest Nilsen knows Lorna Wesley, the girl who edits it. She's English. You should go to meet her; it would be interesting for you if nothing else,' he pointed out.

Dee occasionally looked at the *Tatler*, but its upper-bracket Indian social content did not interest her. However, she was not averse to the idea of writing features. They offered more opportunity for what the subs back home had called 'fancy writing'. Besides, she'd never heard of Lorna Wesley but was intrigued by the sound of her. It would be interesting to meet another woman journalist working in Bombay.

71

'Thanks. That's a good idea,' she told Algy. She could sense him grinning with satisfaction at the other end of the phone as he said, 'I'll get Ernest to fix up an appointment for you then.'

An hour later he rang back. 'Lorna Wesley will see you at eleven o'clock tomorrow,' he told her and added instructions on how to find the *Tatler*.

Dee and Lorna took to each other on sight when Dee turned up in the *Tatler*'s office. Lorna, tall, Nordic blonde and fashion-model thin, contrasted with Dee who was short, curvy and brown-haired. However, it did not take long to discover that they talked the same journalistic language and even had an acquaintance in common – an old Edinburgh colleague of Dee's had worked on *Woman's Own* for a while as a feature writer.

Standing at Lorna's desk, they scrutinised the page proofs for the next edition of the *Tatler*.

'Ernest says I need better features,' said Lorna mournfully, 'but I'm an editor, not a writer. My forte is layout and presentation. The girls who work for me are all amateurs and not professionals. The best layout in the world can't make their stuff interesting.'

Dee nodded. As far as she could see, every issue of the *Tatler* was the same: the same people photographed in the same positions with the same captions beneath the pictures. 'Maybe you cover too many of the same social events,' she suggested.

Lorna sighed. 'We have to. People buy the magazine because of that. If we miss out anyone's party or reception, we lose readers.'

'Then why don't you start a *Month Past* column summing up the big events of the past month? And a *Month To Come* as well. It needn't be all about Bombay events: you could put in bits of international news as well, and funny things that can be picked up from other papers or magazines.'

'That's a good idea,' said Lorna. 'You wouldn't like to do it, would you?'

'I wouldn't mind doing the first one and then you could find somebody else to follow on,' was Dee's reply. She hated to be tied down and didn't want to have to turn up at an office every day or even every week. The freelance life suited her.

'All right. I've just interviewed a Parsee girl who tells me she's a genius. I'll give her a shot at it after you start the pages off,' said Lorna. Whenever one of the young hopefuls on the *Tatler* staff married, another had to be found to take her place but there was never any lack of applicants. The new recruit was a replacement for Miss Anita Officer, whose wedding photographs occupied most of the latest issue.

'A genius? Did she actually say that?' asked Dee with a laugh, wondering if Lorna was being funny.

Lorna nodded. 'Yes, she did, in all seriousness. "Of course I'm a genius", she said. It'll be interesting to see what she can do.'

'What's her name?' asked Dee.

'Maya Bhatia, a name to watch if what she says is right,' was Lorna's casual reply.

'Gosh, I know her. She's the girlfriend of a young chap who's a friend of my husband. She's never struck me as a genius, though she certainly has a good idea of her own importance,' said Dee, remembering how insufferable she had found Maya on the few occasions they had met her with Dadi, Ben's Parsee friend.

Dadi was the son of a diamond merchant in Grant Road and he had met Ben when he had turned up in the Gymkhana club keen to play rugby, a very unusual thing for a Parsee boy to want to do. The last time Ben and Dee had seen him he had been very excited because his family and the rich Bhatias were negotiating a wedding with Maya as the possible bride.

'You might not have her for long,' Dee told Lorna, who only shrugged.

'They all go eventually.' She looked at her watch. 'It's half-past eleven. How about going somewhere for a cup of tea?'

'That's a good idea.' said Dee.

Whistling up her gharry, Lorna quickly climbed aboard and gestured to Dee to follow, which she did after telling an outraged Jadhav to come back for her in an hour.

Dee had never ridden in a gharry before though she'd watched the horses that pulled them with close interest. Horses were one of the loves of her life and she could tell class and breeding in an instant. Jehangir earned her pitying approval because he had obviously been bred for better things than plodding around Bombay pulling a cab.

Ben had warned his wife against riding in gharries because of the size and ferocity of the bugs and parasites that infested their seats and pounced on new blood as soon as passengers got in. With these tales running through her head, it was difficult not to act like an archetypical memsahib and start scratching as soon as she sat down. She felt ashamed at herself for thinking like that because she prided herself on appreciating the Indian way of life but now, having met Lorna, she realised she still had a lot to learn. Lorna was so much at home in India, and so much at ease with Indian things.

They drove to a green-painted tea-shop halfway down Colaba Causeway. Dee had often walked past it, but never been inside before. A hunched old beggar woman in a white sari sat on the step and silently gave the folded-hand greeting when Lorna tossed her a few annas.

In the cafe's dim interior, they sat at a metal table and drank sweet milky tea flavoured with cardamom and cinnamon. It was served to them in thick tumblers by a tousled-headed little boy.

When Dee talked about Ben and the children, her new friend suddenly said, 'You're lucky to have a family as well as interesting work to do. It's difficult for women, especially out here. So many give up all ambition when they marry. I don't ever want to do that.'

Dee nodded. 'Before I married, my work was the most important thing in my life. Now it's only a diversion, but at least I have it. It means I don't have to despise myself for being a drone and I'm grateful for that.'

'I don't think I could ever stay at home and do nothing. But it depends on the character of the man you marry, I suppose,' said Lorna.

'Ben likes to hear about my stories. He's very easy-going and it amuses him,' said Dee.

Lorna nodded and said, 'Yes, people like us need easy-going men – and preferably men who do a different job to ours. I'd never marry another journalist because there'd be too much competition. I think I might have found the right man at last, though. I've only just met him. He's a pilot . . .' Her voice trailed off but her starry-eyed look told Dee that she was talking about someone who meant a great deal to her.

'With an airline?' asked Dee doubtfully. Like Lorna, she was dubious about airline pilots, who were notorious in Bombay for having affairs and breaking up marriages. Spending time away from home in the steamy tropics apparently removed all feelings of fidelity for partners left at home.

'No, thank goodness. He's not with an airline. He has his own plane – quite a small one, I think. He does charters and he's away at the moment but he'll be back soon. I'm counting the hours,' Lorna told her new friend.

Dee grinned and toasted her new friend with her glass of tea. 'May all your dreams come true,' she said, 'What will you do if he proposes?'

'Accept him at once,' said Lorna.

'But what about your magazine?' asked Dee.

'I'm only holding down the editor's job till my father can sell it. As soon as he does, I'm off, whether I'm married or not,' said Lorna solemnly.

When they returned to Churchgate Street they parted and Dee crossed the street to the WWN office where she found Algy in his shirtsleeves lounging beneath a whirling fan and apparently doing nothing in particular.

He introduced her to Ernest, and she thanked them both for putting her in contact with Lorna. 'I don't think there'll be much work for me, but I liked her a lot and we could be friends,' she said.

Algy seemed pleased. 'I don't expect she'll pay much but it's always a good thing to keep your hand in at features and being in that office could turn up other stories for you,' he said, always practical.

She looked at him, reflecting how bedazzled he'd always been by the job of a newspaperman. He lived and breathed his work. The clothes he wore, the way he talked, his love of keeping his own circumstances a mystery had not changed over the years. He was a great play-actor. Now that he'd actually become a world-weary reporter, what other part was he playing? He wouldn't be satisfied without having a secret Algy inside his head.

Who are you now? she wondered.

When she got up to leave, she said, 'I'm off to look in at the Ritz and see how the gold smuggler is settling down to house arrest.' She hadn't checked on Ronnie Weston for a few days but still hoped to get a story out of him.

Algy frowned. 'That's a dodgy business. These guys talk a lot of rubbish. You can't believe half of what they tell you.'

'I'm sure you're right,' she agreed, 'but he intrigues me. He's such an unlikely smuggler – not piratical at all but more like the sort of man who goes round demonstrating vacuum cleaners to bored housewives!'

'That's probably what he does when he's not out smuggling gold,' said Algy. 'Forget about *Frenchman's Creek*. Real smugglers aren't interesting enough to have books written about them.'

Eleven

The man on the Ritz reception desk told Dee that Mr Weston was in the dining room. When she peeped through the archway from the hall she saw him sitting alone at a table for one in a corner by the kitchen door. A blue-uniformed police constable was standing beside it, cradling a rifle in his arms.

Weston caught sight of her and waved with an air of desperation, so she went in and sat down beside him. 'Have lunch,' he said but she shook her head.

'I can't. I'm going home to lunch with my family.'

Though the policeman's face was impassive she could tell that again he was listening to – and understanding – everything being said.

He sighed. 'Lucky you.'

'Have you any family in England? Is there anyone you want me to telephone for you and tell them you're all right?' she asked, for she thought it odd that he'd only communicated with his organisation and not with anyone else, as far as she knew.

'I haven't any family. Only my mother and we don't keep in touch.'

'That's a pity,' she said, scrutinising his weaselly face. Something told her that this was not the first time he'd been involved with the law. *I bet you've been to prison before, too*, she thought.

He shrugged. 'It doesn't bother me.'

'What about your work? Isn't there anyone there who'll wonder what's happened to you?'

'No.'

She took the bull by the horns and asked the question that was in her mind. 'What sort of work did you do at home?'

'Just before I came out here I was a croupier in a gambling club, and before that I sold the *Encyclopaedia Britannica*.' He sounded proud of this job and she almost burst out laughing, remembering her remark about the vacuum cleaners.

'But your passport gave your occupation as a company director,' she said and he looked suspicious, obviously wondering how she'd come to see his passport.

'It was on your charge sheet,' she explained and he relaxed.

'Company director looks good on a passport, don't it?' he said. 'I'm a red-hot salesman though. I can make people who never thought they needed encyclopaedias buy a whole set. I use psychology. I can sell anything to anybody.' He was becoming quite expansive with enthusiasm and she put on her look of blue-eyed naïvety. 'Really?' she enquired.

'Yes,' he said, crumbling a bread roll. 'I pick my mark and work them. I find out their weaknesses and play on them. There's hardly anybody I don't know how to work. I can always tell soft marks. You, for example. I could sell a whole set of encyclopaedias to you.'

She hid her resentment, but she was sure – or thought she was – that he would never get across her doorstep with his box of books.

'Yes,' he went on. 'You'd be easy.'

She sighed as if in acceptance of this but all the while she was thinking that the situation was like the magic men and their tricks. Neither she nor Weston was sure of what they were seeing or saying. They thought they knew, but they would be very wrong. *I'm as big a dissembler as he is*, she thought guiltily.

'Maybe you should have stuck to that line of work, then. You don't seem to have deceived the Customs men,' she reminded him sharply.

'Bringing the gold in seemed easy, and the money was

good,' he said. 'All I had to do was fly here, spend a night in a hotel and then go home.'

She remembered what she'd been told about him coming off the plane wearing a waistcoat loaded with gold bars. 'Didn't it occur to you that you might be searched?' she asked.

A shutter went down over his eyes. 'The people at home said it'd be all right,' he told her. Though he didn't say so, she guessed he'd been told the Indian Customs were in on the racket and she wondered if he suspected that he'd been set up, as Tommy had suggested, for he was almost certainly a decoy. While he was being searched and arrested, someone else could have been walking through Customs with more gold than he was carrying. Did he know that?

She also wondered about the identity of the contact to whom he was to have handed the gold over to if he *had* got it through. It was obviously impossible to ask such a question with the policeman practically breathing down their necks, however.

'You're lucky not to be in the cells anyway. You seem pretty comfortable here at least,' she said.

'Yes, that's been fixed up for me,' he said and she wondered if he meant that his organisation had also arranged for him to be put under house arrest instead of being given jail detention. If that was the case they must have contacts in very high places.

'Are you allowed to go outside?' she asked. Though the Ritz was air-conditioned the perpetually recirculated air smelt stale, and it had no garden where he could stretch his legs.

He nodded at the policeman. 'Yeah, they've said I can go out during the day providing they know where I'm going and he goes too. He walks with me to the cigarette booth on the corner but that's as far as I've gone yet. It's too stinking hot.'

She didn't like him but suddenly felt sorry for him and, of course, there were still questions she wanted to ask. 'Would they let you visit my house?' she suggested.

'During daytime they would, providing I'm back by six o'clock,' he said, visibly brightening.

'Then bring your policeman to lunch on Sunday. Have you still got my card with the address on it? You'll meet my husband and my children if you come,' she said.

It'll be interesting, she thought, *to see if he recognises Ben as the pseudo* Daily Express *man.*

Before giving lunch to Weston, Dee and Ben had to go to dinner with Brian and Phoebe Meredith. Saturday nights to Ben were rugby-club party nights. He'd been going to the same sort of parties with the same people since before Dee married him and was reluctant to change his routine, but she managed to coax him by saying, 'For the eight years we've been married, I've gone to your type of party. I hate rugby-club parties. I hate the songs they sing and I hate the stupid women that join in. But I go. Surely you can spare one Saturday night to go to have dinner with the sort of people I meet?'

'Oh, all right,' he said grudgingly. 'But I bet your British Council man and his wife are a pair of colossal intellectual bores, what with their cultural films and everything. Is it a black tie dinner?'

She remembered Brian's yellow flip-flops and said, 'I shouldn't think so for a minute. I bet it's a bush shirt affair.'

'Pity,' said Ben, who liked the ritual of dressing up.

At eight o'clock they were shown into the Marine Drive flat by a bearer, and immediately presented with ice-cold gin martinis by a beaming Brian, who was indeed wearing a bush shirt patterned all over with block prints of tiny elephants. His lanky wife Phoebe was dressed in a purple sari with a silver border and her dark hair was twisted back into a knot at the back of her head.

Dee felt Ben bristle at the sight of Phoebe and knew the reason. He always said that European women should not copy Indian dress, since few of them could carry it off properly.

Their stride was too long and their gestures too foreign for the sari. When Dee's female Indian friends had tried to get her to wear a sari, he had talked her out of it.

Phoebe's sari was obviously a great hindrance to her and she carried its floating end bunched under her arm as she came forward to greet her guests. Her feet in open sandals looked white and misshapen, not elegantly Indian at all. The sight of them made Dee think of chilblains, an uncharitable thought which she soon repented because Phoebe radiated friendliness and hospitality. Dee was soon won over to her.

They were the only guests and the meal was peculiarly English – clear soup followed by roast buffalo meat with horseradish sauce and Yorkshire pudding in defiance of the stifling heat that gripped the city outside. The dessert was jam roly-poly of which Ben greatly approved because it reminded him of his schooldays.

He also relished the claret which, as Brian had promised, was first class. Dee, who had recently been diagnosed with a delicate liver, watched her husband downing glass after glass with a certain amount of envy mixed with relief. It meant he wouldn't complain too much on the way home.

After dinner they went into the sitting room where the curtains had been drawn and a film projector set up. Fortified with more wine, they settled down to watch documentaries about the glories of the English countryside. Halfway through Dee felt Ben gently snoring by her side.

At ten o'clock the lights were switched on again and Phoebe said how nice it was to meet other British people. Apparently they had met very few so far.

'How long have you been in Bombay?' Dee asked.

'Only thirteen months but we never know how long we're staying anywhere so Brian and I are determined to use our time to the best advantage. We travel around as much as possible and we've been reading up about the interesting places. Both of our children are in boarding school at home so we're free to go away almost every weekend, from Friday afternoon till Monday morning,' she said.

Dee had an enormous love of travelling, which had dominated her dreams since childhood and certainly helped to make up her mind to marry a man who proposed to whisk her off to life in a distant country. Ben, however, was a reluctant traveller and preferred not to stray too far from his familiar surroundings.

'Where have you been?' she asked Phoebe.

'Well, already we've been to Elephanta Island, Ahmedabad and up to Mahableshwar, Matheran, Kandala, Poona, Daman and Deolali. Next we plan to drive to Surat and maybe as far as Goa,' Phoebe replied.

Ben, the stay-at-home, was listening with astonishment. 'Will you drive to Goa?' he asked.

'Oh yes, we drive everywhere. You see so much more that way,' said Brian.

'Where do you stay? There's no proper hotels.' Ben liked his creature comforts.

Brian laughed. 'We don't need hotels. We take our own tent and camping equipment.'

'My God,' said Ben in a heartfelt tone.

Phoebe smiled. 'Why don't you come with us next time? We're planning a trip to the fort of the Marathi warrior Shivaji. It's near a place called Bhor, not too far from Mahableshwar. Have you ever heard about it?'

Ben frowned and said, 'I thought Shivaji's fort was at Sattara. That means seventeen in Hindi.'

This surprised Brian. 'Does it really? I haven't heard about any connection between that number and the fort but I'll try to find out.'

Because neither Ben nor Dee knew much about Shivaji or his fort, Brian launched into a complicated résumé of the Maratha Wars, which had engulfed the area of the western ghats in the seventeenth century. He ended his lecture by saying, 'Shivaji was a ferocious warrior and made the Marathi nation very powerful, defeating even the Moghuls. I believe his fort's still more or less as he left it, and Phebes and I want to visit it. Come with us. We're planning to go next weekend.'

Dee would have accepted without a second thought but Ben said doubtfully, 'What about the kids? It doesn't sound the sort of thing they'd enjoy. It'll be pretty hot . . .'

Brian frowned. 'How old are your children?'

'Katie and Annie are three and five,' Dee told him.

'We took our children camping when they were that age,' said Phoebe. 'They loved it. But you could come with us just for one day and leave them at home. That way you'd be back with them at night.'

'It's much cooler up in the ghats just now. It'll be a relief to get away from the heat of the plains,' Brian added.

Ben still shook his head. 'I don't think the children would enjoy it,' he said, but then he looked at his wife and saw how disappointed she was. 'But if we can make arrangements to leave them with the ayah all day, we might come with you,' he added.

'That would be fine,' enthused Brian. 'We'd enjoy your company.'

He sounded so pleased that Dee said firmly, 'We'll come and we're looking forward to it too.'

As they drove home half an hour later, Ben said, 'I hope you know what you're doing committing us to that trip up-country. It's going to be stinking hot.'

Dee was not to be put off. 'No it won't. He's right. It'll be cooler up in the ghats and we'll leave early in the morning, before dawn, so we'll be off the plains before the sun's up. It'll be lovely.'

Ben groaned. 'I know you. You'd go anywhere. I hope we don't have to travel with them. His wife looked awful in that sari.'

Dee sighed. 'But they were kind and very hospitable. We'll go in our own car of course because we'll have to come back before they do. And you know how much I like expeditions. It's my Viking ancestry I guess. Pure wanderlust.'

Ben scoffed. 'Viking ancestry! So long as you're not planning any rape or pillage. They said they were going to camp out in a tent. You'll not catch me doing that. The locals for miles around'll be out robbing them blind.'

She was looking out of the car window at the sea as she said, more solemnly, 'But he did seem keen for us to go, didn't he? Maybe he wants the company.'

'Yes, he was set on it. He seems to have a bit of a bee in his bonnet about that Shivaji chap too,' agreed Ben.

'I'll go to the Asiatic Library and read up about him before we go,' she told him. 'Then we won't be as ignorant as we were tonight.'

Twelve

On Monday morning Lorna was sitting on a high wooden chair in front of her sloping desk with her head resting on her crossed arms when the door was gently opened and someone looked round it.

'Missy sahib, missy sahib,' hissed a voice and she turned quickly expecting to see an Indian messenger. Instead Rawley was stepping into the room with an enormous bunch of pink rosebuds in his arms.

In her haste to reach him, she knocked the chair over but the noise it made bouncing on to the marble floor didn't bother either of them because they were locked in a tight embrace.

After a long time she stepped back and looked at him. 'Oh, I'm so glad to see you. I was terribly worried because you've been away such a long time and I had the strangest dream the other night—'

He held up his hand. 'Don't tell me about it. I'm very superstitious.'

'It wasn't too bad. You were laughing, but you were walking into the sea and I was standing on the beach watching you go. It made me awfully sad. Now I see you again I realise that what was making me so sad was not being able to speak to you for all those days.'

'And that made me sad too,' he told her. 'I missed you every single minute I was away.'

They clutched each other again and she felt sheer happiness fill her heart like warm honey as she stood with her face pressed into his shoulder. He was wearing a silk shirt and through it she breathed in his musky, intoxicating smell.

It never occurred to her to play the coquette with him, to pretend that he would have to court her.

'I've missed you so much. I've never felt like this before. After I had that dream, I went over to the news agency on the other side of the road every three or four hours to check on their ticker tape in case there were any reports of plane crashes. Why did it take you so long to come back?' she whispered.

He laid his face against hers and said, 'I'm a very careful pilot. I've never taken chances and I'm not going to start now that I've found you. You mustn't worry about that. My trip took longer than I planned because I picked up another job when I was away. That happens a lot. But I'm not going to work for at least three days and I thought that you might like to take a trip with me so you can see what a good pilot I am. I'll fly you down to Goa. Would you like that?'

'I'd love to see Goa. When will we go?' she said enthusiastically.

'What's wrong with now?' he laughed.

She looked at her watch. It was fifteen minutes past twelve.

She looked at her desk, and it was covered with page proofs, all waiting to be corrected.

She looked at her lover and knew that nothing else mattered but going with him. 'All right. Let's go,' she said.

Hand in hand, with the already wilting roses hanging down between them, they went into the front office where five goggle-eyed girls were waiting. The first desk by the window, which used to be occupied by Bubbles Bulabhai, had been taken over by buck-toothed Maya Bhatia, the girl who claimed to be a genius. She'd joined the *Tatler* the previous Friday and had calmly swept Bubbles' things off the best desk before appropriating it for her own use.

A furious Bubbles was planning on presenting her grievances to Lorna at lunchtime but when Rawley Fitzgerald arrived, she realised she'd have to wait for another chance. Silently sulking, she sat in a dark corner and only nodded

when asked to telephone Mrs Wesley and break the news
that Lorna was taking a trip to Goa and would not be back
till the next day at the earliest.

'And Bubbles, be an angel and have a shot at marking
the page proofs on my desk, will you?' said Lorna over her
shoulder as she left.

The employees were silent for a few moments after the
door closed and then all began talking at once.

'Doesn't she look different!' exclaimed one girl who'd
always thought that Lorna with her yellow hair and trans-
lucently white skin was an ice maiden, too chilly to attract
any man.

'What a lovely man! Who is he?' said a plump Marwari
girl whose dreams were full of handsome men, all of them
desperate to marry her. In fact, she had been betrothed since
infancy to the son of her father's oldest friend and that boy
was already ballooning to prodigious size though he was only
nineteen, two years older than she was herself. Their marriage
was to be celebrated in the next marriage season, during the
coming winter.

'I know him,' said Maya, the newest recruit to the staff. All
eyes turned to her, and a Muslim girl called Fatima who was
allowed by her rich and indulgent father to amuse herself by
occasionally going to work, said impatiently, 'Tell us then.'

'His name's Fitzgerald and he has a little plane that he
rents out. My brother Homi hired it last month and I saw
him when he came to our house for his money. Homi says
he's a gun runner,' Maya pronounced.

Bubbles, fierce in her partisanship of Lorna, swung round
in her chair and snapped, 'And what does your brother know
about anything? How can he say who's a gun runner? Your
brother's not a policeman, is he?'

'My brother has extensive business contacts. He knows
everybody who's anybody in Bombay. He's not a common
grocer like the men in your family,' Maya retorted and struck
her adversary to the quick. Bubbles' father and brothers
owned and ran three enormous food emporia, including the

one at the main gate of Crawford Market. Electrical sparks of hatred flashed between the two girls and Bubbles rose to her feet to stride into Lorna's sanctum where she pointedly closed the door with a slam.

Maya shrugged. 'Take it from me, if Homi says he's a gun runner that'll be right. I hope Lorna knows what she's doing,' she told her awed audience.

To get to the airstrip near Santa Cruz where Rawley's Piper Cherokee was waiting, Lorna and Rawley had to hire a black and yellow taxi because the distance was too great for a gharry. Sitting close together on the torn upholstery of the back seat, they held hands and gazed rapturously at each other till Lorna suddenly said, 'I haven't brought anything with me.'

'Like what?' Rawley asked.

'Like clothes . . . like a toothbrush . . . and soap . . . like pyjamas,' she told him.

He laughed. 'You won't need any more clothes. That's a very pretty dress. And we can buy toothbrushes. As for pyjamas, I'd be insulted if you even think you need them.'

She snuggled up beside him and held his hand.

'Have you ever been to Goa before?' he asked.

She shook her head. 'No. It was Portuguese till a couple of years ago when the Indians took it over and we couldn't get in before, but I've always wanted to go.'

'It's still very Portuguese, with lovely old houses. It's like going back in time and being suddenly swept off to Europe. There are little cafes where you can buy wine if the police aren't looking, and men play guitars on the water-buses. You'll love it,' he told her.

She nodded, looking at him with eyes shining like sapphires. 'I'll love it,' she agreed softly and it was obvious that she was not talking just about Goa.

His trim little plane, painted white with broad red stripes along its sides, was drawn up in the shade of a large hangar.

'Oh, it's sweet,' cried Lorna at the sight of it.

Rawley laughed. 'Yes, it looks almost human, doesn't it?'

They were walking towards it as they spoke and when they reached it, Lorna patted the metal of the fuselage, which was very hot to the touch because of the brilliant sun. She said, 'Hello, plane. Nice to meet you.'

Rawley cocked his head and said, 'It says hello back. It's pleased to meet you too.'

Sher Singh, a tall Sikh mechanic in a blue turban and blue overalls, came out of the hangar and said to Rawley, 'Flying out again so soon?'

'Yes, sardarji. I'm taking the lady to see Goa. Is the tank full?' asked Rawley.

'Everything's ready. And the weather's perfect. You should have a good flight. You'd better check in before you go, though, or they'll be wondering where you are.'

'Check in for me and give the propeller a whirl, will you? There's nothing else taking off right now, is there?'

'No. Anybody with any sense is having a nap,' said the Sikh with a grin, and walked round to the front of the plane while Lorna and Rawley climbed aboard.

The engine started sweetly. Soon they were soaring off the ground and out over an aquamarine sea. Sitting beside Rawley in the co-pilot's seat, Lorna gazed entranced out of the window. Far below them, the island of Bombay unfurled itself. As they followed the line of the crowded city, they passed over Colaba Point and the cove where her parents' bungalow stood. She waved down at it.

They followed the coast southwards, past mud flats, tangled mangrove swamps and lines of coconut trees where frothing gently on to golden sands was the brilliant sea, with lazily floating fishing boats and dug-out canoes dotted haphazardly over it.

After about an hour, Lorna turned to Rawley and asked, 'How far is it to Goa?'

'Two hundred and fifty miles or so,' he said. 'Are you tired?'

'No, it's wonderful. I'm loving every minute of it.'

'We'll be there in another forty-five minutes. I'm going quite slowly so you can see as much as possible,' he told her.

She studied his profile – the beaked nose, the high forehead, the laughter-wrinkled eyes. He was a knight of the air with the little plane as his warhorse and she thought she'd never seen a man who pleased her more or who was more romantic-looking. 'You love this, don't you?' she asked.

He looked straight at her as he replied, 'Yes. I love it. I feel out of my element when I'm on land.'

'Does your brother fly too?' she asked.

His expression changed and became more solemn. 'Tim? He used to. We worked together. He had an accident though and hasn't a pilot's licence any more.'

'That's sad if he loved flying as much as you do. What happened?' she asked.

He stared ahead through the cockpit window. 'His plane caught fire. He was badly burned and he's blind now. He'll never recover his sight completely,' he told her.

Her horror showed in her face. 'Where does he live? Is he married? Does someone look after him?'

Rawley's jaw was set as he answered, 'He's in the south of France, in the hills near a place called Draguignan. The climate suits him there. He's not married but he lives with his lover, a woman called Paulina who looks after him. She's quite difficult but she's good to him and that's all that matters. They love each other a lot, I'm glad to say.'

'Were you in the plane with him when he crashed?' she asked.

'No. I was working somewhere else. They told me when I got back. And he didn't crash. His plane never left the ground before the fire started,' he said bitterly.

'Where did it happen?' she wanted to know.

'Calcutta.'

His voice was crisp and something told her not to probe further, so all she said was, 'I'm very sorry.'

He looked at her again and said in a bitter tone, 'Please don't worry about it. He crashed because someone – not him – made a mistake. It was avoidable.'

He was adjusting the controls as he spoke and she realised that they were gradually dropping down in the sky. Once more she looked out of the window and saw the outline of a promontory sticking into the sea with a half-moon harbour sheltering behind it. In the deep blue water of the harbour several big ships were at anchor. 'That's Goa, there's Panjim,' said Rawley, pointing down.

'Do we land there?' she asked excitedly.

'No, we come down at an airstrip near Marmagoa. It's not far away. Fasten your seat belt, we're landing now.'

He brought the plane down so lightly on the sandy airstrip that she was not aware of the moment the wheels hit the ground. When the engine was switched off, she turned and flung her arms round him. 'You're a marvellous pilot!' she said.

Hand in hand they walked through another hangar to a tumbledown shed of an office where Rawley went in with his papers and chaffed the clerks for a few moments. When he came out he was grinning. 'One of the clerks told me the address of a good place to stay in Old Goa. It's kept by his mother apparently,' he told her as they climbed into an ancient Chevrolet taxi. 'We'll find a good room and when it's cooler we'll explore,' he went on, but all she could think was, *When we've found that hotel we're going to make love.* Her stomach lurched in eager anticipation at the thought.

The room they were shown was on the first floor of an old-fashioned, lime-washed guesthouse called *Casa Lisboa* in Old Goa. The sweet-faced woman who owned the hotel opened two long windows on to a wrought iron balcony that overlooked a courtyard garden which was full of purple bougainvillaea and scarlet hibiscus. A fountain trickled in the middle of the patio and the sound of water splashing into a stone basin were the only noises that they heard during that somnolent afternoon.

91

An enormous four-poster bed dominated the immaculately clean room. The bed had stiff white linen sheets, a crocheted bedcover over the hard mattress and starched white cotton covers on a pile of pillows. It stood so high off the floor that they had to climb up three carpeted wooden steps at the side to get in. Hanging round it were gauze mosquito curtains looped in huge falls as if they were encircling a stage.

And the play performed that afternoon was a romance.

Silently and solemnly, they undressed each other and then, very slowly, began to make love behind the dropped mosquito curtains. Carried away in ecstasy and delight, they never noticed when the sunlight began to fade and darkness crept in like a spying cat. At last, exhausted and satiated, they sprawled side by side in the huge bed and fell asleep.

Lorna woke first. She was lying on her side, facing him, with her hand on his hip. When she opened her eyes a brilliant silver moon was glowing in a square of purple sky beyond the open window. The light it reflected was strong enough for her to see clearly and she propped herself up on her elbow to watch him as he slept.

A lock of dark hair had flopped over his face and his broad shoulders loomed above her like a sheltering rock face. Very gently she stroked her hand from his armpit to his waist and then along the tight slope of his hip to his leg. He was smooth-skinned and almost hairless except for a sprinkling of dark hairs on his chest and his springy pubic bush. There was a scattering of tiny dark brown moles over his right hip and leading into his belly that looked like a constellation of stars in an astronomical chart. With a fingertip she traced them, one by one, counting, 'One, two, three, four, five, six, seven—' Then he woke and caught her hand in his.

'You're tickling me,' he whispered.

She laughed. 'You've got all those little moles. I couldn't resist them.'

'I can't resist you,' he said, and kissed her. They made love again, then lay in each other's arms, staring out at the watchful moon. 'It really has a face, hasn't it?' she whispered.

'Yes, it's like a huge silver coin with a Roman emperor's head engraved on it,' he said. 'We could use it as a ransom payment for love.'

From the courtyard below they heard the sound of people talking and a guitar softly playing. 'You're right. It's not like being in India here,' she said.

'It's still Portuguese. I wonder how long that will last,' he agreed.

'We've probably come at the right time to catch the last of old Goa,' she said. 'Maybe this is what it was like when Vasco da Gama stayed here.'

He laughed. 'I wonder what he ate? I'm starving. Let's go and find some food.'

Their landlady smiled beneficently on them when they appeared downstairs. It was obvious that she knew how they'd spent the afternoon and that she approved. When she'd told them where to go for good food, she put her hand on Rawley's arm and said earnestly, 'I hope you are going to see our saint when you are here.' Her English was heavily accented but understandable.

He looked down into her black eyes and asked, 'Which saint, madame?'

'St Francis Xavier, of course. He's in the church of Bom Jesus not far from here. If you pray at his shrine, he will protect you. He is a very great saint and has performed many miracles,' she told him.

He said they would try to see the saint and then, hand in hand, they walked out into the stone-flagged street, past arches and wrought iron gates that led into patio gardens like the one at their hotel. Some of the archways were guarded by ancient iron cannons with triangular heaps of stone cannonballs piled up beside them, waiting for a siege that did not come until cannons were obsolete. They had stood no chance against the guns of the Indian navy in 1962.

The lovers ate grilled fish and drank acid red wine, which the cafe owner produced from his cellar. 'It's all I have left,' he said with a mournful expression. 'The Indians don't allow us to drink any more. They take away our pleasure as well as our nationality.'

When they paid the bill and rose to leave, he too urged them to visit the shrine of St Francis. 'It is most marvellous place,' he said with an expressive gesture of the hands that seemed to encompass the world.

'We really must go to see that saint if everyone's so set on it,' said Lorna to Rawley as they walked away.

He looked at his watch. 'It's ten o'clock. Will he still be able to perform miracles at this time of night?'

'Let's go and see. Churches never close, do they?' she replied.

Rawley ran back to ask the cafe owner how to find Bom Jesus and came back grinning. 'He's sent for a taxi to take us there,' he told her.

The taxi was a grunting, rattling Ford decorated inside like a shrine itself with holy pictures, crucifixes and rosettes of paper flowers tied with coloured ribbon. The driver sang to himself for the entire journey, part of which was negotiated on river buses where lounging men with guitars played Spanish-sounding music. The sense of moonstruck unreality was heightened in Lorna who found it increasingly difficult to remember that she was only a two-hour flight away from Bombay.

At last they arrived at their destination, an ornately decorated church standing tall in the middle of an empty stretch of ground. When the taxi drew up at the main door, it looked to be firmly closed but the driver gestured with his hand for them to go in and when Rawley turned the embossed metal handle, the door swung open and admitted them. They found themselves staring up an enormous, cavernous nave that seemed to stretch to infinity. A few candles were burning in sconces along the nave and at the far end there was a more concentrated blaze of candlelight which was reflected back at them from a wall entirely coated in embossed gold and studded with jewels.

They both gasped in amazement as they walked forward,

drawn to the golden glitter like moths to a flame. 'These jewels can't be real, can they?' asked Lorna in amazement.

'I reckon they are. Look at the guard,' said Rawley.

As they neared the dazzling shrine, a soldier in khaki had stepped out of the shadows with his gun pointed towards them. They both stopped dead and held up their hands. Swinging the gun muzzle in an alarming way, he hustled them through a little door beneath an overhanging arch and along a narrow passage.

They kept walking, hands still aloft, till they found themselves back in the silver moonlight in a cloister garden full of citrus trees. A fountain was flowing here too and the drops of falling water sparkled like diamonds against the dark foliage of the trees.

At the far side of the patio, a light glimmered in an open window and they were prodded towards it. Before they got there, however, a priest in a dark soutane stepped out of a door alongside the window and said something to the soldier. Then he turned to Rawley and they saw that he was European, a middle-aged man with receding hair. His face was very pale, almost yellow, as if he had recently been ill.

'What language?' he asked in halting English.

'English, French and Spanish,' said Rawley.

Lorna chipped in with, 'Hindi and Marathi too.'

The priest smiled and seemed to relax. 'I speak a leetle English and of course good Portuguese and Spanish because I come from Spain, though I have forgotten much of it. What have you come for so late at night?'

'We want to see the shrine of St Francis Xavier. We are only passing through Goa and everyone tells us it is magnificent, something we must see. I apologise for disturbing you so late,' Rawley told him.

The priest made an expansive gesture with his hands. 'It is no trouble. I do not see many people from your country. You were right to come to see our saint. His shrine is magnificent because the Medici family paid for it and they were very magnificent people. You have heard of them?'

When they said they had, he smiled and gestured with his hand. 'Then let me take you there. Come, come.'

'We don't want to inconvenience you. We've seen the golden wall and all the jewels. That was very splendid indeed,' Rawley apologised.

'But you haven't seen the saint, have you? Him you must see,' insisted the priest.

Lorna gave a little sigh and whispered into Rawley's ear, 'I don't like relics, old bones and things,' but he gently pulled her along because they were not being given the chance to refuse. The priest in his billowing cassock hurried in front of them, carrying a hissing Tilley lamp, obviously intent on giving them a private tour.

Back inside the church, the soldier, friendly now, scuttled from candle sconce to candlestick, lighting wax tapers one after the other till the whole place seemed to blaze with light that was reflected back off the gold and jewels with dazzling effect. The magnificence was made mysterious and awesome because dark shadows still lurked in the unlit aisles and side passages.

The priest stopped by a high glass reliquary in the middle of the floor, and there, raising his lantern high, he said, 'Look, look at him. There he is. The saint himself.'

They stepped forward and saw, lying on a bed of folded linen, a tiny shrunken man, with his bony hands crossed on his chest and his skeletal feet sticking out beneath a white habit. A rope was tied round his waist. The skin on his face had weathered to the colour of parchment and was stuck to the bones, for the flesh that once covered them had long ago wasted away.

'It is three hundred years since he died but you can still see what he looked like. He had a big nose like yours,' said the priest, pointing from the saint's face to Rawley's. Involuntarily Rawley put his hand to his own face and said, 'So he did.'

The priest was looking at the shrivelled little body with reverence. 'He was a Jesuit like me, and a Basque as I am too. He was a very holy man, which I try to be, but I do not succeed as well as he did. People come here to say their prayers to him and he has performed many miracles. I have seen people who were dying walk out of this church completely well after they have prayed to him.'

Then he turned to Lorna and said, 'I will take him out of the shrine so you can touch him, if you like. Then you will be forever blessed.'

It was impossible for her to conceal the shrinking of revulsion this offer caused her. Shaking her head, she drew back, saying, 'No, please, no. I mean I don't want to disturb him. It is enough to be allowed to see him . . .' The words fell awkwardly from her mouth and she could not stop talking, apologising.

Eventually Rawley squeezed her hand tight and said to the priest, 'You have been very kind. We apologise for coming here so late. It was thoughtless of us. Thank you for letting us see the saint. Now we must go back to Old Goa.'

The priest was almost reluctant to let them go, as if he were starved of human contact and conversation. 'Wait. Have coffee. Tonight I am staying awake till morning because we watch over our saint all the time,' he said, and when they backed off down the aisle, he followed them, still speaking. 'So few visitors come now.'

'It is late. We must go,' said Rawley firmly and then the tall priest stopped, a gaunt shadow in black among the gathering darkness. 'Then say a prayer to our St Francis before you leave, and I too will pray for you,' he said.

Impressed by his sincerity, they stopped and bowed their heads while he muttered some Latin words over them. While they were shaking hands in farewell, Rawley put some folded notes into the priest's hand as an offering before they parted.

'Go in peace. May your sins all be forgiven,' he called after them as they climbed into the still waiting taxi.

They were silent and subdued for a long time as they were driven back to the town, but before their hotel came into view,

Rawley turned to Lorna and said, 'There's something I must tell you. I've been meaning to say it all day. I'm thirty-four years old and I've been around a lot.'

She smiled and said, 'I'm twenty-four and I'm planning to be around you a lot.'

His face was very solemn as he went on, 'You don't understand. I'm trying to tell you I'm married. My wife and I parted ten years ago – it only lasted two years, for we were too young when we married – and I haven't seen her since. She's called Rachel and she's Irish and very devout, like that priest, so she'll never divorce me. I'm sorry. I should have told you long ago. But I've fallen in love with you and I couldn't bear the thought of losing you.'

'Why are you telling me now?' she asked quietly.

'Because of the priest and that church and the saint. I knew I had to unburden myself of lies.'

'Are you Roman Catholic?' she asked.

'I was, but I'm not any more,' he said.

She turned her head and looked out of the car window. 'I'm not either. I suppose I'm more of a believer in Hinduism than anything really and Hindus are not into guilt very much. I'm sorry you're married. I sort of guessed you must be because some woman would surely have caught you by now. Have you any children?'

'No,' he said.

She sighed. 'You being married doesn't change the way I feel for you. I love you too, you see, and I'm not worried if we never marry provided I can always have you.'

'Oh God, Lorna,' he said, putting his arms round her, 'you'll have me forever. I'm so sorry.'

'What for?' she asked.

'For not telling you the truth straight away.'

'Then we might never have got together. We might never have come to Goa and seen that poor saint. He was a *man*, Rawley, with a nose like yours! He walked about and prayed and ate and fought with his conscience. I was so overcome when I saw him. It made me realise that we should take happiness when it is offered to us.'

At that point the taxi drew to a juddering halt before the guesthouse archway, and she took his hand, saying, 'Pay the fare and let's go back to that marvellous bed again.' She knew without doubt that they were living through a night that would never be forgotten by either of them.

It was three o'clock the next afternoon when they touched down again in Bombay. The Sikh was waiting on the tarmac for Rawley as he stepped out of the plane. 'There's a man been here to see you. He left a telephone number,' he said, passing him a slip of paper.

Rawley stuck it in his shirt pocket and helped Lorna out of the plane. 'It looks like work,' he said. 'I'll ring him now.'

When he came out of the office inside the hangar, he looked solemn. 'I was right. It's a job. He wants me to fly some stuff to Delhi this afternoon.'

'You must do it,' she said. 'I can go back into town in a taxi.'

'Are you sure?' he asked.

'Of course. I'll be all right. You go to Delhi and take care. Come back soon,' she told him.

He grinned. 'As soon as possible. Tell me your home address so I can find you if the office is closed when I get back.'

She told him where she lived and sat back in the taxi as she was driven off. It was only as she was out of sight of the airstrip that she realised she had no address or telephone number for him.

He was absent for five days, and once more they were days of agony for Lorna, who never left the office during working hours, or her home in between times.

As the hours ticked by she became more and more distressed, unable either to eat or sleep. Her parents watched her pacing the verandah with disquiet and became convinced that she was keeping a terrible secret – even a pregnancy – from

99

them. If they asked what was wrong, however, she exploded in fury.

The last day of his absence was a Sunday and, while her parents attended service in Bombay Cathedral, she sat in a garden chair with her knees drawn up to her chin and a look of desperation on her face. At twelve o'clock a taxi drew up at the garden gate and Rawley stepped out. Immediately she burst into tears, and ran towards him with her hands bunched into fists. Furiously belabouring him, she cried, 'Where have you been? Why were you away so long? You should have told me . . .'

He caught her flailing arms and held them still. 'I couldn't let you know. I didn't know myself. At Delhi I was told to go on to Peshawar and then the weather broke so I couldn't get back.'

Still sobbing, she said, 'Peshawar? Pakistan? You could have been shot. They're at war with India.'

'But not with me. I'm an Irish citizen,' he reminded her. 'Calm down, darling, I'm back now.'

When Mr and Mrs Wesley returned from church, their bearer told them that Missy Sahib had gone out with an Englishman but left a message to tell them she would be back soon.

'An Englishman?' quizzed Ella Wesley.

The bearer nodded.

'White?' she repeated.

The bearer nodded again and she said to her husband in a resigned voice, 'At least he isn't a native. I suppose we can only wait till she decides to tell us what's happening. Lorna has always pleased herself and nobody else.'

Thirteen

If Ronnie Weston recognised Ben Carmichael as the man who'd passed himself off as a *Daily Express* correspondent, he gave no sign when he turned up at the Walkeshwar Road house for lunch.

With him he brought his police escort who was taken into the kitchen to be fed and cross-questioned by the Carmichaels' staff, who took it upon themselves to find out as much as possible about everyone who crossed their employers' threshold. Like Jadhav, Babu had his favourites among Ben and Dee's friends and took no trouble to conceal his feelings. One woman who was a heavy drinker, and particularly fond of gin, was always announced by him as 'the gin memsahib' for he pretended he could not remember her name, though he knew it very well.

After a fairly strained lunch, Ben and Dee, with their children playing beside them, sat under a leafy canopy in the garden and listened to Ronnie talking. He was far more loquacious than usual and Dee wondered if he had been drinking before he arrived because he had had only one gin and lime at lunch. Throughout the meal, however, he smoked several hand-rolled cigarettes, and by the time they'd finished eating he was rambling on about his skill at selling encyclopaedias and his adroitness as a dealer at the blackjack table.

Several times she tried to steer him towards the subject of gold smuggling, but he avoided answering her questions. She could not decide whether he knew very little about the people who'd sent him on his wild goose chase, or if he was exceptionally good at keeping secrets.

101

His case had once again been postponed for several days, which did not bother him because living in semi-imprisonment in the Ritz was infinitely better than serving time in jail. He was not alone in his house arrest because a young French journalist, who had just been released from Poona prison after serving eighteen months for smuggling gold, was also in the Ritz awaiting deportation to Paris. This fellow, said Ronnie, was almost out of his mind from sexual starvation, and talked of nothing but women. His organisation was not as generous as Ronnie's and he had no money with which to buy the services that would assuage his problem.

When not fantasising about sex, the journalist had been a good source of information on Indian jails. He advised Ronnie to go shopping for things like toilet paper, bug sprays and anti-louse powder. Ronnie no longer seemed so worried by the prospect of serving time, providing his sentence was not too long, and Dee's conviction that he had been inside before strengthened as she listened to him. He said that Oliver Grace had assured him that the sentence would be light if he was found guilty, but in the meantime he preferred to drag things out by still pleading 'not guilty'. He was putting off the evil day, as if waiting for a miracle to happen.

Dee sat back in her chair and through her opaque sunglasses watched him leaning forward to talk to Ben. He was obviously much more comfortable with men than with women, so prison would not be as big a strain for him as it was for the amorous Frenchman.

Is he homosexual? she wondered. No, somehow he was asexual, like an earthworm. It was not a flattering comparison but it suited him, for it was difficult to imagine him being roused to passion by anything but encyclopaedias, and those he would probably appreciate only because of their size and gold-tooled bindings, not for any information that could be found in their pages.

The sun was hot, making her yawn. After a while Mary, the ayah, came down to take the children off for their afternoon naps. Dee wished she could follow them but Ronnie showed no sign of leaving. Now he was confiding in Ben, telling him that the cigarettes he smoked so lavishly contained cannabis. 'They make you feel fantastic. Don't you ever buy them?' he asked, waving one about.

Ben shook his head. 'I prefer gin. Where do you get them?' he asked.

'You don't know and you've been living here how long?' asked Ronnie in surprise.

'Ten years,' said Ben.

'Huh! All the cigarette booths in the city sell them. I'm amazed you haven't tried smoking them. They're much cheaper than alcohol and have the same effect,' Ronnie explained, bringing out a squashed bundle of hand-rolled cigarettes tied in a little twiglike bundle with pink string. He offered one to Ben but it was not accepted, for Ben was very suspicious of anything too exotic. Ronnie shrugged, dismissing him as an unenterprising stick-in-the-mud. 'Suit yourself,' he said.

At last it seemed he'd run out of conversation and was about to go when there was a clattering of feet on the garden stairs and Algy Byron appeared. 'I thought I'd find you in,' he cried. He was wearing a white shirt and white trousers which set off a deep tan that testified to hours spent lounging by Breach Candy pool. Obviously he was not killing himself with overwork.

He strolled across the grass towards them and sat down beside Dee who introduced him to Ronnie, and added in explanation, 'Mr Weston's living in the Ritz because he's awaiting sentence for gold smuggling.'

Algy leaned forward and said, 'I've heard about you. Is that your policeman upstairs? I wondered what he was doing here.'

'Yes, I get out during daylight hours providing I take him with me,' said Ronnie.

'Very liberal,' said Algy, 'What do you think they'll give you?'

'My lawyer says I might have to serve a year, less the time I spend waiting for sentence,' was the reply.

Algy laughed. 'You'll be lucky. The average is three years. They're getting tougher on you guys.'

Ronnie blanched. 'There's a French journalist flying out tomorrow who only got eighteen months,' he said.

Algy nodded. 'Yeah, I know him. He was working in Bangkok when I was there, a bit of a nitwit. He got off lightly because he wasn't carrying a lot. You had much more than him if I recall.'

Ronnie's voice cracked as he said, 'I can't do three years! I hate the bloody place. I lie awake at night listening to the cockroaches scraping about in that hotel room – what would prison be like! There's a rat in my bathroom and it's been eating my *soap*. They'll have to fix it for me.' He sounded as if he was on the verge of hysteria and Dee wondered if she should suggest he lit himself another cigarette. Instead, however, he leapt to his feet and started heading for the garden gate, saying over his shoulder, 'I can pick up a cab on the street, can't I?' It was obvious he did not want to be around Algy any longer than he could help.

When he'd gone Ben said to Algy, 'That got rid of him. Telling him he could do three years just about blew his mind.'

Algy was unrepentant. 'It's his own fault. They're all stupid and greedy, these guys. They do it for the money and when they're caught they cry for their mothers. It's the bosses that are interesting, but the police never get near them. They're clever.'

'I was hoping to get a story out of him,' said Dee but Algy frowned and said, 'Don't waste your time. He won't know anything important. He's just a pawn. Stay away from him. You don't want to get mixed up in it.'

'In what?' she said. 'It's all very boring as far as I can see.'

'Keep it that way,' said Algy. 'You're an old friend and I don't want to see you getting hurt.'

He accepted some coffee and after a short while left, saying he was going to the pool for a swim. After he'd gone Dee said to Ben, 'I wonder what he came for? He didn't seem to have any particular reason, did he? You don't think he knew Weston was here and came in to see what was happening?'

Ben laughed. 'For Pete's sake, Dee, don't let your imagination run away with you. He only dropped in to say hello, that's all. You read too many novels.'

It was not easy to write two columns for Lorna.

Dee wanted to make the October column fairly light-hearted in tone, but the war between India and Pakistan was still boiling away and causing great anxiety. During September, bombs had been dropped by the Pakistanis on Amritsar, the holy city of the Sikh religion. Some had even fallen on the Bombay suburbs but no fatalities were announced, which did not, of course, mean there were none. By the end of the month it looked as if peace might be negotiated.

In England the news was equally gloomy for the chief item was about the Brady-Hindley murder case involving the bodies of children that had been found buried in moorland near Manchester. Among the month's obituaries was ninety-year-old Albert Schweitzer, and thirty-six people had been killed in a plane crash at London's Heathrow Airport.

Writing another column about November, the month to come, should have been even more difficult for it was dangerous to attempt forecasting the future, especially since current conditions were so unsettled both politically and economically. However, most people were taking the trouble with Pakistan in their stride, and there would be plenty of events in Bombay's social calendar because November was the start of the cool weather. Soon people would feel more energetic and sit out in the evening with stoles or sweaters draped over their shoulders.

It was also the start of the Indian wedding season when solemn-looking bridegrooms in gold lamé turbans were led through the streets on white horses decorated with flowers and ribbons, behind discordant brass bands playing tunes like 'When the Saints Come Marching In'. That column could be padded out by Lorna who was well supplied with details of upper-class marriages by socially conscious parents eager to see their children's names in print.

When Dee spread her typed sheets out on the office desk, Lorna began to read and after a bit looked up to say, 'It's good, though there's not much to laugh about at the moment, is there? Did Ernest warn you that we're poor payers? I can either give you a hundred chips or take you out to lunch.'

Dee did not really care about the money. Ben was earning well and she didn't have to count her small change any longer. 'I'll settle for a lunch,' she said, 'but not at one of your cafes, if you don't mind. Food that's too spiced upsets my stomach.'

Lorna grinned. 'I could give you a cure for that. It never fails and it's far better than the drugs they hand out to you in Breach Candy hospital. I never go there. My favourite doctor has a room in Chor Bazaar and he only uses traditional medicines. For stomach trouble he prescribes a drink of seeds that dissolve in water like jelly and it works wonders.'

'Ugh,' said Dee. 'In spite of that, I'd still prefer to have chicken tandoori in Gaylord's, or an ice-cream sundae in Bertorelli's. Which will it be? You're paying.'

They went to Gaylord's in Lorna's favourite gharry to sit and chatter like old friends.

Lorna was full of her trip to Goa. 'It's the most beautiful place, so out of time, not twentieth-century at all but that's bound to change soon. Go and see it now if you can,' she told Dee.

'I'd like to,' Dee said, 'but it's difficult enough to get Ben to go to Poona far less to Goa.'

Lorna leaned across the table and said, 'If you get there, make sure you see the saint.'

'Which saint?'

'Francis Xavier. He's lying in a huge church like a little

shrivelled-up mummy in a glass case. He's so pathetic. The priest wanted to open the case so we could touch him but I couldn't.' As she spoke, Lorna's skin prickled, half in sensual pleasure as she remembered making love to Rawley and half in superstitious awe as she recalled the strangeness of their night in the Cathedral of Bom Jesus.

'Is St Francis Xavier really down there?' asked Dee. 'I thought he died in China.'

'They must have brought him back then for he's certainly there,' Lorna told her.

'How did you get to Goa?' Dee asked.

Lorna's eyes shone as she said, 'Rawley flew me down in his plane. It was the most marvellous trip of my life. I'm so in love, I can't do anything but think about him. I can't work, I can't eat, I can't sleep. I just wish my father would hurry up and finish his deal with the people who want to buy the magazine and then I can go away with him.'

Dee knew what it was like to be hopelessly in love and smiled in sympathy. 'Where will you go?' she asked.

'I don't know. It could be anywhere. My father's promised I'm to have half of whatever he gets for the *Tatler* so I won't be hard up. I don't think Rawley's very rich but we won't need a lot of money. Maybe we'll go to Australia – or more likely to France. He has a sick brother there and seems very fond of him.'

Dee was sitting with her folded hands propping up her chin as she looked at the exuberant girl on the other side of the table. Lorna was glowing with health and love, and a golden future lay in front of her.

'How old are you?' she suddenly asked.

Lorna looked surprised. 'I'm twenty-four. How old are you?'

'Thirty-two,' said Dee. 'I've been married for seven years.'

'So you were twenty-five when you got married,' said Lorna.

'That's right. And the advice from an old married lady is not to take the plunge too young,' was Dee's reply.

'Do you think twenty-four's too young?'

'No, I don't suppose it is in your case. You seem a lot older than your age – not in looks, I mean, but in experience and poise,' explained Dee.

'Even if I wasn't, there's no need to warn me against marrying. I'm not getting married. Not now and probably not in the future,' said Lorna boldly.

Dee was surprised. 'But you're crazy about this pilot fellow.'

'Yes, I am, but we're not getting married. Between you and me, we can't because he's married already.'

Dee sat back in her chair and shook her head. 'Gosh, that's not good news. Do be careful. What will your parents say?'

'They don't need to know. Frankly, they don't bother a lot about what I do. They washed their hands of me when I went off to boarding school. Neither of them is particularly child-obsessed. As long as I don't make any scenes or disturb my mother's bridge games, they're quite happy,' said Lorna.

Dee felt a twinge of envy as she remembered the critical attention paid by her parents to everything she'd done. Despite her feelings about her parents' interference, however, she felt that someone should warn Lorna about precipitate action in matters of the heart.

'That's all very well,' she said, 'but what if you get pregnant? What'll happen then?'

Lorna reached across the table and patted the other girl's hand as she said, 'Don't worry, grandmama. I won't get pregnant, and if I do, I know what to do. Ayurvedic medicine has cures for everything, you know. At the moment I'm not in the least broody. Perhaps I never will be.'

Dee snorted. 'At your age I wasn't broody either. I was never one of those women who go all soft-eyed when they see babies, but one morning I woke up and wanted one of my own! Even I was surprised. It creeps up on you, this maternity thing.'

'How many have you got now?' asked Lorna.

'I have two little girls, Annie and Katie – and I'll tell you something I've not told anyone else, even Ben. I've a funny feeling that I might be pregnant again.' A strange thing had happened to her for, though she had no physical symptoms yet, she'd sensed deep inside herself that she'd conceived on the night they came back from seeing the magic men. She would not be certain for a few more weeks, however.

'Are you pleased about it?' asked Lorna curiously.

'Yes, I think so. I'm usually very well when I'm pregnant, with lots of energy and all that sort of thing, and having babies out here is better than having them at home where I'd have to do all the nappy washing and changing myself. Employing an ayah means I can really enjoy my children,' said Dee.

Lorna laughed. 'Does that mean you're telling me to start breeding before I leave India?'

'No, I'm advising you not to start breeding at all, especially if the chap you have your eye on as the father has a wife already. Does he have children too?'

Lorna shook her head. 'No. He says he hasn't and I believe him because he didn't have to tell me about his wife. She lives in Southern Ireland and he hasn't seen her for ten years.'

'She must be hoping that he'll come back to her or she'd have divorced him and found someone else by now,' said Dee.

'She's a Roman Catholic,' was Lorna's reply. 'It always amazes me what people do because of their religion.'

They both sighed because neither of them had much in the way of religious conviction. Dee had first questioned Presbyterian doctrine in her schooldays when, partly as rebellion, she went through an agnostic 'don't know' phase, which eventually hardened into atheism. Lorna had been telling the truth when she told Rawley she was more of a Hindu than a Christian. The symbolic Hindu gods with their multitude of faces and influences on different aspects of human life gripped her far more than any Christian beliefs.

Their lunch was almost finished but both nibbled on the aromatic scraps left over from their chicken tandooris before they pushed the plates away. Then Lorna said, 'I'd like you to meet Rawley, Dee. He's such a wonderful man. I feel as if he's come down to me in a chariot from heaven like the god Krishna! Except in his case his chariot's a little plane.'

'Does he earn enough to keep you?' Dee asked, because she'd observed how marriages sickened and died when a couple lived on the wife's money.

'I don't know. I've never asked him. He charters his plane to people. The other day he flew to Delhi and then to Peshawar,' said Lorna.

'Pakistan? Just now?' asked Dee.

Lorna nodded. 'I said the same thing but he has an Irish passport and so he gets through when someone with an Indian passport wouldn't.'

'Still, it all sounds a bit dangerous,' said Dee doubtfully.

'Don't worry me! I know it is. He's told me that his brother used to fly out here as well but he had a terrible accident and can't do it any more. His plane caught fire in Calcutta and he was blinded. I can't bear the idea of something like that happening to Rawley,' Lorna said with a visible shudder.

Dee crumpled up her napkin and threw it on to her plate. 'I'm sorry, I didn't mean to upset you. Stop worrying. Just be happy. I'm glad for you. Enjoy every moment of being in love and don't worry about what might never happen . . . Come on, those girls in your office will be sitting around gossiping and varnishing their nails. Nothing'll get done till you're back there.'

Lorna stood up, cheerful again. 'You're right. Did you enjoy your lunch? I wish it was as easy to pay the rest of them.'

They left the restaurant laughing and in the street Lorna said, 'Come back to the office with me and I'll give you a few books to review for the next issue.'

'Great! I love books. I can never get enough of them,' enthused Dee.

In the *Tatler* office the girls were all suspiciously busy, so busy that it was obvious that they'd only started to work when they heard Lorna's footsteps on the stairs. There was tension in the air too because the war between Bubbles and Maya was still raging and they had been spending their time trying to win over the others to their respective sides. In this Bubbles was the winner, because Maya's supercilious and snobbish attitudes and her conviction that she was by far the cleverest person ever to have set foot in the *Tatler* did not win her many supporters.

Dee and Lorna went into the inner office and closed the door while Lorna sorted out some books for review. When Dee was leaving the office with her bundle, Maya stood up and waved to her.

'Is your car waiting, Dee?' she asked in her high-pitched, sing-song voice. She was obviously trying to make it obvious to the others that she was on friendly terms with Lorna's visitor.

Dee shook her head, thinking Maya was looking for a lift. 'No, I sent him home, Maya, sorry. I'm going to take a taxi.'

'Don't do that. I'm leaving now too because I've a big party to attend tonight. I can give you a lift,' said Maya grandly.

Dee was flustered. She did not like Maya but, because of knowing Dadi so well, she could not rebuff her. Walkeshwar Road was on Maya's route home, and it would be churlish to say, 'I'd rather get a taxi.'

'Thank you, that's kind,' she said instead and they went down to the street together. The Bhatia family car was an enormous old silver Dodge that looked more like a battle tank than an automobile. The driver was a solemn fellow in a turban with a decoration like a silver lightning flash pinned on the front.

Maya climbed into the back, which was immaculately upholstered with pale cream linen seat covers, and patted the space beside her for Dee to sit down. They were not even at the end of Churchgate Street before she started on the subject that was uppermost in her mind.

'You seem very friendly with Lorna Wesley. She's such a *nice* person, isn't she?' was her opening gambit.

'Yes, very,' was Dee's cautious reply, now realising why she'd been offered this lift home.

'Some people my father knows are trying to buy the magazine. I wonder what Lorna will do then?' said Maya.

'I expect she'll be rich enough to do anything she wants,' said Dee.

Maya shook her head. 'I doubt it. Mr Wesley's selling to Sindhis and Sindhis always end up on the right side of any deal. They're wearing him down, always promising to finalise and then backing out at the last minute.'

'That sounds rotten. I hope they don't succeed,' said Dee, thinking of Lorna's dream of having enough money to go anywhere in the world with Rawley.

'Let's wait and see,' said Maya darkly. She had piercing black eyes that seemed to bore into anyone on whom she concentrated her attention. *Like a snake hypnotising its victim,* thought Dee with a shiver.

As the car was proceeding at stately pace into Marine Drive, Maya leaned nearer to Dee and said confidentially, 'Has she told you about her new man?'

Dee shook her head. She wasn't going to discuss Lorna's love affair with this girl.

'Hasn't she? She's involved with a gun runner, you know. A real crook according to my brother,' said Maya.

Dee's heart went cold with apprehension. *Oh no, poor Lorna,* she thought. It was a struggle for her not to press Maya to tell her more, but she soon found she did not have to bother because she was going to be told anyway.

'My brother Homi knows some people who export rhesus monkeys for medical experiments,' Maya said. 'Sometimes they use that man of Lorna's to fly them across to the Gulf. They load the cages into the back of his plane apparently.'

'That's not gun running. Ferrying monkeys doesn't sound a very pleasant trade, but does it make him a crook?' asked Dee icily.

'Of course not, but Homi's friends say he also runs guns up to the North-West Frontier for the Pathans. You know what they're like about firearms. They're always fighting each other up there. Fitzgerald's brother took guns to Nagaland too, and the authorities stopped him – rather drastically, I believe,' said Maya darkly.

Dee remembered what Lorna had told her about Rawley's blind brother in the south of France and her heart sank. 'I heard his brother had an accident,' she said, hating herself for listening to this.

'An arranged accident,' was the hissed reply.

At that point, Maya's driver drew up at the end of the lane leading to Dee's home. 'My car is too big to turn in your driveway, memsahib,' he said solemnly over his shoulder.

She put her hand on the door handle and said hurriedly, 'That's perfectly all right. I'll get out here.' Before the driver could open the door for her, she leapt from the car, glad to get away from Maya, who so relished being the purveyor of bad news.

Fourteen

Two days before the planned expedition to Shivaji's fort, Dee phoned Brian Meredith to say that she and Ben wanted to take their children on the trip and would travel in their own car.

He was not a bit put out. 'That's a good idea,' he boomed. 'I always think it's an excellent idea to expose children to interesting things from an early age. Phoebe and I did that with ours and they're very academic now. Let's meet at Kemp's Corner at six o'clock on Sunday morning. It's cooling down a lot now so we don't have to worry too much about travelling during the day.'

'How long will it take to get there?' Dee asked.

'Five hours. Not much more,' he said. 'We'll take food and a tent because, if you're travelling separately, Phoebe and I'll definitely camp up there and stay away for a couple of days.'

Dee shuddered at the thought of sleeping out in the Indian countryside in a tent.

'You did say you'd camped out up-country before?' she asked cautiously.

'Oh yes, all over the world,' was the confident reply.

Oh well, it's your choice, she thought as she hung up.

Dawn was breaking in glorious Technicolor when a very disapproving ayah and two sleepy children were loaded into the back of the car. Because of the rapidly cooling temperature, Mary was ostentatiously shivering in a woolly cardigan and the flaxen-haired children were wrapped like caterpillars in tight chrysalises of blankets. In the boot Ben put an icebox with bottles of beer and a dozen Coca-Colas, and a second one full of the family's favourite picnic food – cold chicken, fruit and chunks of cheese. Dee stowed away sun tan oil, calamine lotion, sun hats, a large golf umbrella to provide shade, and a book – she never went anywhere without something to read.

For the up-country expedition she selected Laurence Durrell's hilarious diplomatic sketches *Esprit de Corps* because, she thought, Brian resembled some of the bumbling functionaries in the book. She was looking forward to reading it while lying on a rug beneath her umbrella in the sun while the others climbed what Brian had said was a difficult ascent to the fort.

When faced with doing something strenuous that she did not relish, Dee excused herself by referring to a slight heart irregularity which had persisted with her ever since she'd nearly died from a bad attack of pneumonia as a child. Even Ben, who suspected that her heart was often a convenient excuse, refrained from forcing her into what she considered unnecessary over-activity when she reminded him about her heart.

The Merediths were waiting at Kemp's Corner for the Carmichaels to arrive and Ben and Dee gasped when they saw their friends' car because it was so stowed with camping gear that it was hardly visible. There were boxes and tightly wrapped bundles tied on to a roof rack and what looked like tent poles were sticking out of the windows on both sides. The boot, over-full with boxes, was tied down by a fraying rope.

'My God,' said Ben, pointing to the roof rack. 'That's not a bicycle he's got tied on up there, is it?'

Dee leaned forward and looked. 'Yes, I believe it is,' she said.

'Where's he going to park all that gear while he climbs up to the fort?' said Ben. 'The locals'll clean him out the minute he turns his back.'

'I'll stay and guard it,' said Dee in a self-sacrificing tone.

Ben grinned as he glanced at her. 'You'd do anything rather than climb hills, wouldn't you?' She laughed.

Once off the island of Bombay, the road deteriorated rapidly because huge holes caused by the recently ended monsoon had not yet been filled in and driving over them was a spine-dislocating experience. After two hours, Brian, who was leading their cavalcade, drew on to the verge and signalled for them to stop too.

In spite of their protests that they were not hungry, he insisted on hauling out a paraffin camping stove and brewing tea, while Phoebe opened one of their food hampers and produced sandwiches filled with crisply fried bacon. They had no sooner sat down for their breakfasts than a group of four villagers supporting an ancient man popped out of the undergrowth behind them. 'Baksheesh, baksheesh,' they all whined.

Ben got rid of them by distributing coins and telling them in Hindi he'd get violent if they didn't go away. They withdrew about thirty feet and continued to whine but they were easier to ignore from that distance.

When Ben bit into his sandwich he gave a gasp of delight. 'It's real bacon!' he exclaimed, for that was a commodity that was unavailable in Bombay since it offended both the Muslim religion and orthodox Hinduism as well.

Brian beamed. 'It's diplomatic bag bacon!' he said.

For the second half of the journey, Ben, who had been very unenthusiastic about going up-country, was considerably more mellow as he speculated about what else Brian might have in his diplomatic food and drink store.

Eventually, just when the children were beginning to grizzle, their destination hove into view. From below it looked like a tiny citadel perched on top of a dizzyingly high pinnacle. 'God, does he really expect us to climb up there?' said Ben as he pulled on the handbrake.

They climbed out, stretching and yawning, while Brian and Phoebe bore down on them with enthusiasm shining out of

116

their faces. 'There it is. Shivaji's fort,' said Brian pointing. 'It's magnificent!'

'It's a bit ruined, isn't it?' said Dee, contemplating the crumbling battlements high above her head.

'Well, it's three hundred years since it was last fully occupied. The temple's still in use though. It's well worth visiting. You'll see why when you get up there. I've found out a lot of fascinating information about it,' said Brian, and Dee mentally kicked herself for not bothering to pursue her intention of researching Shivaji's fort. In fact she'd been deliberately lazy because she knew the Merediths would do all the necessary reading and she could just listen to Brian telling them about it.

Looking even more he-manlike than ever, he was standing with his hands on his hips surveying the lie of the land. He was wearing his usual blue Aertex sports shirt and khaki shorts but on his feet were massive climbing boots, the sight of which filled Dee with dread. Phoebe had on similar boots, khaki shorts and a white shirt. On her head was a floppy white sun bonnet that made her look like a cross between Little Bo-Peep and Sir Edmund Hillary, for she was very tall and muscular for a woman.

Surreptitiously Dee looked down at herself and then at Ben. He almost passed muster because he was wearing rope-soled espadrilles, a pair of white shorts and a rugby shirt, but she looked ridiculous in bright pink slacks and a skimpy red halter top that tied in a bow behind her neck. On her head was a fetching pink cotton hat that she'd bought in St Tropez, and her footwear was even more ridiculous because she was wearing sandals held on to the feet by a thin leather thong between the toes.

'How do we get up there?' Ben asked, screwing up his eyes as he stared at the rugged rock face where there was not a trace of any path or roadway.

Brian produced a map from the driver's pocket of his car and spread it out on the bonnet. 'There's only one path. The Marathis meant this place to be impregnable and it was, because enemies never captured it. According to my map, the path starts from near here, behind that clump of trees I think.'

He set off walking in the direction he'd pointed to and Ben went with him. Phoebe looked at Dee and asked, 'Coming?'

Dee frowned. 'I don't think so. I can't leave the children . . .' As if to back her up, a mutinous-looking Mary started hauling boxes out of the car and setting up a temporary camp in the shade of some trees for Katie and Annie.

'They'll be all right. We won't be too long,' said Phoebe. 'You shouldn't miss this. It's unique.'

'I can't climb up there in these shoes,' protested Dee again.

'What size are your feet?' asked Phoebe. She was obviously about to offer the loan of more suitable footwear.

Dee panicked and understated the truth. 'Four,' she said, though the true size was five. Judging by Phoebe's boots she took at least size seven.

'Mmm, that's a bit small, but perhaps it would be possible for you to wear my spare boots if you put two pairs of socks on. Let's go and see what the path's like,' said Phoebe. There was no alternative for Dee but to do as she was told.

When the women reached the other side of the thicket Dee almost burst out laughing because, true to form, a group of natives were gathered there, haggling with Ben and Brian. Even in the middle of the wilderness, you could rely on the locals to turn up and try to get your money off you.

Ben was interpreting and told Brian, 'They're porters. They're offering to carry us up.'

'Carry us!' Brian was outraged. 'We're not decrepit!'

This was Dee's chance. If she had to go up to the top of that hill, she was going to be carried. 'They can carry me,' she cried out in relief, and added to Phoebe, 'I don't like to talk about it but I've a bad heart, you see.' She always felt guilty when she exploited what was really a minor ailment and hoped the gods wouldn't punish her by really giving her a bad heart in the future.

She began to have second thoughts about the wisdom of agreeing to be carried up the hill when she saw that, for eighty rupees, four men would bear her aloft on an armless wooden kitchen chair tied to two long bamboo poles. They all crowded round, assuring her she'd be quite safe, so, overcoming her misgivings, she climbed on to the seat and sat there holding on fiercely with both hands. Then, swaying horribly, the chair contraption was hoisted on to the men's shoulders.

Before she could change her mind, they set off at the sort of half trot she'd seen coolies doing when they carried grand pianos through the streets of Bombay. The trouble was that her porters were not all the same size. One of them was considerably shorter than the others and her chair tipped dangerously in the rear right corner.

Screaming, '*Slower, slower. Let me off!*' she was borne away, leaving her companions laughing helplessly behind her. True to type, Brian had a cine camera, which was whirring away, recording her humiliation for posterity. She fervently hoped that he wouldn't include this sequence in one of his film shows at some future posting.

The path was vertiginous and terrifying because it was hardly wide enough to allow two men to walk abreast in it and on the right-hand side there was a steep drop down a precipice to the flat land below. Unfortunately the shortest chair-bearer was on that side too and Dee was always being tipped towards the void. The higher they climbed, the more terrifying this drop became until, when they were about five hundred feet up, she was too scared to shout or even to look at the spectacular view below.

Her legs were shaking so badly that she could hardly stand when they at last reached the top and she was lowered to the ground.

Behind her, puffing and groaning, the others tackled the ascent. Brian was the first to appear. Wiping his brow he said, 'My God, those porters must be fit to run up the way they did. It's even steeper than it looks.'

Phoebe came next, followed a few moments later by a

purple-faced, puffing Ben who lay flat on his back on a stretch of green sward and said, 'Just let me die. Just let me die.'

Brian laughed. 'Come on, get up. There's a lot to see. From the battlements you can see right across the plains to the sea. What a view! There's no way any enemy could creep up on you here.'

They all walked to the edge of the battlements and stared down into the plain where, far below, clusters of trees looked like green powder puffs and two long straight roads crossed the flat plain like tracings on a map. Above their heads, in a cloudless blue sky, the black shapes of predatory kites, wings outspread, were slowly cruising in the air currents.

From the back pocket of his shorts Brian produced a fold of paper and started to read some notes to them. 'The local name for this fort is Rajghar,' he said.

'Which means "the king's house" – but I thought it was called Sattara,' interrupted Ben.

Brian shook his head. 'That's the name of the nearest town, where Shivaji died. The temple here is most interesting because it's very ancient. Even after Shivaji's army left this fort, the temple continued to be used. People say it still is. Let's go and see.' And off he strode with the others trailing behind him.

The temple was a squat, stone-pillared building fronted by a deep stone tank full of green, slimy-looking water. The stone from which it was built looked like black basalt and it was surprisingly unadorned. As she walked towards it, Dee noticed a bundle of marigolds, still fresh and tied round with tinsel thread, tucked into a corner of the steps leading to the entrance. That meant someone else had either just been there, or was still lurking in the shadows watching the strangers.

Glancing back over her shoulder she saw the chair porters sitting in the shade of some trees smoking and chatting, waiting to see if any of the party wanted to be carried back downhill. They did not look the sort who gave offerings to the gods.

Disquiet seized her. 'Must we go in there?' she said, staring into the darkness of the inner temple.

'Of course,' said Brian stoutly. 'We've come all this way, we must see everything. There are some good carvings of dancing girls inside apparently.'

The interior of the temple smelt of recently burned incense but there was not a soul to be seen or a sound to be heard. It was as if the place was holding its breath. Their party seemed to make a lot of noise as they walked across the first court and through a range of more pillars into the second.

'Hey, I think there *are* seventeen pillars in this temple,' said Ben suddenly.

'Let's count them,' said Brian eagerly and dashed about counting them. Ben was right. There were seventeen exactly, all of them delicately fluted.

'Which god was worshipped here, I wonder?' asked Phoebe.

'I know. It's in my book,' said Brian. 'It was Kali.'

'Oh no, not Kali. She's the goddess of cruelty and death,' whispered Dee.

'Yes, and her followers were the Thugs, the ritual stranglers. There's some suggestion that they worshipped here. It would be a good place for them, well out of the way, wouldn't it?' said Brian, who was obviously revelling in the sinister aspect of the place.

For Dee the dark, musky-smelling temple suddenly became a place of evil and horror. With a cry, she turned on her heel and ran back to the open air.

When the others finally emerged, they found her sitting on the stone pavement by the water tank, staring into its viscous surface where large flat leaves and pink flowers of lotus plants floated.

'I'm surprised at a newspaper woman like you being so nervous,' said Brian jovially when he saw her.

'I can't help it. That temple's full of evil. I can feel it. I wish you hadn't told me about the Thugs worshipping there. They were awful. They used to join bands of travellers and strangle them while they slept. Then they offered their booty to Kali. I read a book called *The Deceivers* about them once. John Masters wrote it. I think it was his best . . .' Dee knew she was rattling stupidly on but couldn't stop herself.

Brian nodded in bland agreement. 'I've read it too. A great book. There's some suspicion that the Thugs might still be around, like so many of the things in India that the British thought they'd stopped – suttee for example,' he said.

'If they're around, they're probably still worshipping here,' said Dee. 'It's a horrible place. I'm going back down now. I don't like the children being on their own down there.'

'You're just ultra-sensitive, my dear,' said Phoebe kindly, putting a hand on Dee's arm. 'Don't worry. There's no one here but us.'

'What about those flowers?' said Dee pointing at the temple steps. The others' eyes followed where her finger pointed but the flowers she'd seen lying there earlier had vanished.

'There were flowers there when we first arrived. I saw them!' she exclaimed.

Brian was revelling in the drama. 'I think you've picked up on the atmosphere. Undiluted evil!' he said happily. 'It's very rare to find a place like this. Shivaji is a great Hindu hero, but he was also a ruthless killer. The stories about him are terrifying.'

'Really?' said Phoebe, his faithful back-up woman, and he was happy to oblige her by going on.

'In this fort Shivaji arranged a meeting with his Moghul rival, Afzal Khan. They'd both pledged to come unarmed, but Shivaji secretly carried what he called his tiger claws hidden in his palm. They went over his fingers with rings like a knuckleduster, and had two terrible claws. When Afzal Khan opened his arms in a gesture of friendship, Shivaji *tore his heart out!* Afzal Khan's men were all in a tent pitched down there on that slope below the fort. Shivaji's men rushed down to it and stabbed them through the canvas. Apparently it was scarlet with blood.'

As he spoke Brian pointed over the battlements to the green ground where their cars were parked. 'I can just imagine what it looked like . . . Stained with red on that green grass!' he exalted.

That was too much for Dee. 'That's where the children are! Oh God!' she cried, distraught. 'I'm going back. I've had enough of this.'

Her distress was so genuine that Ben put his arm round her in reassurance. Brian realised that he'd gone too far. 'I'm sorry I scared you,' he said. 'I didn't mean to. It's just that I love old stories like that. Look down, the children are playing beneath the trees. They're perfectly all right.'

Wiping her eyes Dee allowed herself to be calmed but still insisted on going back to the cars. The rest of the picnic was an awkward anti-climax and the Carmichaels set out for home much earlier than they'd planned, leaving Brian and Phoebe busily erecting their tent and making camp in the shadow of Shivaji's sinister fortress.

It was Dee who spoke first during the drive home. 'I think Brian's a bit crazy. He really loves that sinister treachery stuff,' she said to Ben, as she lifted the Durrell book off the floor where it had lain unread. *How badly I've misjudged Brian!* she thought. He was no bumbling fool. It was all that appearance and reality stuff over again.

'Well, he's certainly not what he seems to be,' agreed Ben. 'I'm glad you made us leave. I didn't fancy staying there much longer myself. I hope if he ever invites you to join another one of his expeditions, you'll have the presence of mind to refuse.'

'You have my word on it,' she told him.

Fifteen

A few days later Brian telephoned Dee to apologise for frightening her when they were at the fort. 'Phoebe said that you went quite pale when I told you about the massacre in the tent,' he said.

By that time her disquiet had faded a little and she told him not to worry about it. She did not want to have a deeper discussion about the subject. Privately she thought that her reaction to the fort and its temple might have been due to her possible pregnancy. Perhaps it was making her ultra-emotional, though she hadn't been bothered that way when carrying the girls. Maybe this one was a boy. Ben would like that.

'I hope us leaving so early didn't spoil your trip,' she said to Brian.

'Oh, not at all. It was splendid, really splendid. Very atmospheric. Phoebe and I stayed at the fort for another two days,' he told her. 'We climbed up to the top every day but never saw anyone at the temple. I think you must have imagined there were people about.'

By now she was doubtful if she had actually seen a bundle of flowers on the temple steps. She preferred to think they were imaginary because she didn't really want to consider the possibility of unseen eyes watching them. Normally loiterers would rush out asking for baksheesh and anyone who remained hidden must have had a good reason for doing so.

'Next month Phebes and I are planning to go up to Daman. It's very picturesque up there apparently. Would you like to come with us?' Brian said.

She remembered her promise to Ben and did not hesitate. 'What a pity! We're fully booked up for every weekend next month,' she lied.

'Never mind,' said Brian, unabashed. 'I've developed the photographs we took at the fort. We can drop them in one evening if you're going to be at home.'

Dee remembered his camera whirring away as she was carried off on the airborne chair and flinched, but it was impossible to tell him not to come. 'That would be lovely. Come to tea the day after tomorrow,' she said, accepting the inevitable.

When she hung up she wondered why the Merediths were so eager to be friends with her and Ben. Perhaps she ought to make it a project to introduce them to other people who would suit them better.

On Friday afternoon, before the Merediths arrived, Ronnie Weston turned up unexpectedly and sat out in the garden with Dee, staring across the silken stretch of Back Bay to the lighthouse on the tip of Colaba Point. Because she now found prolonged conversation with him a strain, Dee was glad to be able to point out a sportive dolphin that turned up in the Bay every winter and performed acrobatic tricks a few hundred yards out from the garden wall. It was high tide but as they watched its plunging gambols Ronnie's face showed only a glazed lack of appreciation, which told her that he was well under the influence of his exotic cigarettes and beyond conducting a reasonable conversation.

By now she had given up on the idea of obtaining inside information about gold smuggling from him. When she had broached the subject he told her a collection of contradictory facts and she'd decided that he knew little or nothing about the major movers in the game.

As they sat in the garden watching the dolphin, he lit another of his strongly scented cigarettes and said in a despairing voice that quavered as if he was about to burst into tears, 'If I can't get out of here soon I'm going to do myself in.'

'Don't be silly,' she said firmly. 'Even if you do get sentenced, it won't be too bad. That Frenchman came through it all right, didn't he?'

'He wasn't like me. I'm sensitive. I worry about things,' said Ronnie plaintively.

She knew she did not sound as if she believed this when she said, 'I don't think you have a lot to worry about.'

'That's all you know,' he said darkly.

'What's Mr Grace saying?' she asked.

'He thinks the worst that can happen to me is to be sentenced to six months, less the time I've spent on remand. The longer he can drag out my time in the Ritz, the less I'll have to spend up in Poona jail, but even six months is too long!' he told her.

'How do you know that you'd be sent to Poona?' she asked.

'That's where all first-class prisoners go and it's an easy regime there if you've money, apparently,' was his reply. As he talked about it he seemed to cheer up a little.

'How often do you see Mr Grace?' she asked, wanting to keep his mind running in a positive direction. The prospect of watching him weep or, worse, having him leap to his death off the sea wall was too awful to contemplate.

'Every now and again. He gives me money.'

'Your organisation must have left him quite a bit. The Ritz isn't cheap,' said Dee.

'The people I work for look after their employees,' said Ronnie grandly.

'Their profits must be pretty spectacular, then,' Dee replied, but he did not rise to that.

She was prevented from asking more by a shout from the garden gate. To her surprise Algy appeared through it, calling out, 'Hello there!'

For a second she wondered if the two of them meeting in her garden again was more than a coincidence, but when Algy's eye lighted on Ronnie his smile turned to a look of distaste. Nevertheless he threw himself down in a garden

126

chair and accepted Dee's offer of tea. Ronnie he studiously ignored.

'You've a nice place here,' he said to her, putting on his dark glasses as he stared out over the glittering sea that lapped against the garden wall.

'We're lucky to have it,' she said. 'There were people from the American embassy after it, but by some miracle the Shahs chose us.'

Algy laughed. 'The poor Americans get it in the neck from everybody these days, don't they? It's because of that book *The Ugly American*. But they're not as black as they're painted. Lots of them are very decent people.'

'Do you know many Americans?' interjected Ronnie in a sneering way.

Algy turned cold blue eyes on him. 'Yes, I do as a matter of fact. Do you?'

'A good number and the ones I've met I haven't liked.'

'Then you've been moving in the wrong circles. Let me guess. You've only met the kind that hang around London gambling clubs or strip joints,' was Algy's reply. It silenced Ronnie.

In spite of the obvious dislike between them, however, neither seemed to want to leave. Each was determined to outsit the other.

'Had any good stories for your paper recently?' Algy asked, deliberately turning his attention to Dee.

She shook her head and said, 'Nothing's happening to interest the people at home apart from the war and I don't cover that. The next story I'll send will probably be when Ronnie here comes up in court.'

'That'll make two lines if it's lucky,' said Algy dismissively and Dee had to admit that he was probably right. She was afraid that Ronnie would start on again about his intention to commit suicide if things didn't go his way and she could imagine Algy urging him into it. Loyal to his friends, Algy could be poisonous to people he disliked and he certainly disliked Ronnie.

'I might be more important than you think,' Ronnie unwisely ventured.

'You?' said Algy rudely. 'You're only a fall guy. The big guns in London set you up, chum. The Customs men were tipped off about you coming and they hauled you in as they were meant to do. Ever since they got you, the gold's been coming in like an avalanche. The Customs are sitting back, taking it easy, because you're their alibi for having done good work. They'll make sure you get a big sentence just to show how clever they've been. The only one who wasn't in on the plan was *you*. A lamb to the slaughter, that's what you were. You'll do your time and when you go home, nobody'll want to know you. Mark my words.'

Ronnie's ferrety little eyes became bloodshot with rage as he leaned forward and hissed, 'What do you know about it? I was carrying a lot of gold. They wouldn't let all that go down the drain.'

'Of course they would, especially if there were another two people on the same plane as you who were carrying in fifty thousand quid's worth between them in the false bottoms of their suitcases.'

'That's rubbish!' Ronnie almost screamed.

'Is it? Do you remember seeing a little old lady in a sari who was so nervous about flying that the stewardess had to give her double brandies? Do you remember an American college boy who read *Playboy* magazine and sat in a seat across the aisle from you? They were better mules than you.'

It was obvious from Ronnie's face that he did remember these particular people but what he said was, 'Someone who was on the same plane as me told you all that.'

'That's right,' agreed Algy, 'and I'm telling you they were carrying gold too, and because of you walking the plank, they got away with it.'

Dee sat silently and watched animosity flare between them. How had Algy found all that out, she wondered? He'd told her the smuggling story wasn't worth following up, but all the time he must have been working on it himself. *Well, that's journalism*, she thought. *Every man for himself.*

Ronnie was again the first to crack. Jumping to his feet, he said something about having to get back to the Ritz and bolted up the garden stairs, calling for his policeman as he went.

Algy, leaning back in his chair, impassively watched the precipitate departure, then shrugged as he reached into his shirt pocket to bring out a packet of cigarettes. Very casually he took one out, stuck it into his mouth and lit it. 'Little rat,' he said happily as he inhaled.

'Yes, he is a bit,' agreed Dee. 'But I hope you've not driven him to try to kill himself. He was threatening to do it before you arrived.'

'Huh, no chance. His kind don't kill themselves. They only talk about it,' was the dismissive reply.

'And how did you find out so much about his smuggling story? You said to me it was run of the mill,' she accused.

'So it is. It's happening all the time. Gold comes in by dhows and on planes. The Customs guys pull in somebody every now and again, but hardly ever Europeans. They needed a big catch, so London tempted that stupid little rat with a thousand pounds and fixed him up. The arrest of an Englishman would make the British papers. You played your part, sent over your story and that was all they needed. A big catch made the Customs look efficient. Nobody gives a toss what happens to him now.'

'Are *you* writing this up?' Dee asked.

'What's the point? You're doing it. I've no names, no proof. Just rumour and bazaar talk – which is usually highly accurate, by the way,' he told her.

'Who do you get your bazaar gossip from?' she wanted to know, envying him for being a man because doors opened for him that were closed to a woman.

'Sitting in drinking dens listening to people talking,' he told her and she sighed. Women reporters, she thought, were still destined to write pleasant little features or book reviews while men like Algy prowled the night-time streets looking for real scoops. She felt condemned to triviality by her sex.

'Don't look so down in the mouth,' he told her. 'You're good at what you do. Just don't get out of your depth. Don't get taken in.'

An angry riposte sprang to her lips and she would have delivered it if they had not been interrupted yet again, this time by Brian and Phoebe Meredith who Dee had forgotten all about. They appeared through the garden gate, smiling all over their faces.

'We've brought you the photos,' said Brian.

Glad for the diversion, Dee collected herself and made the introductions.

'This is Brian and Phoebe Meredith,' she said to Algy. 'Brian's with the British Council. We went up to Shivaji's fort with them last weekend.'

To the Merediths she said of Algy, 'This is Al – I mean Adam Byron.' She'd almost forgotten he didn't like being called Algy any more. 'He's an old friend and work colleague of mine from Edinburgh days. He's running a news agency here now.'

Brian gave his usual response. 'How interesting! Which agency?'

'World Wide News – WWN,' said Algy and Brian nodded.

'I've heard of it. American based, isn't it?'

'Yes,' was the short reply.

A beaming Babu, who loved entertaining, came trotting across the garden bearing a tray loaded with tea things. Following him was Prakash who was carrying an enormous teapot. Prakash was followed by Katie and Annie, who had just wakened from their afternoon nap and looked lovely, spruced up in fresh dresses by Mary, who also liked to impress visitors.

The little girls created a huge diversion and it was not until after tea was served that Phoebe and Brian had a chance to show their photographs of Shivaji's fort. There were some spectacular shots from the fort battlements and of the sinister temple. Somehow, although the pictures had been taken in bright light, the temple looked very dark and, if anything, more sinister than it had done when they were there. A little shiver swept through Dee as she looked at the photographs. She could almost swear she saw the outlines of figures standing in the dark shadows.

What caused the most interest were the shots of Dee looking panic-stricken in the high chair. While her daughters were squealing with delighted laughter at their mummy being carried in the air by four running men, however, Algy was examining the photographs of the fort and temple. 'Where's this?' he asked after Mary had taken the children, who were showing signs of becoming over-excited, upstairs.

'Near Mahableshwar, on an outcrop of the Western ghats,' Brian told him.

'Pretty sinister-looking, isn't it? Not my idea of a good place to go for a Sunday trip,' said Algy, laying them down.

Brian leaned forward and said earnestly, 'It *is* sinister. That's what makes it so interesting. It's a place of treachery.' Then he retold the story of Shivaji's murderous rendezvous with Afzal Khan, and finished by saying, 'And afterwards the temple in the fort was used by the Thugs for the worship of Kali. People still go up there to pray and make offerings to her.'

'Did you?' asked Algy, looking the other man straight in the eye.

Brian threw back his head and laughed heartily. 'Of course not. A good Church of England man, that's what I am.'

Just as he'd outsat Ronnie, it seemed that Algy was determined to outstay the Merediths, who left at about six o'clock. 'When we see you again we'll give you more prints of the photographs. I'll develop them for you tonight,' said Brian.

After the sound of their departing car was heard, Algy said, 'I wonder why he's so keen to hang around you.'

'I expect he doesn't know many other people,' said Dee.

'Maybe. But you know he's a spook, of course. They don't usually waste their time with people who aren't going to be useful. Who or what do you know that interests him?' Algy enquired.

She was surprised. 'What do you mean?'

'Come on. Those British Council chaps are nearly always spies.'

'Spies! That's ridiculous. He's not the spy type,' she protested.

He smiled sardonically. 'What's the spy type? If there *was* a recognisable type they wouldn't be very effective, would they? He may act like a bit of an idiot, lolloping around in flip-flops and baggy shorts, but he's up to something.'

'He runs the British Council library in Marine Drive,' Dee said feebly.

Algy was not impressed. 'Huh. Who ever goes in there except a lot of students with time to waste? That's only a front. It'll be amusing for you to keep an eye on him – it'd be a better story than that smuggler – but watch your step,' he said.

He stayed for supper and finished a bottle of gin with Ben. Dee was asleep in bed before he left.

Next night, Brian and Phoebe invited Ben and Dee to dinner. Surprisingly their hosts had dressed up for the occasion – Brian in a white dinner jacket and black tie, Phoebe in a long green dress with beading round the neckline that made her look very elegant.

'Oh, we're not dressed up,' cried Dee when they were met at the door. She was in an old cocktail dress but Ben was wearing a bush shirt and white trousers.

'We thought it would be nice to do you the honour,' said Phoebe graciously, kissing Dee's cheek.

Another bottle of Brian's special claret helped the evening pass very convivially and after the meal they sat on the sea-facing balcony enjoying a fine brandy which loosened all their tongues.

Dee talked about how Shivaji's fort had frightened her and

they all reassured her that her fears were imaginary. Then Brian leaned forward in his chair to say confidentially, 'You know, often the things that you think are frightening are not the things you should be worrying about, Dee.'

'What do you mean?' she asked.

'I think you should be more careful about the company you keep. Your friend Byron is a suspicious character, I think.' Brian's voice was very solemn.

Dee laughed, 'Algy? Oh, no. I've known him for years. We met when we were kids and he's always been a friend. I met him again by accident in Breach Candy about a month ago and it was great to see him. He's not a danger to anyone.'

'How long since you last saw him?' asked Brian.

'Maybe twelve years. He left Edinburgh before I did. He got a job in Fleet Street. I'll never forget his farewell party – we were all hung over for a week.'

'What do you know about anything he's done since then?'

Dee frowned, slightly disconcerted by Brian's cross-questioning. 'I know he's worked in Australia and New Zealand and in Hong Kong. He came to Bombay from there, I believe.' She didn't say anything about Algy's unfortunate marriage record. That was nobody's business but his own.

'Oh, dear,' sighed Brian. 'Don't you know that chaps like him are nearly always spies?'

How funny, she thought. *Algy said the same thing about you.* She fought back the impulse to laugh but did allow herself a smile. 'Oh, come on,' she said. 'Who's he spying for?'

'Who knows? He could be spying for us, the British, or for the Americans, or even for the Russians. They all recruit journalists. It's the perfect cover,' was Brian's solemn reply.

'Nobody's ever tried to recruit me,' sighed Dee.

'Be glad of that. I'm warning you to watch your step. Your friend is up to something,' said Brian solemnly, unaware he was using almost the same words about Algy as Algy had used about him.

Sixteen

That weekend Lorna and Rawley decided to spend three days at Marvi, a long strip of golden beach eight miles to the north of Bombay Island.

He told her that an Indian friend of his had offered to lend him a beach house there and they drove off on Friday morning with an icebox full of beer and bags full of beach towels and bathing suits. 'Won't we need bedrolls and food?' she asked.

He shook his head. 'The house has got everything we'll need and the people in the fishing village will sell us food.'

When she'd been to Marvi before, her stay had been in a primitive bamboo-thatched shack with sand on the floor and a cold-water shower, so she was unprepared for the luxury of the house Rawley had found. It was solidly built, with whitewashed stone walls, and though the roof was still bamboo thatching, it was well tied down and very thick. The building snuggled down in a sandy hollow among a grove of coconut palms that swayed and rustled above their heads all night making wonderful midnight music to lull them to sleep.

There was nothing primitive about it: it had a proper bathroom with a flush lavatory and a shower that was heated by a gas cylinder. The refrigerator and the cooker ran on gas as well. The sitting room had a long window that opened on to the beach and the furniture was all very modern – low settees and lounging chairs upholstered in oatmeal-coloured material. On the walls were abstract paintings by Indian painters, all in brilliant, stinging colour.

Lorna was astonished by the luxury and opulence. 'Goodness!' she exclaimed. 'This has to be the grandest house for miles. Most people who come out here for the weekend camp in basha huts.'

Rawley grinned. 'My friend's only recently finished building it.'

'He must be a millionaire,' said Lorna.

'I guess he is,' admitted Rawley.

'What's his name?' she asked.

'His name's Advani and I do some flying jobs for him.'

'What sort of jobs?' she persisted.

'Oh, bringing in things he can't get in Bombay . . .' Rawley's voice trailed off.

'Liquor?' she asked.

He grinned. 'Sometimes.'

'You'll be in big trouble if you get caught,' she said doubtfully.

'I won't get caught, so don't worry,' he told her.

She believed him and they made love, then went to swim in the pounding, white-tipped surf of the Arabian Gulf, drank beer, made love again and slept with the windows wide open during a silent afternoon. Time passed without them being aware of it and, when they were hungry, an impassive-looking woman from the fishing village a mile down the beach turned up at the door with a huge basket full of freshly caught shrimps which they boiled in a pan full of sea water. They both thought they had never tasted anything so delicious.

Around midnight, when they were sitting on the terrace playing cards, two Indian men in European dress walked up the path to the house and bent in greeting with their hands folded before them. Rawley sat up from his lounging chair and recognised one of them. 'Hey, Pedro,' he said. 'How are you?'

The man called Pedro came forward into the light. He was young, with carefully combed and oiled black hair that was twisted into a quiff like Elvis Presley's. Round his neck he wore several gold chains, from one of which dangled a large crucifix.

'The fish woman told me you were here,' he said in English. 'I came to pay my respects. Do you want some brandy?'

'I don't think so. I've plenty of beer,' said Rawley. 'Anyway, your brandy is always dodgy.'

'This isn't. It's very good Spanish brandy. From the Gulf, as you know.' Pedro laughed, showing magnificent white teeth.

'No thanks, I still don't want it. Are you well? Is business good?' asked Rawley.

'I am well. My family is well. The police aren't giving me trouble. Business is good,' said Pedro. After exchanging a few more pleasantries, he and his friend melted into the darkness of the night beneath the swaying trees.

When they had gone, Lorna looked at Rawley and said, 'What was that about?'

He grinned and sat down by her chair holding her hand. 'Pedro was just paying a call on us. He's the chief smuggler round here and he works for the Advanis too. Dhows from the Gulf moor offshore and he sends out dugouts to offload the contraband. I do the same job as him but I use the plane. Sometimes I land on the sand about five miles up the coast and Pedro and his pals bring the stuff down to this beach and bury it in the sand. If you were to start digging out there now you'd hit treasure in no time at all. There's hundreds of bottles hidden away right there on the golden beach.' He laughed in open delight at the idea.

Lorna knew that liquor was continually brought into Bombay to supply the thriving bootlegging business. It was a fact of life. But, till now, she'd never given much thought to the people who did the smuggling or about the extent of their operations.

She put her hand on Rawley's cheek and said, 'I wish you'd not told me. I'm going to worry about you so much.'

'Don't. It's quite safe. Advani has the police in his pocket.

How else would Pedro walk about like that? Did you see his necklaces? A suspicious policeman would run him in just for the size of his crucifix.'

'Is liquor running the most dangerous thing you do?' she asked him.

He looked into her eyes and said, 'Do you really want to know?'

'Yes, tell me or I'll worry even more. I won't talk out of turn.'

'I'd trust you with my life,' he said solemnly, 'so listen. First of all I swear to you that I don't take part in any of the really dirty games. I don't fly little girls out to the Gulf to be forced into prostitution. I don't carry drugs. Other people do that but not me. I bring in liquor and I run guns up to the Frontier. I do two or three trips every month. I hope you realise how crazy I am about you for me to tell you all this.'

'Gun running's more dangerous than bootlegging,' she whispered.

'Not if you're careful, and I am. I land the plane on a paddy field on the mainland beyond Thana, or I go to Bangalore. The consignment's always waiting at an arranged point. It's loaded on to the plane and I take off. It's like doing a shop delivery really,' he told her.

'How can you trust the people you work with?' she asked.

'I just do. For the guns, I work with a Pathan called Mustafa Ali. He's very trustworthy and pays on the nail. If I go on doing his run for another year, I'll have enough cash salted away to go back to France to collect Tim and Paulina. Come with me and we'll all live the good life in Ireland. I'll fix up our old house. I can't imagine anything better, drinking Guinness and eating oysters, fishing and hunting, making love to you and growing old together.' His face glowed as he contemplated the prospect.

She was not to be diverted from her serious thoughts, however. 'Was your brother running guns when he had his accident?' she asked.

She knew she had hit on a sore point when his face changed and he said, 'Yes, he was, but he was running them to the Burmese border and I think his people stitched him up. Somebody got greedy or jealous. He's not sure either but he's almost certain the plane was sabotaged. I always check and double-check mine before I take off now, and I trust my mechanic Sher Singh. Remember him? He was the guy who saw us off when we left for Goa.'

'He knows what you're doing?' she asked.

'Yes, he's part of the operation. He's saving up to go to New York. He's got some relatives living there and he wants to see the Statue of Liberty.'

Lorna groaned. 'You sound like little boys playing war games.'

He kissed her and said solemnly, 'Believe me, we're deadly serious.'

She put both arms round his neck and pulled him towards her as she said, 'My father's selling the magazine. He's promised me half of the money when he does. There's people negotiating with him now. If it comes off, you and I can go to fetch your brother without waiting a year. I've been thinking a lot, making plans.'

'Any money you get must be yours,' he told her. 'Because I can't marry you, you've got to be secure on your own. I'll make my pile and you make yours and we can indulge each other.'

'But I wish I could make you stop living the way you do. I wish I could be sure that you're safe when I'm not with you,' she whispered.

'Just trust me,' he said.

In the middle of the night, she wakened and lay listening to the dry rustling of palm branches in the trees outside their open window. They were living like lotus eaters, and so the best thing to do was to enjoy life as they lived it, to savour the moment.

'I love you and I'll always love you,' she whispered to him but he did not hear her.

*   *   *

138

On Monday morning they parted at her office door. 'Where are you going?' she asked. It was the first time she'd felt disquiet since their discussion on Friday night.

'I'm going out to the airstrip to see if any work's come in. Sher Singh takes the messages,' he told her.

'Will you let me know if you're going to be away for more than a day?' she asked.

'I will,' he promised.

At eleven o'clock Dee arrived with the book reviews she'd done, but Lorna could hardly concentrate on them and only ran her eye swiftly down the typed sheets. 'That's fine,' she said shortly.

Dee looked disappointed but did not protest. 'You're very brown, Lorna,' she said. 'Have you been sunbathing?' She could not imagine Lorna grilling herself like a lamb chop as the Breach Candy wives did.

Lorna stuck out her bare arm and looked at it. It was very tanned. 'A combination of sun and sea. It always browns you faster,' she said.

'Where were you?' asked Dee. 'Goa again?'

'No, we went to Marvi, to a marvellous beach house, like something out of California,' Lorna told her.

Dee laughed. 'Lucky you. This man of yours is really making things happen, isn't he?'

Lorna's brow was furrowed as she replied almost doubtfully, 'Yes, he is.' Then she pulled herself together and asked, 'What did you do this weekend?'

'Nothing much. Sat in the garden, played with the children, took them for pony rides at the Bandstand . . . family stuff. It wasn't like last weekend when we went to Sattara to see Shivaji's fort. Did I tell you about that?'

'No. I know that fort but I've never climbed up to it. Did you go up?' Lorna was surprised because Dee did not strike her as the mountaineering type.

'Not exactly. The others climbed. I got myself carried by four coolies,' admitted Dee, and Lorna laughed.

'That's the way to do it. What's it like?'

139

'Horrible! Very scary. Humming with evil; I can't explain it. There's a sinister temple up there dedicated to Kali and the man who took us said that the Thugs used to worship there. Probably still do,' said Dee very seriously.

'Shivaji was a tough piece of work, but all the important men were at that time, weren't they? It was dog eat dog. The place seems to have worried you, though,' Lorna said.

'Yes, it did. Maybe the fort wasn't as sinister as I thought it was. Maybe I didn't see what I thought I saw. You see, about a month ago Ben and I took the kids for a trip up-country and we met some travelling magicians. They did a trick that completely bamboozled us and I've thought about it ever since.'

'Some of those magicians can do amazing things,' Lorna agreed. 'Which trick was it?'

'I asked them to do the Indian rope trick but they couldn't. Instead they made a mango seed grow into a little mango tree, right in front of our eyes!'

'I've seen that one. It's spectacular. I expect they hypnotise the people watching,' Lorna said.

'Ben and I wondered about that, but we both saw it. Could they hypnotise us both? The children were half asleep so they didn't appreciate what they were seeing but Ben's a pretty tough nut and would be hard to hypnotise,' said Dee.

'I think they could probably hypnotise a room full of people if they put their minds to it,' Lorna told her.

'Well, anyway, there was something about Shivaji's fort that really worried me. It was the effect it had on the man we went with. He seemed to relish the blood lust and treachery, but he's not normally like that. Do you know him? He's Brian Meredith, the British Council man in Bombay.'

Lorna shook her head. 'These people change so often. None of them stay around very long.'

'Brian and his wife haven't been here long, just over a year,' agreed Dee.

Just then the telephone on Lorna's desk rang and she

lifted it quickly from its cradle, saying sharply into it, '*Yes?*'

A quacking sound came from the other end and Dee turned away so she could not overhear while Lorna nodded her head several times, then burst out laughing as she said, 'That's great. I'm very happy. Be good. See you then.'

When she turned back to Dee her previous air of abstraction had disappeared and she was smiling like a child at Christmas time. 'That was Rawley,' she said. 'He's flying out tonight with a cargo of oysters for a big hotel in Calcutta. He'll be back tomorrow morning.'

'You really love him, don't you?' said Dee.

'I adore him.' The reply was completely definite.

Dee's face clouded as she remembered what Maya Bhatia had said about Lorna's lover. How true was it, she wondered? And if it was true, did Lorna know?

'Have you still got that Bhatia girl working in the office?' she asked suddenly.

Lorna looked surprised at the change of subject. 'Yes, she's still here but she comes and goes as she pleases.'

'I didn't see her when I came through,' Dee said.

'Oh she'll turn up eventually I expect. I can't get worked up about it any more. Why do you ask?' Lorna wanted to know.

'She gave me a lift home the other night and it seems that her brother – who sounds a rather unpleasant piece of work judging by anything I've heard about him – knows your friend Rawley,' Dee told her.

'What did she say?' Lorna's voice was sharp.

'Nothing much . . .'

Dee's voice trailed off but Lorna glared at her and said, 'Come on, tell me. I want to know.'

'She said he'd flown a cargo of rhesus monkeys someplace for her brother.'

'Monkeys? Is that all?'

'Oh, well! She said he also ran guns.' Dee came out with it because she couldn't bring herself to lie.

141

'Do you find that awful?' Lorna asked.

'Well, I think it could be dangerous – and I thought that if he does, it's not good if Maya's going around talking about it. Perhaps you could warn Rawley to stay away from Homi,' said Dee, who was more worried about Lorna being hurt than about the implications of gun running.

'I'll pass the message on,' said Lorna, 'and thanks for telling me. Why don't you have lunch with us tomorrow and meet Rawley properly? We'll be at Gaylord's at one o'clock.'

As Dee walked into Gaylord's restaurant next day, she saw Lorna sitting at a window table with a handsome, dark-haired man. They were leaning towards each other, totally absorbed and oblivious to what was going on around them.

Dee had a failing for handsome men and this one was very good-looking indeed, boyishly frank-faced, wide-shouldered and clean-looking, as if he'd just washed. His mouth was humorous and his eyes pleasantly quizzical. His slight Irish accent and ready laugh enhanced his appearance. He seemed like a man who could see the funny side of almost anything and she could understand why Lorna had fallen for him, especially since he carried with him the frisson of being engaged in dangerous and illicit work. He was the buccaneer type, a middle-class man who had ambitions but no pecuniary prospects at home. His type invaded England with William the Conqueror; sailed the Spanish Main with Drake; voyaged to India in search of a fortune in the days of John Company. Long ago he would have ended up commanding a native regiment for some rajah, or sailing the high seas as a privateer.

Men like him were magnets for risk-taking women, and Lorna was certainly not the sort to play safe. Dee admired her for that. The three of them soon launched into a bantering conversation and their laughter rang out in the crowded restaurant.

When they parted on the pavement, they shook hands with real enthusiasm, because they liked and were well disposed to each other. As she was being driven away by Jadhav, Dee turned in her seat to watch Lorna and Rawley walk off hand in hand. Their obvious happiness pleased her and she hoped that everything would turn out well for them, but somewhere in the back of her mind there was a little black cloud of dread. She was worried for her friend – not because of what Rawley might do but because of what fate might do to Rawley.

Seventeen

Jack Wesley was entertaining three men in his study at the Colaba bungalow. Gopalchand Advani, a grizzle-haired man in his sixties, was flanked by his two sons, Raju and Madan, sleek characters dressed in well-cut sports clothes that were obviously not the product of any Bombay tailor.

With them they had brought a bundle of papers tied up in a large cardboard file. This was laid on the coffee table beside them as they launched into general chit-chat, but all their eyes continually flicked towards the file.

After half an hour, the oldest of the trio began to touch on the subject that was on all their minds. 'It is a pity that trading conditions are so poor these days,' he said, pulling a long face. 'The time of making fortunes has gone, I'm afraid.'

Jack was used to the convolutions of dealing with Indians in business, and nodded in agreement but added, 'It depends on what trade you're in. Fortunately my magazine is still doing quite well.'

'Is the circulation up?' asked one of the sons, who spoke with a strong American accent, a legacy from his period of studying at the Harvard Business School.

'It's selling much the same number as it has always done,' said Jack.

'And what is that?'

'About eighty thousand a month,' Jack exaggerated. The true figure was not much more than fifty thousand but he gave away a lot of free copies to make the returns look better on paper.

'And your cover price is?' asked Advani senior.

'Five rupees, as it has been for several years now,' was Jack's reply. He suspected that the Advanis were as well versed about the magazine's details as he was himself. That file probably contained exact up-to-date figures.

'And the advertising revenue is?' was the next question.

Jack reached into his desk drawer and pulled out a sheaf of papers, which he leafed through as if searching for something before he said, 'Very healthy. Our advertisers are faithful, I'm happy to say. Each issue earns about eight hundred thousand rupees.' This was also an exaggeration.

The three men facing him nodded together and the father gave an oily smile. 'So after deducting rent, printing costs and staff wages, it is all profit, yes?'

Jack smiled. 'I'm glad to say it is.'

'It is a pity that government regulations make it so difficult for you to send money out of India,' Mr Advani sighed.

Jack, who had been illegally buying currency on the black market for ten years, shifted on his seat. 'Yes, it is difficult, but my wife and I are happy to live here,' he lied.

'We were led to believe that you are going back to England soon,' said Mr Advani, looking surprised.

'England? I'm afraid the climate there does not suit us after living so long out here. We're thinking of retiring to Portugal,' said Jack airily. In fact he had a house there which was bought and paid for. What he needed from the sale of the magazine was enough money to provide for Lorna and give him and Ella an income for the rest of their lives.

'You are fortunate,' said Mr Advani and his sons sighed in agreement, as if regretting their failure to own property abroad. The youngest son let his eyes rest on the folder that lay in front of his father.

Jack wanted to fidget, to get up and stride about the room, because he was impatient to know where this was leading. After weeks of hinting, had they come to make a definite offer for his magazine or not? He knew that he had to control himself, to sit still and wait for them to come to the point, however long that took.

145

It came at last. Old man Advani shook his head and reached for the folder at the same time. 'We would like to have bought your magazine but we are afraid that this new publication might take away its readers and its advertisers.'

From the top of his papers he pulled out a sheet and handed it to Jack who said in bewilderment, 'What new publication?'

'It's written down there. *Bombay's Social Register*. Haven't you heard about it? A local consortium is launching a new title. They've raised a lot of money and they're out to take over the market. The people who advertise with you have been approached and offered cut-price terms to switch their ads to the new magazine.' In unison the Advanis shook their heads in sorrow.

'There's often rumours like that,' said Jack carelessly. 'They never come to anything.'

'This one will. They're planning their first issue for February. They have premises and an editor, everything. As well as promises from the advertisers. When January comes, you'll find none of them will commit to continuing with you.'

Jack tried desperately to think of something to say but only came up with, 'Who's putting up the money for this new magazine?'

'The Bhatia family, with the backing of several other investors. They've arranged for the printing to be done by *The Times of India*, and one of the Bhatia daughters is to edit it. I understand it was your daughter who trained her and she's been making lists of all your advertisers while she's been in your office.'

'Lorna trained her?' It was only a croak.

'Yes, the Bhatia girl has been working for you and supervising the editing of the *Tatler* when your daughter is out of the office, which she has been a lot recently. Last week she was away from Friday till Monday and the Bhatia girl was left in charge. She is very talented, was educated in England and has wonderful social connections, I believe,' said one of the brothers.

'I've heard nothing about her or her magazine,' said Jack.

'They've been keeping their plans very quiet. It was only by good luck that we managed to hear about it before we committed ourselves to buying the *Tatler*. The Bhatias want to spring it on the public at the last minute with much publicity – cinema ads, billboards, newspaper advertisements. It'll be spectacular,' said Mr Advani with a certain relish that warned Jack that he himself probably had a finger in that particular pie.

'And I take it that because of this new magazine you no longer want to invest in mine,' said Jack bravely.

The three of them looked at each other. The youngest and slyest said, 'We might still buy, but at a newly negotiated price, of course.'

'How much do you have in mind?'

'Eight hundred thousand rupees.' It was stated flatly.

'I'm expecting five times that much,' said Jack. He knew that the Advanis were only floating a figure so that bargaining could start, but, even if they trebled their offer, which was unlikely, he would still be left short. He had hoped to sell the magazine for the equivalent of £90,000 of capital, which represented £30,000 for Lorna and £60,000 for himself and Ella.

Currency bought on the black market cost twice as much as its face value. To be able to export £90,000 you had to have the equivalent £180,000 in rupees at a rate of thirteen and a half rupees to the pound. He had worked out that he needed nearly two and a half million rupees for the magazine, a very far cry from the Advani offer. His expression showed his consternation.

Mr Advani stood up. 'The situation is different now, isn't it? If you don't accept our offer, it's unlikely that you'll be able to sell for half our price in three months' time. If the Bhatia magazine captures the market, the *Tatler* will be finished. All you'll have to sell is the office furniture and your butterfly collection.'

The sons shook their heads in silent agreement and Jack groaned. 'But what about my daughter?'

The brother called Madan raised an eyebrow. 'But Miss Wesley will be marrying soon, surely?'

'I expect she will in time, but she has no plans at the moment,' said Jack, who barely noticed whether Lorna was in the house or not.

'But she has plans. She and an Englishman called Fitzgerald were at my beach house recently and they are very much involved with each other,' was the reply.

Jack's blank expression showed clearly that he had no idea who Fitzgerald was. 'I don't know anything about that,' he said.

Madan Advani smiled. 'Really? Well, Fitzgerald's not exactly the sort of man I'd wish my daughter to marry. He's a pilot with his own plane – a Piper Cherokee. He flies *consignments* in and out.'

It was patently obvious what he meant and Jack did not miss the inference. He was hardly able to keep his mind on what they were saying as they made their farewells. When their car vanished from the drive he sat silent at his desk for a good five minutes before he was able to get up and pour himself a stiff drink.

After he'd downed it, he called for his own car and was driven to the office. Lorna was surprised to see him because he'd given up attending their place of business some time ago.

'Is something wrong?' she asked anxiously because his face was drawn and his lips trembling as he walked into her office. He leaned against the first case of butterflies and asked, 'Do we have a girl called Bhatia working for us?'

'Yes. She's been here for several weeks. She's a rather unpleasant Parsee girl,' Lorna said.

'Is she here now?'

'I don't know. I'll ask.' Lorna opened her office door and called for Bubbles, who came running. 'Is Maya Bhatia in the office?' Lorna asked her.

Bubbles shook her head. 'No, she called in this morning

and said she's sick again. Last week she was at the dentist and today she's sick!'

Lorna closed the door and said to her father, 'You heard that. She's not here. Why do you want to see her?'

'I don't. I just wanted to know why you've been training a girl who's going to start up a magazine that'll put us out of business.'

'Training her? Of course I haven't. She's a troublemaker and I was going to fire her soon. How can she start a magazine? She doesn't know the first thing about it,' protested Lorna.

Jack groaned. 'Apparently she's been learning all she can, especially when you've been out of the office. The Advanis came to see me today and cut their offer for the *Tatler* by four-fifths. They said if I don't accept it, I might end up with nothing because a group of investors are launching another magazine with this Bhatia girl as its editor.'

Lorna's face showed that this news was as big a bombshell to her as it was to her father. 'I can hardly believe it. The people who want to buy from us told you that? Is their name Advani? You never told me that before.'

'Yes, it's Gopalchand Advani and his two slimy sons. One of the sons said you'd been in his beach house last weekend with a man – a smuggler. He said you've been out of the office a lot recently and that Bhatia girl's been doing the editing in your absence. What's happening? Everything's going wrong at once.'

Lorna flushed. 'I've only been away from the office for three or four days at the most, and I didn't leave that girl in charge. Bubbles is my deputy. I'll ask her what happened.'

Again Bubbles was summoned. She stood with her back to the door as Lorna questioned her. 'On the days I was away, who sat in this office?'

A red tide rose in the other girl's cheeks. 'That Bhatia girl came in here last time and locked the door. There was nothing I could do. She took over your work, and she said you'd told her to do it. I was very hurt.'

Lorna and Jack looked at each other. Both of them knew that it was unlikely Maya Bhatia would ever show her face in the office again. Her current illness was only an excuse. Locked in Lorna's office, she'd had ample opportunity to scour the files and the list of their chief advertisers. 'So she got you out of the way, and now she's going to ruin us,' said Mr Wesley to his daughter.

'I think they're bluffing,' she said, after she'd waved Bubbles away.

'Perhaps, but not entirely. If I don't accept their offer, I suspect they'll lend their weight to this other magazine. We haven't the capital to sustain a circulation war. I've exported all my available money – and I imagine they know that as well. You can't keep secrets from Sindhis. Who was this man you went away with? Advani took a lot of pleasure in telling me you stayed in his beach house.'

'He's a friend,' said Lorna stonily.

'Advani said he's a smuggler. Perhaps he was in this plot too, getting you out of the office while that girl snooped about,' suggested her father.

She turned away from him and walked to the window, staring down into the crowded street outside. *Surely not, surely not*, she thought over and over again.

When her father dragged himself home, she left the office, locking the door of her inner sanctum behind her, and ran downstairs to find a taxi because her destination was too far for any gharry. 'Santa Cruz, and hurry,' she told the driver.

Rawley's plane was drawn up on the tarmac and she ran past it to the hangar where the tall mechanic was wiping tools with an oily rag and swaying to ear-piercing sitar and drum music coming from a tiny transistor radio.

She had to pluck at his sleeve before he noticed her. 'Where is Rawley Fitzgerald?' she asked.

He smiled. 'He only flew in an hour ago. He said he was going to his house to bathe and sleep.'

It struck her then that she had no idea where Rawley lived. 'Where is his house?' she demanded and Sher Singh looked slightly surprised. She sensed that he was working out whether he should tell her, so she pleaded, 'I must see him. It is most important.'

He decided in her favour. 'Number twenty-seven, Seventh Avenue, Parel. He rents rooms from people called Gonsalves. Mr Gonsalves works in Air Traffic Control.'

Thanking him, she ran back to the waiting taxi and gasped out the address, which was not too far away.

The two-storey house was painted sherbet pink and stood in its own garden behind a concrete wall and a closed wrought iron gate. On the roof terrace she could see a line of gaily waving laundry, mostly shirts and underwear. The gate was unlocked and she pushed it open. A red path of trodden earth led to the front door.

A little servant boy in khaki shorts and a loose white shirt answered her knock. In Hindi she asked him to fetch the lady of the house. The woman who came in response to this summons was plump, middle-aged and motherly with a sweet, chubby face and strands of grey in her lustrous dark hair. She was wearing a cheap daytime sari but there were many valuable golden bangles decorating both her arms.

'Are you Mrs Gonsalves?' Lorna asked.

'Yes,' said the woman in a surprised tone.

'My name is Lorna Wesley and I've come to see Rawley Fitzgerald.'

'Raw-ley is sleeping,' said the woman, pausing between the two syllables of his name.

'Please. I must speak to him,' Lorna begged and this time her urgency met with success.

'Raw-ley has talked about his Lor-na. Please come in,' said Mrs Gonsalves, holding open the door.

The big room that took up most of the ground floor was sparsely furnished with chairs and a sofa upholstered in red plastic. On the walls were religious pictures of rose-decorated crucifixes. Lorna was asked to sit down while the small boy was sent upstairs to wake Rawley.

Very soon Rawley came stumbling in. He was wearing a

sweatshirt and a brightly coloured South Indian lunghi was knotted round his waist. His hair was uncombed and standing on end. When he saw Lorna his jaw dropped in surprise, but he ran towards her. 'What's wrong, darling?' he asked.

She stood up, very stiff, and did not touch him. 'I must speak to you. Is there anywhere private we can go?'

He looked at Mrs Gonsalves who said, 'Take your lady on to the verandah. The swing seat is out there.' It was obvious that she would not think it proper for him to take Lorna upstairs.

They walked side by side across the room and through an open door at the back on to a covered verandah. In the middle of it, staring out into a garden full of red hibiscus and banana trees, was a green, shaded swing seat for two people. They sat gingerly down in it and still did not touch each other.

Lorna stared ahead while she said, 'Did you know that your friends the Advanis were negotiating to buy my father's magazine?'

'No,' was his firm reply. 'All I know about them is that they buy the liquor I bring in for Pedro. I also do some legitimate commercial runs for them from time to time, carrying car parts and things like that.'

'My father thinks that they arranged with you for me to be absent from the office during the time we were at Marvi. Did you?' Her voice was perfectly controlled.

He sounded rattled. 'Why should I do that?'

'Because when I was away, a girl called Maya Bhatia got into my office and raided the files. The Advanis have now greatly lowered their offer for the *Tatler* and my father may not be able to sell it at all. He'll be ruined.' This time her voice cracked.

'Christ, Lorna, I wouldn't do a thing like that to you. I didn't know anything about your father's deal being with the Advanis. I only ever meet one of the sons and I've never discussed you or the magazine with him – not ever.'

'They knew I was in the beach house and they knew who I was with. They told my father,' she informed him.

'They'd get that from Pedro or the village people. You know how curious they are. They find out everything,' he said. She could not deny that was true.

When she looked at him her eyes were full of tears. 'You didn't arrange for me to be away from the office, then?' she asked.

He leant towards her and took her hand. 'I swear to you I didn't – but I can understand why your father thought I might. They'd also tell him I smuggle stuff sometimes. To him that would mean that I'm a criminal type. But I don't know anything about their intention to buy your magazine. Tell your father they're probably only twisting the screw on him. The fact they're trying it on shows they really want the *Tatler*. If they didn't, they'd not waste time going to see him and pouring poison into his ear, like Hamlet's stepfather did to his father. If you like I'll go to see him myself.'

'Oh, Rawley,' she said. 'That won't be necessary. I just had to ask you. I just had to be sure.'

'Then be sure,' he told her with absolute conviction, putting his arm round her. 'I swear to you I didn't.' Their heads were so close together it was inevitable that they would kiss.

Eighteen

R onnie Weston was gradually losing his grip. Smoking dope-laden cigarettes from morning till night, he quickly drifted out of reality, through episodes of exhilarated optimism to deepest paranoia which usually had him in thrall by mid-afternoon. That was the time he called up taxis and took himself and his police guard off to Walkeshwar Road to pour out his worries to Dee Carmichael.

The trouble was that she had lost interest in him. As far as she was concerned, he'd become nothing more than a responsibility. Only if she could dig up some juicy facts about the London end of the operation would her newspaper think of running the story. 'Get some names and addresses out of him or else give the story up,' ran the latest cable she'd received.

She was not disappointed, because she had lost interest in the Weston story. His coy reticence and continually mulled-over problems had become a nuisance as far as she was concerned.

She wanted to forget about him and move on to the next project, which promised to be very exciting for news had just broken that Pope Paul VI was to visit Bombay that winter and would conduct Mass before thousands of people on the Maidan. It would be the first time ever that a pope had visited India, where there was a large Roman Catholic population, especially in Bombay.

The press from all over the world would be following the story, and Dee, as a resident of the city, was in a position of advantage. Her pregnancy, if she was correct in thinking herself pregnant, which as every day went by seemed more certain, would not be so far advanced as to hinder her pursuit of the Pope.

Besides, Ben's career was soaring. Since returning to India, he'd built up the Indian branch of his engineering company, Macintosh Foulis, till it was challenging, and taking contracts from, the biggest international concerns. From his old Indian company, two experienced planners, two project managers, and, most valuable of all, a brilliant Brahmin accountant called Mr Rangan, had come with him. Mr Rangan was not only scrupulously honest but utterly devoted to Ben. Inside the office safe he kept a little shrine dedicated to Ben with his photograph on a tiny plinth. Incense was burned and offerings of sweetmeats and marigolds were made to it from time to time.

Due to good teamwork and immense enthusiasm Ben's company swept all before it. Every contract was completed well within time and with marked success and significant profit, so more customers were always knocking at the door. Within the last two years, Macintosh Foulis had built two rayon manufacturing plants, erected a factory for photographic print making, a pharmaceutical plant, and a soap powder manufacturing unit, as well as successfully bidding for refinery contracts.

Recently Ben heard that an influential London businessman, Lord Affleck, was coming out to Bombay to investigate the mismanagement of a big Indian contract in which his construction company, a rival of Macintosh Foulis, had been involved.

'He's sent me a cable saying he's been told I was the most effective construction engineer in India and if he comes out here he wants to pick my brains about his contract,' Ben excitedly told Dee.

'If he arrives we'll invite him to dinner and see what he's like,' she said. A great deal of Ben's business was contracted around their dining table and she enjoyed the stimulus of the conversations. Ben relied on her opinion about the people with whom he came into contact in business.

She was sitting in her garden planning a dinner party with a menu with which to impress the business tycoon from London, if he ever did arrive, when Weston came reeling through the garden gate. He was weeping and maudlin.

'I've had enough!' he exclaimed, throwing himself down in a chair. 'I really am going to do myself in this time.'

She pulled her dark glasses down on her nose and stared at him over the top of the frames. He would have made more impact if he hadn't threatened the same thing before.

'Really? What's brought it on this time?' she asked.

'It's living in that bloody hotel, being watched all the time. It's not being able to contact anybody at home. It's because I've a sentence in an Indian jail hanging over my head,' he said brokenly. Under his arm he was carrying a ragged-looking brown paper parcel which he brandished at her, saying, 'I've brought all my papers. I want to burn them. Can I do it in your garden? There's no place I can do it in the hotel.'

She looked at his papers with a jaundiced eye. It was obvious that he wanted her to ask what was in them so that he could refuse to tell her. *Quite frankly*, she thought, *I don't care what you've got there. I bet it's all rubbish anyway.*

She rose to her feet and said, 'OK, I'll send Babu down with a charcoal sigri and you can burn them on it.'

He looked taken aback. This was not what he'd expected. She stalked past him and shouted up the stairs towards the kitchen door where the servants sat taking their ease in the afternoon sun. 'Babu,' she called, 'bring down a sigri so Mr Weston can have a bonfire.'

The sigri was a little iron tub full of burning charcoal that was kept in the kitchen and very quickly Babu and Prakash arrived in the garden carrying it between them by a long stick passed through the two handles in its top. Giggling at the unusual request, they laid it down on the concrete slabs of the sitting-out area and a drift of smoke rose from its red heart.

Dee turned towards Weston and said, 'Right, burn away then. Try not to make a mess. Let me know when you've finished.' Ushering the servants before her, she left him to it. His expression told only too clearly that he'd hoped at least for a dramatic little scene with her attempting to talk him out of suicide – certainly not this.

After about twenty minutes he appeared in the upstairs sitting room with small soot smudges spotting his face and the front of his white shirt. 'I've done it. I've burned everything,' he announced.

She did not ask what had gone up in smoke. 'Too bad,' she said in an even tone. 'Won't you need any of it?'

'I couldn't risk leaving anything behind,' he said dramatically.

'Then it was best to get rid of them,' she agreed.

He stuck out his hand and said in a deflated tone, 'It's goodbye, then. You'll not be seeing me again. I've left instructions with Mr Grace.'

She shook his hand. 'Make sure you take enough of whatever it is you're planning to take. You don't want to be left a vegetable,' she callously advised. She was sure that he'd no intention of killing himself.

When Ben came home, she told him, 'Ronnie was burning papers in the garden this afternoon. He's threatening to do away with himself again.'

Ben was as unimpressed as she had been. 'He's not the self-sacrificing sort,' he said. The news he'd brought was much more exciting. 'It's definite that Lord Affleck is coming out here. He sent me a cable at the office today to say he'll be in Bombay next week staying in the Taj and he hopes that we can meet.'

She was pleased because it was flattering for Ben to be sought after for advice by a man of such consequence. She'd play her part and back him up. 'I'll tell Alex and Babu to put on an extra good show because we're having a lord to dinner,' she laughed.

In spite of her irritation at Ronnie's histrionics, when she

157

was driving into the city to call in at the *Tatler* office two days later, she told Jadhav to stop at the Ritz. It was no surprise to find the would-be suicide sitting in the front hall, staring at the door. When he saw her, he only nodded as if he'd been expecting her to call.

She walked across the marble floor and sat on a chair facing him. 'So you're still with us?' she asked.

He was completely unabashed, and some of his original cockiness and irritating air of superiority had returned. 'Yeah, something good's happened,' he said loftily.

'Really? Have you got a date for your hearing?' she asked.

'Yeah, but it's not that. It's something better.'

She glanced at the burning cigarette between his fingers and noted that it was an ordinary one, not a reefer, so he probably knew what he was saying. 'That's good,' she said idly, unprepared to coax information out of him.

Perversely, he was eager to share the news and went on, 'The Customs men picked up another carrier yesterday. Mr Grace thinks he'll be sent here tonight.' His tone was jubilant so there was more to this than he was telling her.

'Somebody you know?' she asked.

'Yeah, somebody I've heard about. He's from the same organisation,' he said, rubbing the end of his cigarette into a full ashtray. 'He's a big fish too. He won't take to being messed about. If you ask me, they'll make sure to get him out and there's a good chance I can make him take me with him.'

'Don't count on it,' she warned.

Intrigued in spite of herself by what she'd heard, instead of going on to the *Tatler*, she went to the WWN office and climbed the stairs to Algy's eyrie. He was there with Ernest and, as usual, their ticker tape was spewing out paper.

Accepting the offer of a bottle of Coca-Cola, she sat down and said, 'I've been to see Ronnie Weston in the Ritz and he tells me another European's been picked up for gold smuggling. Do you know anything about it? My office usually sends me a cable about things like that but I haven't heard a word.'

Her concern at not hearing from London was partly based on the fear that the *Sun* had dispensed with her services. They were under no obligation to give her notice and, though she didn't need the money, she'd miss the interest and excitement of being on the fringes of the press world. Her spasmodic transformations back into a newspaper reporter gave her a life of her own, distinct from her role as wife and mother.

Algy looked at her with a mild expression. 'They wouldn't cable you about this guy because they won't have heard about him. He's an American passport holder. Ernest got the story last night and we sent it to New York.'

Of course, she thought, *news agencies send their information to outlets that will be interested in them. There's no reason to cable London with details of an American smuggler.*

'Weston knows him, though. He's from the same group or syndicate, or whatever you call a collection of smugglers,' she said.

Algy and Ernest looked at each other. 'What did he say?' they asked in unison.

'He said he knew of him and that he's a really big wheel in the organisation. So big that he seems to think this guy'll get away and he might take Ronnie with him.'

'He's dreaming,' said Algy shortly. 'The new one's up in court today. If Grace gets his case deferred he'll be lodged in the Ritz as well, but that's as far as he's going.'

'I wish you could see the change in Ronnie Weston. Two days ago he was in my garden threatening to commit suicide and burning papers, and today he's bouncing with joy,' she told them.

'He's a nut,' said Algy. 'I'll let you read the story we sent to the States yesterday about this new one.' He passed a sheet of flimsy copy paper across his desk and she read the short bulletin it contained.

Enrico Santos, 29, of 1123 Twelfth Street, New York City, was picked up by Bombay Customs tonight for attempting to smuggle in ten kilos of gold. Santos was taken into custody and will appear in court tomorrow.

She read it twice and then asked a question. 'Ten kilos?'

Ernest spoke up. 'Not on him. He had it in the false bottom of his suitcase.'

She looked at the paper again. 'Enrico Santos?'

'He's a Puerto Rican, a real mobster,' said Ernest.

'Was he on an American plane?' she asked.

'No, he travelled Air India from London like your friend did,' was Algy's reply.

'Do you think he could be part of the same gang?' she asked.

'I've no idea. It really doesn't matter, does it?' Algy told her.

'I don't suppose it does. It's only that I'm intrigued by the way Weston's reacting. It's as if he's won the Irish Sweepstake,' she said and the men laughed.

'Will you follow this story up?' she asked Algy, remembering how dismissive he'd been about Weston.

'I don't think so. He was carrying a bit less gold than the other one, and even if he's a bigger wheel, in the end it's just another smuggling story. We'll send back details of any sentence he gets and that'll be that,' was his reply.

When she left their office, she walked across the street to Lorna's office and found her friend looking beautiful and starry-eyed.

'You're blooming. Love obviously agrees with you,' Dee said.

'Am I? It's just that Rawley's such a gorgeous man. I can't find one single thing wrong with him. We're driving up to Poona at the weekend to see a friend of his who lives there. I took my courage in both hands the other day and took him home to meet the parents. They liked him!'

'Of course they did. He's charming,' said Dee.

'They don't know he's married, of course, but they don't need to,' Lorna told her.

'Did you tell them what he does for a living?' was Dee's next question.

'Not really. Just that he has his own plane and ships things for people. I suspect my father knows about the liquor smuggling though because he dropped a couple of hints about looking for the odd bottle of gin.'

Lorna's eyes were dancing. She was resolutely opposed to seeing any obstacles in the path of love. Her sheer determination would win through.

'What have you been doing with yourself?' she asked Dee.

'Nothing much. My husband's very excited because a big wheel in the engineering world is coming out next week from London and has asked to see him,' she told Lorna.

'What does that mean? That he might be offered another job?' Lorna asked.

'No, I don't think so but it does mean that Ben's reputation is getting back to Britain. Maybe one day he'll be a big wheel himself. He's very pleased and I'm delighted for him,' Dee told her.

Lorna sighed. 'Even women who are quite capable of making their own way in the world have to accept second place for their careers when they get married, don't they?'

Dee frowned. 'Yes, I suppose that's true. But you would for Rawley, wouldn't you?'

'I suppose I would but I'd prefer it if we were equals. He's not the sort to insist on me always being at home to serve his dinner though. I'm going to ask him to teach me to fly so I can do the same job as he does when the magazine's sold,' Lorna replied.

Dee laughed. 'I can see you doing it, too! What news of the sale? Is it coming along?'

Lorna told her about Maya Bhatia's involvement with the new consortium wanting to start a rival for the *Tatler* and Dee listened, open-mouthed. When Lorna finished, she said,

'I wouldn't worry about Maya if I were you. She's all hot air. The wedding with our friend Dadi is almost finalised now. You know how long these things take. Dadi thinks it'll take place in February if everything goes through. Even Maya can't start a new magazine and get married as well. Anyway, she's not half as clever as she thinks. She has an account with the Strand bookshop and the man who owns it tells me that she buys all the latest highbrow books – philosophy and stuff like that – but never reads them properly, if at all. When he asks her to tell him what's in them, she changes the subject. If it comes to actually bringing out a magazine, she'll wriggle out of it somehow.'

Lorna nodded, 'That's what Bubbles and I have decided too. I'm a lot more optimistic now and so's my father. He thinks the Advanis were just trying to scare him into accepting less money. He won't get as much as he originally hoped but that doesn't matter any longer. I've told him I just want *out*. Rawley's going to take me to Ireland to see his family house. He loves it and wants me to love it too.'

'Won't his wife be there?' Dee asked.

Lorna shook her head. 'Apparently she never goes near it. Her own family live on the other side of the country and Rawley's house is in very bad condition. He's saving up to restore it and then he and his brother will leave France and share it – and so will I.'

'I hope it happens for you soon,' said Dee.

'I'm sorry I don't have any work for you today,' said Lorna. 'But I wonder if you'll stay for a short while and help me with something.'

'Yes, I'm not in any particular hurry. I just came for a chat,' Dee told her.

Lorna opened her desk drawer and brought out a big iron key with which she indicated a cupboard door set in the wall on the other side of the room. 'Help me sort out my great-grandfather's stuff. It's in that cupboard over there and my father says I can have anything I want and throw the rest away. I don't just want to throw out the trunks without knowing what's in them first though.'

'I love sorting out old rubbish,' said Dee. 'Let's get started.'

There were two dome-topped, iron-bound trunks in the cupboard. They still bore the labels that had been stuck on them almost a hundred years ago when they were first shipped out from England. The keys were in the locks and they turned smoothly.

'What do you think is inside?' Dee asked excitedly as they prepared to lift the first lid.

'I don't know. My father says his father and his grandfather were great collectors. All those butterflies in the glass cases outside were caught and mounted by them, but I don't know what else interested them. Father says his father used to check on these things regularly, but since he died Father hasn't looked and he says he doesn't want the stuff, whatever it is.'

She was struggling to lift the heavy lid as she spoke. When Dee lent a hand, they managed to throw it back.

A layer of printed cotton cloth lay on top and when that was lifted a collection of small carved statues was revealed, each one nesting like a baby in an old stitched quilt. Dee lifted a figurine out and held it gently. It was a five-inch-tall bronze dancing girl with emerald-coloured eyes. The movement of her body was so fluid that she seemed almost alive and about to break into dance.

'Isn't she lovely?' Dee sighed.

Lorna said nothing because she was busy lifting out more figures of dancing girls, gods, noble carved heads, and a few animals, mostly snakes or Brahmin bulls. There were also two Chinese horses made of pottery. Some of the Indian carvings were made of metal or stone, but there were others of ivory and soapstone as well as translucent quartz.

'There's dozens of them,' said Lorna. 'Keep that one, Dee, if you like it. I have plenty more.'

She swayed back on her heels and wiped her forehead

with the back of her hand. 'Gosh, I feel funny. My head's swimming,' she gasped.

Dee pulled her friend to her feet, saying, 'Come back into the office and sit down. You've gone very white.'

When Lorna was settled in her chair, Dee soaked her handkerchief in the earthenware water cooler and laid the cloth on the other girl's brow. Her face was worried as she said, 'You nearly fainted, you know. Does that sort of thing happen to you often?'

Lorna sat forward to lay her cheek on the top of her desk and said faintly, 'No, never, but I've a funny feeling that I know why. I think I'm pregnant. My breasts hurt and I've vomited two mornings running.'

Dee remembered their previous conversation about having children and her face was solemn as she asked, 'Are you going to do anything about it?'

Lorna's head was lifted and her blue eyes were dancing. 'Remember what you told me about suddenly wanting a child? Well, that's happened to me too. I want this baby. I don't care if it's a bastard. It's Rawley's and mine and I want it.'

'Does he know?' Dee asked.

'No. I haven't said anything because I'm not really sure yet. I might tell him when we go to Poona.' Then she sighed and put her head down on the desk again.

'Oh Lorna, I told you to be careful,' said Dee anxiously.

'I've abandoned being careful for ever. From now on I'm going to live dangerously,' was the defiant reply.

Dee looked distractedly around the room, walked across to the cupboard and closed the open trunk before locking the cupboard door again and taking the key back to Lorna. 'Let me take you home in my car. You should lie down,' she said.

The answer was a firm negative. 'No. No, I'll stretch out on the floor here. That's always very relaxing. Rawley's picking me up for lunch at half-past one and I'll be fine by then. I'm awfully sleepy suddenly and I can have a quick nap if I lie down now.' She climbed out of the chair, went down on to her knees and then arranged herself elegantly on a cotton mat behind the desk.

'Off you go and let me sleep. Don't forget to take that figurine I gave you,' she said firmly.

'I can't take it,' Dee said. 'It's probably valuable.'

'Don't be silly. If it was valuable my grandfather would have sold it years ago. Father says that these two trunks are only full of rubbish, just old bits and pieces, that the old man thought unimportant. He's given them all to me so please accept my present, don't be churlish.'

Faced with that attitude, Dee could only accept graciously, and while Jadhav was driving her home she sat with the figure resting in her cupped hands, stroking the delicate planes of its dancing body and admiring the flash of green from the roguish eyes. It was really lovely, a masterpiece of artistry.

Nineteen

A dark blue police van with metal mesh over all the windows and two armed guards hanging on at the back step clanged through the evening rush-hour roads from Byculla to the centre of Bombay, and stopped in the parking area before the Ritz Hotel. A crowd of street beggars – three boys and two girls, a haggard woman with a sick-looking baby, and a legless man on a trolley – clustered round the van, curious to see who was going to emerge from it.

One of the armed policemen swung open the door and shouted inside in two languages, 'Come on, hurry up! Jilde, jilde!'

Enrico Santos, a slim young man with a mop of curly black hair, wearing denim trousers, a cotton sweatshirt and a black satin zippered jacket, casually stood up from an interior bench and strolled towards the door.

'Jilde!' said the policeman again, brandishing his rifle nervously.

'Keep your hair on,' said the prisoner. 'I'll come at my own speed.'

Arrogant and defiant, he jumped down from the van step, stretched his arms high above his head and yawned, showing a pink tongue and an impressive set of white teeth. Staring with distaste at the beggars, who drew back from him as if they were well aware there was no point begging from this character, he swaggered across the strip of pavement to the double glass doors of the hotel, which were swung back at his approach. He entered with the second armed policeman following him, rifle at the ready.

166

Before he disappeared, he turned and waved at his other police escort and the man driving the van. 'Byee, boys!' he called mockingly.

There were several people waiting inside the hotel. Ronnie Weston was installed in his usual chair in the hall. He'd been there for hours, scared to leave in case he missed the moment of arrival. When Santos stepped into the lobby, he jumped to his feet and ran forward, crying out, 'Rico! Great to see you! Come and sit down. I know the guys here and they'll look after you well.'

The new arrival stopped and stared at Ronnie from the top of his head to the tip of his toes. 'You know me? You a friend of mine?' he asked. His accent was pure New York, as heard in movies about gangsters, and his attitude told the same tale.

'We know the same people. I work for them too,' said Ronnie, taken aback.

'That don't give you no reason for bugging me,' was the reply and Enrico shouldered him out of the way as he headed for the reception desk. 'Gimme the key,' he snapped to the desk clerk. 'And don't let no visitors come to my room without ringing me on the phone first.'

Ronnie sat down again, looking around to see if anyone had seen Enrico giving him the brush-off. There were quite a few other people in the foyer but none of them appeared to be paying any attention to him, and he relaxed a little, managing to light a cigarette before he gathered enough confidence to get up and go back to his own room.

There *were* eyes watching, however. Sitting motionless behind a potted palm in a dim corner was Ernest Nilsen, and in the adjacent verandah restaurant, where he had a position of advantage, able to see without being seen, sat Oliver Grace. He was sharing a table with an elegant Indian woman wearing a magnificent silk sari of deepest purple, shot through with green. Though she was no longer young, her beauty was of a classical Indian type with pale cream-coloured skin and elegantly arching eyebrows over flashing eyes that were skilfully outlined in kohl. They were drinking tea and seemed to be totally unaware of what was happening in the foyer.

About ten minutes after Santos disappeared, Nilsen rose to his feet and wandered over to the desk. He was wearing a white suit that was crumpled and shabby-looking and he looked deathly tired. The concierge knew him and leaned on the desktop to listen to his whispered question. A bank note was surreptitiously passed over and Ernest was told Enrico Santos's room number. Very casually, he wandered to the lift and was whisked away out of sight.

Twenty minutes passed before he came down again and headed for the street. Not long after he left, Oliver Grace and his companion wiped their lips with folded linen napkins, stood up and graciously exchanged farewells. He escorted her to the front door and bowed over her hand, saying, 'Goodbye again, Mrs Advani. It was very kind of you to take tea with me today.'

She smiled beneficently. Though no longer young, she was very beautiful and cool-looking. 'It was most enjoyable, Mr Grace. I'll tell my husband that you send him your good wishes,' she told him. Her English was impeccable with only a hint of a lilting Indian accent. Then she climbed into the long white Cadillac that waited, with a servant holding open its back door, at the hotel entrance.

Grace did not leave, but went back inside and announced himself at the desk as a caller on Mr Santos. Like Ernest, he was told the room number; he then entered the lift and disappeared upstairs.

Darkness had fallen before he emerged from the hotel and whistled up his waiting car. This last departure was noted by a man with a beard who was sitting in the driver's seat of an Ambassador car drawn up in a patch of light cast by a flickering street lamp on the other side of the road. When Grace had been driven away, Brian Meredith turned the ignition key in his car and with much relief started on his way home.

Before dinner time Ronnie Weston walked up the hotel

stairs and looked along each corridor until he spotted a policeman squatting on his heels by the door of Room 240. He hurried along to it and knocked. The door was opened by Santos, who scowled and said in a hostile questioning tone, 'Yeah?'

'I thought I could be a help to you. I've been here for nearly a month and I know my way around.'

'Yeah?' Still hostile.

'Let me in. We should talk.' Ronnie's voice was pleading.

Santos was obviously debating with himself whether to bang the door closed or not. Suddenly he relented, stood back and let the other man enter.

When the door was closed, Ronnie said, 'Like I said, I know my way around here. Have you been able to contact London yet?'

'Why d'you want to know?' Santos fixed his eyes on Ronnie. They were very dark brown with translucent whites and had a strange power of transmitting menace.

Ronnie shivered a little, but pulled himself together before saying, 'Just interested. When did you leave London?'

'Two days ago.'

'How was it?'

'How was *what*?'

'London. How was London? I miss it.' Ronnie was floundering now.

'Like it always is. A shitheap.'

'You prefer New York?'

'Who wouldn't?'

Ronnie wasn't prepared to argue the point. 'Did you have a good flight?' was his next effort at making conversation.

Santos stared hard before he snapped, 'You got any other half-assed thing you want to say? Get to the point.'

'I want to know if London's going to do anything about you.' Ronnie sounded desperate.

'They know what's happened, if that's what you mean,' was the reply.

169

'Who told them?'

'My contact, I guess,' said Santos as he strolled across his room and poured a measure of whisky into a glass from a bottle of Johnnie Walker.

Ronnie's eyes widened slightly when he saw it. 'Where'd you get the whisky?' he asked.

'You can get anything if you're prepared to pay,' said the other man, sipping his drink and pointedly not offering any to Ronnie. 'And what can you do to help me?' he continued sarcastically.

Ronnie floundered a little but managed to come out with, 'I can show you around, tell you where to buy reefers, put you in touch with a lawyer, that sort of thing.'

'Gee!' said Santos, pouring himself out a second measure before he went on, 'I already got myself a lawyer but I don't think I'm going to need him. I'm getting out.'

'Huh,' snorted Ronnie. 'That's what I thought too when I first landed here. That's what they promised me, but it hasn't happened. Don't count on it.'

Santos shrugged as if Ronnie's affairs bore no comparison to his. 'I'll get out,' he said. 'I'll be out of this dump within a week. Want to bet on it?'

Ronnie's brow was furrowed. 'Have you fixed it up already? Will you take me with you?'

Santos laughed. 'Why should I?'

'Because we work for the same people. They owe it to me. If they're getting you out, I should go too,' said Ronnie. A whine was beginning to show in his voice by this time.

Suddenly Santos seemed to take pity on him. 'You shouldn't have jumped on me like that downstairs. You shouldn't have shown you knew me,' he said.

'I didn't want to miss you. No one was watching,' said Ronnie.

'Yeah? That's what you think. The lawyer was watching for one,' was the reply.

'Your lawyer?' Ronnie asked.

'Mr Oliver Grace, a real smooth guy. London got in touch with him when I was pulled in,' said Santos.

'I know him. He's my lawyer too. When's your next hearing?' Ronnie asked.

'Next week, but it don't matter. Like I told you, I won't be here,' said Santos firmly.

Ronnie visibly brightened. 'How will you get out?' he asked.

Santos shrugged. 'That's not fixed yet, but it will be. With enough money you can get anything you want.'

'I've found that they promise anything to get you to bring the stuff in, but if it goes wrong, you're on your own,' Ronnie told him. He stared at Santos for a moment before he said, 'When I was picked up someone suggested that the organisation shopped me. Do you think they did the same to you?'

Santos frowned. 'If I was shopped it would have to be someone high up that did it. When I get back, I'll find out, and then . . .' He slid an index finger along his throat expressively.

The thought of exacting revenge seemed to cheer him up and he relented enough to give Ronnie a drink. It was real Scotch whisky, not bootleg hooch, Ronnie was gratified to discover when he took his first sip.

Santos sat down on an easy chair and flung one leg over the arm. 'Now, tell me again what you can do to help me,' he said.

'I can show you around. I know where to buy reefers. I've made a few friends too. There's a family with a nice house on the Bay. I could take you there. The wife's a journalist for a London newspaper. She thinks I'm going to tell her about the smuggling organisation,' said Ronnie.

'Which you won't, of course,' said Santos pleasantly.

'No way,' agreed Ronnie and sipped his drink.

'And how else can you help me?' was Santos's next question.

'You've only got to ask,' said Ronnie expansively.

'Where can I find a woman, then?'

The question was direct and Ronnie blanched.

'Tonight?' he enquired, looking at his wristwatch.

'Sure, tonight, and maybe tomorrow and the night after
. . . as long as I'm here.' Santos was watching Ronnie with
a sarcastic grin on his face.

'You should ask the hall porter for that,' was the reply.

'Don't you know? You've been here over a month and
you don't know that? What you been doing with yourself?'

Ronnie drained his glass. 'I don't take chances. You never
know what you might catch.'

Santos laughed. 'I've had everything you can catch from
a woman already so I'm not worried. You a pansy boy then?
We wondered about that.'

A red flush rose up in Ronnie's cheeks. 'No, I'm not. It's
just . . .'

'Just that you're scared. You'd rather smoke dope, wouldn't
you? If you want me to look after you, you'd better do what I
ask. Ring the hall porter and get a woman for me.'

Ronnie was going to be forced to work for any effort Santos
made on his behalf.

Twenty

At noon the next day Ronnie was sitting in the hall as usual when Santos came strolling through and went to stand in the open doorway, breathing deeply as if in need of fresh air.

Ronnie rose to go and stand beside him. 'Everything all right?' he asked in a man-to-man fashion.

Santos grinned. 'Sure, great. I've been speaking to my contacts and we're working things out.'

A strange trembling gripped Ronnie when he heard that. 'You mean about getting away?' he said in a low voice, looking over his shoulder as he spoke.

'Sure thing. Want to take a stroll so we can talk about it?'

Followed by their policemen they walked in a leisurely manner down Churchgate Street to the big cinema on the corner where they stopped and stood together studying the stills for a Hindi epic movie.

'What's going to happen?' Ronnie hissed.

'They think they can get us out before the end of next week,' was Santos's reply.

'How?' Ronnie's throat was dry with excitement.

'They'll take us out by boat in the middle of the night to a French merchant ship anchored out in the roads beyond Bombay harbour. My contact knows the skipper. He's taken people away before.'

'Any idea when?' Ronnie asked.

'The boat's arriving in about three days' time, unloading and then leaving again two or three days later. They'll let us know but not till the last minute. You'd better keep this to yourself. If it gets out I'll know who to blame,' said Santos menacingly.

'Where will the ship take us to?' asked Ronnie.

Santos shrugged. 'That ain't fixed. Maybe Italy, maybe Marseilles. Either way it'll be easy to get to London from there. I'll let you know when it's fixed. In the meantime we'd better not be seen together too much. You ain't good for my reputation!'

Not knowing if this was meant to be a joke, Ronnie gave a nervous little laugh. 'What are you going to do with yourself now?' he asked.

'What do you think? When I'm not doing that I'll go to the swimming pool and get myself a nice tan.' Santos turned on his heel and walked quickly back to the hotel, leaving Ronnie staring after him.

The thought of escaping dominated Ronnie's thoughts and his jubilation was hard to hide. He decided to take a taxi to Walkeshwar Road and tantalise Dee Carmichael with dropped hints about the gold smuggling business. He enjoyed leading her on and had been disappointed recently because she had showed signs of losing interest in him and his secrets.

When he arrived at her house that afternoon, she was in the garden as usual, stitching a tapestry panel, and did not look overjoyed to see him. Through courtesy, however, she offered him tea. Before it arrived she eyed him and said, 'You're looking a lot more cheerful than the last time I saw you.'

He bounced in his chair. 'Perhaps I am!'

'Good news from home?' she asked.

'You could say that.' He longed to come out with his story about the merchant ship. It was burning on his tongue.

'At least you're not threatening to kill yourself any longer,' she said.

'Well, I'm not on my own any more,' he said.

'Oh, you mean the new smuggler. What's-his-name, the American. He's in the Ritz too now, isn't he?'

'Yes. He's called Santos. He's big time, really big time,' said Ronnie.

'That's good,' said Dee, carefully pricking the canvas with her needle.

'Drop in to the Ritz and meet him,' was Ronnie's next remark.

'I don't think so,' Dee said. 'My paper won't be interested in him. He's from New York, isn't he?'

'He's a New Yorker but he's been in London for three or four years now. He's important,' insisted Ronnie, knowing he shouldn't be pursuing this subject but unable to stop.

Dee looked at him. 'You've met him before?'

'Not actually *met* him, but I knew about him before I came out here. He normally doesn't do the runs. He organises things.'

'Why did he do this run, then? Was he shopped too?' Dee was convinced Ronnie had been a convenient sacrifice and had stopped pretending that he wasn't.

'They wouldn't shop him! Anyway he'd be shopping himself! This guy's big time.' He wanted her to realise Santos's importance.

'Maybe the Customs just got lucky, then,' said Dee.

'If they did, they needn't start celebrating yet. He's not likely to go to jail,' Ronnie snapped.

Dee sighed. She'd stopped even considering that he might be telling the truth.

'You said that your organisation would get you out long ago and that hasn't happened,' she said wearily.

He was nettled. 'But it will. It's being organised now. Just you wait and see. We'll both be off – Santos and me. He's promised me that.'

Dee stood up and folded her tapestry. 'That's good. Now you'll have to leave, I'm afraid, because I'm going out.'

She was angry because she knew he was only trying to make her react. He hated the idea that he was no longer of interest to her. Any day now, though, he'd be sentenced, sent to Poona Jail and out of her life. It wasn't as if they'd send

175

each other Christmas cards for years to come, she thought. Once he went to Poona, she'd never see him again.

After he left she collected her children and took them to Breach Candy swimming pool. It was very quiet there, with only a few people lounging in the long chairs or ploughing up and down the blue water. She knew most of the sunbathers around her but there was one stranger, a young man with a mop of black curly hair, who was showing off to the watching women by bouncing on his toes on the diving board and turning somersaults before he hit the water. There was something unpleasantly arrogant about him that compelled her to keep watching. It was when she heard him speaking in a marked American accent that she was hit by the notion that she knew who he was – Enrico Santos.

How had he got in to the pool? His house arrest rules, like Ronnie's, probably allowed him out for certain periods of time, but only with his police guard and there was no sign of a policeman at the pool. Her idea that she had identified him hardened into certainty when she was leaving, however, and spotted an armed constable sitting at the entrance gate with the pool guards.

That evening she persuaded Ben to go to the Ritz for a drink. They had once spent a lot of time in the hotel bar, but since Ben's elevation in status they did not go there so often. It had been the haunt of their youth and they were past that stage now. However, the barmen, Thomas and Raju, were pleased to see them and put up their favourite drinks without being asked.

Sitting in a booth at the far side of the bar, Dee saw the same dark-haired man as she'd noticed at the pool, and she leaned over the bar to nod at him and ask Thomas, 'Who's that?'

He whispered, 'Gold smuggler. He's waiting to come up in court. He arrived the day before yesterday.'

'What's he like?' she asked.

Thomas rolled his eyes expressively. 'A bad man, a badmash,' he said.

Dee sat back satisfied she was right. *Badmash* meant

villain, and broad-minded Thomas was so used to playing host to smugglers and people on police bail that he would not automatically apply that word to them. He must have taken against Santos for some other reason.

At dinner she talked to Ben about the change in Ronnie Weston. 'Last week he was suicidal, but today he's as cocky as ever. Another smuggler's been arrested and they seem to know each other. Ronnie's dropping huge hints that the other man will be helped to escape because he's so important to the organisation. He says if the other chap's going, he's going with him. I don't give much for Ronnie's chances though. The other man's a very different type from him . . . much more dangerous.'

Ben nodded solemnly. 'It's not as easy to get away from here as those villains seem to think. I don't know about the new arrival but I suspect our friend Ronnie's going to be around for quite a while.'

Dee laughed. 'And I hoped we'd be shot of him! He's becoming a bit of a nuisance, I'm afraid.'

Next morning, which was Friday, she went down to the Fort to call on Algy and Lorna. Unfortunately Lorna was not in and Dee remembered that her friend was planning a trip to Poona that weekend. She must have gone away earlier than planned, Dee supposed.

Algy was alone and looked hung-over. She smiled when she saw several torn-open packets of Alka Seltzer on his desk. 'Heavy night?' she asked.

He nodded. 'I went out with Ernest and that's always a mistake. I can't imagine how he can put away the amount of drink that he does. Too much of his company and I'd be a dead man. It's a good thing I'll be leaving here soon.'

'Will you? That's a pity. It seems that all my friends are planning to leave,' she said, thinking of Lorna.

'I've been here almost long enough. Ernest's been given a scare and he knows that if he starts backsliding again, he'll be out. We could always shift all of the India operation to Calcutta. We've a good man there too.' Algy sighed.

'Won't you be staying to cover the Pope's visit?' Dee asked. Sami, the cable clerk, had told her that government organisers were expecting the arrival of hundreds of press people from all over the world. 'Even *Time* magazine!' Sami had said, deeply impressed.

'I've got my official accreditation already,' she told Algy, who shook his head dismissively and said, 'The best of luck. I'm leaving it for Ernest to handle. It'll all be too organised and you'll have to cover the story from official handouts. No reporter'll ever get near His Holiness.'

Dee looked at him critically, wondering what exactly he wrote about, if he still wrote at all. What sort of story would get him excited? He'd pooh-poohed her smuggling story and now here he was pooh-poohing the Pope! His prediction about the Papal visit was probably accurate, though, she admitted to herself, because there would be too many people chasing too little news.

He grinned when he saw how crestfallen she was and said, 'Cheer up. You'll enjoy driving about in the official cavalcade. Just churn out a bit from his programme every day and your Foreign Desk'll be happy. I can't be bothered any more with that kind of stuff. Nothing big'll come out of it unless somebody tries to kill old Pius.'

'You're a cynic, Algy, and anyway his name's Paul,' she said, and they both laughed. His crack about an assassination attempt on the Pope was a good example of the irreverent attitude of newspaper people, be they from *The Times*, *Newsweek* or the *Brighton Argus*. Normal people would be shocked to hear such things said and only journalists would laugh at it. Algy and she talked the same language. They would both have been astonished and vastly intrigued to be told that one day not too far away there would be an assassination attempt on a Pope.

She decided to share Ronnie's most recent indiscretion with Algy. 'Remember the American gold smuggler? He's in the Ritz arranging a getaway. He's going to take Ronnie along too.'

Algy of course was unimpressed. 'Hot air,' he said with a shrug.

'I don't know about that,' she said. 'I've seen this Santos person and he's a much tougher character than Ronnie. He really looks the part. Maybe he will get away.'

'If he does, you can bet your life he won't take your friend with him,' was Algy's cynical reply.

Twenty-One

R awley's friend lived in a huge rambling bungalow in the middle of Poona cantonment. It was more than a century old and stood in a lush garden, staring down one of the long straight roads that criss-crossed that part of town.

After the 1856 Mutiny, the nervous British army had laid out geometrical carriageways in all their garrison towns to that they could fire cannons straight down the road and annihilate advancing squads of rebellious sepoys. There was something about Poona, even a century later, that made it seem as if the Mutiny had only happened yesterday, and might break out again at any moment, even though the British army had withdrawn from India nearly twenty years ago.

Rawley's plane was grounded because it needed some repairs and he borrowed a snorting little Fiat car for the trip. When it drew up at the bungalow gate late on Friday afternoon, Lorna looked out of the window with delight. 'What a wonderful house! It's straight out of a history book,' she exclaimed.

He leaned across and kissed her. 'I thought you'd like it,' he said. 'It's the sort of place your ancestors might have lived in when they first came out to India.'

'And your Wellesley relations too!' she exclaimed. 'Who lives here now?'

He grinned. 'A chap I've known for years. My godfather, in fact. He's Irish too and a bit older than my father – eighty now, though he doesn't look it. He's retired now but he was in the ICS, and the Indian government allowed him to stay on after Independence.'

She was impressed. The ICS, or Indian Civil Service, was an elite selection of highly intelligent men, nicknamed 'the heaven born', who had administered British India during the years of the Raj. After Independence, few of them had been permitted to remain in India by the new government because they had wielded Imperial rule. Those who were allowed to stay were highly respected by the Indians for fairness and incorruptibility.

She asked Rawley, 'Was your father ICS?'

He shook his head. 'No, he was army. All his life he hoped to save up enough money to go home and fix up the old house in Ireland but never managed it on his army wages. He died in London five years ago when he was sixty-eight. He thought of England as exile but he had to stay there because our mother was ill and couldn't cope with the problems of living in a falling-down house. She died a few months after him. Come on, let's get out of this apology for a car and stretch our legs.'

He lugged their two travelling grips from the back of the car and pushed the wooden gate open. The green paint on it was peeling and it creaked a lot but it gave them entry to a miniature Garden of Eden where small orange and lemon trees heavy with fruit flourished in old wooden tubs ranged along a paved terrace. The rest of the garden space was full of tangled rose bushes, luxuriant clumps of scarlet geraniums, and the ever-present bougainvillaea climbing over a thicket of large-leafed trees, from the branches of which hung enticing purple figs.

Tall glazed doors leading into the main house were standing open and they stepped into what looked like a museum. In one corner stood a harp, with its gilding badly chipped and flaking. Facing it was a grand piano, over which was draped a brilliantly coloured cloth with silver tassels hanging from its edges.

There was a square of dark red Persian carpet in the middle of the marble floor. Grouped around it, facing inwards, were spindly Edwardian settees and high-backed armchairs with bits of stuffing hanging out here and there in feathery little clumps as if an army of moths was making gradual inroads into them. Occupying the centre of the carpet was a beautiful oval rosewood table with a tall paraffin lamp on it. The lamp had a rose-coloured bowl and a brass base. Overhead, hanging from high rafters, was an immense crystal chandelier that tinkled gently when Rawley and Lorna stepped through the door.

In the wall spaces between the open doors – for there were no windows, only doors on both sides of the room – hung large oil paintings showing romantic scenes with knights on white chargers rescuing naked maidens in distress.

'Goodness!' exclaimed Lorna in astonishment, gazing around, and Rawley laughed, as if he had anticipated this reaction. 'He likes junk. He collects it,' he said.

'What's your friend's name? What do I call him?' she whispered.

'It's Patrick Bryant, but everyone calls him Paddy,' he told her and then raised his voice in a shout. 'Hey, Paddy! Anybody about?'

From somewhere above their heads came an answering shout. Soon they heard the shuffle of slippers and a thin, white-haired old man appeared, leaning on a walking stick. 'Aw Rawley, my lovely boy,' he cried and hurried across to hug the new arrival. Though stooped he was still very tall, and he towered over Lorna when he turned to shake her hand.

'Welcome, my dear,' he said and sharp eyes of a faded blue ranged over her face for several seconds before he turned back to Rawley and said, 'I can see why you're so entranced by her, my boy. She's a lovely girl.' His Irish brogue was very marked.

He then laid his stick across the tabletop and sharply clapped his hands to summon two young boys in khaki shorts and white shirts, who grabbed the travellers' bags and bore them away.

'Where's Ajit?' Rawley asked his host as the boys disappeared.

'He's at the market. We've planned a fine dinner for you tonight and he's gone to buy everything fresh,' was Paddy's reply.

Turning to Lorna, he said, 'You must be tired and dusty, my dear. Go and have a bath. The boys have been heating water for you for hours. Then take a rest and I'll see you again at dinner. We dine at eight thirty.'

Rawley stayed downstairs while one of the boys showed Lorna up to an enormous bedroom on the floor above the salon. It contained a four-poster bed shrouded in mosquito net and, like the bed in Goa, had a set of carpeted steps to climb up in order to crawl in and lie on the deep feather mattress.

At the back of the bedroom, through an open door, she could see an old-fashioned bathroom with a thunderbox lavatory, which had a white china pot under a thick wooden seat. Behind it was a tiny hatch. After using the lavatory, the user opened the hatch and shouted for the waiting sweeper to take the used pot away. The sweeper was always a low-caste harijan, an untouchable, because only untouchables did that sort of work.

Standing in the middle of the red-tiled floor of the bathroom was a large enamelled hip bath, and beside it were two metal buckets full of steaming hot water and brass ewers to be used for pouring water over the bather. There was a pile of snowy white towels on a cane-seated chair and a flickering oil lamp to provide illumination.

Lorna *was* sweaty, and felt as if the red dust thrown up from the roads during their journey had worked its way into every fold of her skin. Grabbing her soap bag, she ran into the bathroom, stripping off her clothes as she went. There was a shallow level of warm water already in the bath and she climbed into it, leaning her head against the high back. Then, slowly and luxuriously, she washed, pouring more warm water over herself from the ewer, sliding her hands down her legs and arms, gently soaping her tingling breasts. As day after day went by she was becoming more and more convinced that she was pregnant. Her breasts, she noticed, seemed to have grown in size and itched slightly when she touched them.

But her period was only seven days late. Perhaps she was wrong. She decided to wait until she was absolutely sure before she told Rawley.

She was leaning forward soaping her hair with her eyes closed tight when she felt his hands on her back, sliding lovingly down her spine as if he was counting the vertebrae. Her stomach contracted with desire as he climbed into the bath beside her. It didn't bother either of them that their lovemaking covered the tiled floor with soapy water.

At eight fifteen they went downstairs to find the salon aglow with a soft light from dozens of candles in the chandelier and an intense ruby glow from the paraffin lamps. Lorna's beauty was transfixing in the flattering, flickering light and she looked like one of the damsels in the paintings, stepped down from her gilded frame.

Paddy, who was wearing a long white robe with scarlet trimming round the neck and the edges of the sleeves, stood up to offer her a glass of wine. 'I regret it's not French,' he said. 'It's our home brew, made from our own fruit. Ajit is skilled at making it.'

She sipped at her glass. The wine was chilled and slightly sweet but not sickly and she smiled as she said, 'It's delicious. What's in it?'

Paddy laughed, 'Don't ask, my dear. It's a secret, but I suspect mangoes and pineapples play their part.'

In an ante-room off the salon, a table was laid for dinner with a long white cloth and hibiscus flowers arranged in a tall epergne in the middle. Starched white napkins, folded into the shape of water lilies, stood beside crystal glasses at each place. Here the lighting came from candles burning in tall candelabra at each end of the room. There were four chairs set round the table and a servant pulled one out for Lorna, while Rawley sat down facing her.

Paddy took his seat at the head of the table as a door swung open to admit a portly, middle-aged Indian in white trousers and a black, high-collared Nehru jacket. He was carrying a large china soup tureen with a silver serving ladle sticking out of it.

When he laid his burden on the table, he sat down in the fourth chair and solemnly started ladling soup into the plates. While this was going on, Paddy gestured to the soup server and said to Lorna, 'Let me introduce you to Ajit, my companion.'

Ajit looked up to give her a dazzling smile of infinite sweetness and she smiled back. He had a plump, kindly face and his black hair was sprinkled through with silver. 'Ajit doesn't speak much English, I'm afraid,' said Paddy.

'Which languages does he speak?' she asked.

'Hindi and Marathi,' was the reply.

She smiled. 'I can speak those languages too.' She turned to Ajit and addressed him in his own language, complimenting him on the comforts of the house.

Paddy clapped his hands in delight and said to Rawley, 'How lucky of you to bring us such a clever girl!' He too spoke to Lorna in fluent Marathi, saying that he hoped she really loved Rawley because he was a man much in need of love.

Her eyes filled with tears as she answered in the same language. 'I love him with all my heart,' she said fervently.

The only person at the table who did not know what was being said was the man they were talking about.

It was a delightful dinner for all of them because they revelled in each other's company, changing languages as they leaned across the table to talk or interpret for Rawley. They ate delicately flavoured chicken soup followed by grilled river fish and mango fool. Toasts were pledged in home-made wine; they laughed and joked, and after the dishes were cleared away they went back into the big salon to listen to old-fashioned gramophone records played on a wind-up gramophone. The selection included piano playing by Charlie Kunz, 'Old Man River' sung by Paul Robeson, and cabaret numbers from pre-war London shows

185

performed by Cicely Courtneidge, Gertrude Lawrence and Jack Buchanan.

'This is the music of my youth,' said Paddy with a sigh. 'When I went home on leave to London in the thirties I used to go to the theatre every night. I saw all those people. They've never been outclassed.'

Lorna leaned forward and asked him, 'Do you miss your own country?'

He sighed again. 'Sometimes I do, but I'm not like young Rawley, I have no family house left in Ireland. Mine was burned down in the twenties, during the Troubles. I've still got some photographs of it if you'd like to see them.'

'I'd love to. I've never been to Ireland,' she said.

'It's a beautiful country, but fickle, isn't it, Rawley?' said Paddy as he rose to cross over to an armoire, which he opened. He took out a large, leather-covered volume, laid it on a low table in front of Lorna and said, 'I'm not going to bore you with all the pictures, just some of our house – and I've got some of your home too, Rawley, that were taken in your grandparents' time. I don't think you've seen them before.'

Rawley sat down on the floor beside Lorna and said, 'It breaks my heart to look at the old house.'

'There's no need to feel sorry,' said the older man. '*You'll* be seeing your house again.' His hand was firm, however, as he flicked through the pages till he paused with his index finger pointing to a large sepia and white photograph. It showed a group of people on horses gathered in front of an elegant, ivy-covered house which had tiny turrets at both ends of the façade.

'That's my family at the opening meet of the local foxhounds, in 1900 I think. There's me, aged fifteen, on a bay pony called Thisbe, and my father on Achilles, his big grey,' he said. Lorna leaned forward to see more clearly. The lad on the pony had a cheeky face and looked as if he would be up to all kinds of mischief.

'I bet you were a real scamp,' she said with a laugh. Ajit asked her what she'd said and she translated for him.

186

'He still is,' was the Indian's fond reply.

A few more pages were turned till they were looking at another, older house, built in the Georgian style with two ranks of windows, six on ground level and eight on the floor above, as well as a line of peeping attics along the roof. It had a pillared entrance with a circular sweep of carriage drive in front of it. Drawn up at the front door was an open landau with two women in huge hats seated in it. On the box was a coachman in livery and a cockaded top hat.

'That's your grandmother and her sister at Killygrattan,' said Paddy to Rawley.

'I don't remember her. She died before I was born,' said Rawley softly.

On the opposite page was a photograph of three young men in the uniform of army officers standing in front of an ornamental Chinese screen and a potted palm. They were all handsome, tall and proud, grinning broadly as if they were about to set off on a great adventure.

'That's your father and his two brothers before they went to Flanders,' said Paddy again.

'And only my father survived,' said Rawley sadly. 'The loss of her sons killed my grandmother and spelt the beginning of the end for Killygrattan.'

'At least it wasn't burnt to the ground,' said Paddy.

'It might as well have been. It's got wet rot, dry rot, holes in the roof, bats in the eaves; whatever makes a house fall down, Killygrattan has it,' Rawley sighed.

The old man closed the book with a thud and said, 'I hope I didn't make you sad. Killygrattan's still there and one day you and Tim'll get back to it. Aim for that.'

'I am aiming for it,' Rawley told him. 'But you'll never go back, will you?'

'I've chosen not to. This is my country now and I'll stay here till I die,' Paddy told him.

Seeing how the showing of the photographs had sobered Rawley, Lorna slipped her hand into his and clasped it tight. Soon Ajit began to extinguish the candles and they bade each other goodnight. Lorna was still holding Rawley's hand as they climbed the stairs and when they were in bed together she held him close as if she was trying to protect him from sad memories.

'You love that old house, don't you?' she whispered.

'Yes. I want to take you there. Tim loves it too. We were blissfully happy when we were boys. It's like looking back to a golden age when I remember those times.'

'Were there only the two of you?' she asked.

'Yes. Just the two of us. Tim thinks I should have a son to inherit the house – he can't have any children because of the accident,' Rawley said.

Lorna's heart gave a huge leap when she heard this. Should she tell him about her suspicion that she was pregnant? But it mattered so much to him, she decided to be sure of her pregnancy before she broke the news. It wouldn't matter that any child they had was technically a bastard. It would still be his. It would still be a Fitzgerald. To raise his hopes of having a child and then disappoint him would be too cruel. To quieten her own tongue as much as anything else, she pulled his face towards her and kissed him.

Much later, they lay side by side talking the talk of lovers who are drifting in and out of sleep. Words were exchanged between them in fits and starts. 'I like Paddy,' she said softly.

'He's a good sort,' he mumbled.

'Why did he stay in India?' she asked.

'He stayed because of Ajit, of course,' Rawley said.

'Ajit?'

'They're lovers, darling. They've been together for years. That sort of thing's much more accepted here than it would be at home. In fact they could go to jail for it there.'

'I never guessed,' she said.

'I hope you don't mind,' he told her.

'Of course not. They're lovely people. I hope they're very happy together.'

'I'm sure they are. They first met about thirty years ago

when Ajit went to work for Paddy. I remember my mother being a bit shocked but she accepted it in the end. Now they're like an old couple who've been married for ages,' said Rawley.

'I hope we'll be as happy as they are when *we're* an old couple,' she whispered.

'We will be. I'm sure of it,' he told her.

Twenty-Two

Lord Affleck, Ben's business contact from London, arrived on the following Monday morning and rang him from the Taj Mahal hotel.

'My God, this is a terrible place,' he groaned. 'Every time I put my foot over the doorstep, I'm besieged by beggars. And I can't buy a bottle of gin.'

Ben laughed. 'I can't do anything about the beggars but I can give you some gin. I'll send it over to you now if you like.'

'No, no, I brought a bottle off the plane and what's left in it will keep me going till tomorrow. I want to meet you, though. This contract my company's running is in a terrible mess. It's going to cost us a fortune.'

'It would probably be best to discuss that in my house,' said Ben. 'Come to dinner tonight. I'll send a car to pick you up at half-past seven.'

When he phoned Dee to tell her, she exclaimed, 'Oh heavens, I didn't expect him so soon. You said he wouldn't be here till next week and I was going to invite some people to have dinner with him.'

'He's come early. Don't worry, he sounds like a good sort even if he is a lord,' her husband reassured her.

He was a good sort. Large, shambling and distraught by the problems of trying to do business in India, he was driven to Walkeshwar Road by Jadhav, and received at the front door by Babu who had decked himself up in a ceremonial turban and a red sash over his white jacket for the occasion. The dinner was Alex's special – jellied consommé, roast mutton and rice pudding with raisins. Those were all Ben's favourite dishes and they met with approval from the guest as well.

After dinner they sat in the garden with their coffees and quickly found that they had no need of other company to keep the party going. Affleck's sense of humour tended to be black, like Dee's, and he entertained them till two o'clock in the morning with hilarious anecdotes. In spite of his worries about his contract, they all enjoyed themselves so much they never actually got round to discussing it.

When he was returned to the Taj, Ben and Dee knew that they'd made a friend. It didn't matter who he was, they liked him and looked forward to seeing him again. That would be soon too because he'd invited them to lunch next day in a big new hotel at Juhu beach. 'We'll really have to get round to talking business,' he said.

The second meeting was as enjoyable as the first. They sat under beach umbrellas by the side of the hotel pool and ate grilled langoustines. Ben and Lord Affleck talked and Ben laid out his ideas about what could be done to try to rescue the ailing project, which was a plastics factory under construction at Nagpur. A silent Dee sat back in the sun with her eyes closed behind dark glasses, listening intently.

Ben sounded very impressive, and she could tell that the visitor from home admired his mastery of his business. Some of the questions he asked Ben seemed to be very leading – 'Do you plan to stay in India much longer? Have you ever thought of applying for a post back home?' – and she was suddenly convinced that this stranger had an ulterior motive in coming to Bombay. He was sounding out Ben; in fact, he was interviewing him.

When they were alone at home that evening, she said to him, 'Lord Affleck is going to offer you a job. What'll you do when he does?'

He was surprised. 'Do you really think so?'

'I'm sure of it,' she said.

'It all depends on what sort of job he has in mind,' he said. 'Let's worry about that later.'

191

'Would you want to leave here if the job was in Britain?' she persisted.

She had lived in Bombay for six years in total, but Ben had been there longer and she couldn't imagine him anywhere else because India suited him so well. He had superb relations with everyone who worked for him, from labourers to the top executives. He could read and write Hindi and Urdu and had total sympathy with the country. So well suited was he to India that she often teased him by saying that when he died, he'd have to be burned on a funeral pyre on the banks of the Ganges and his ashes scattered over the river. He didn't object to that idea.

'I don't know. I'd miss India. I'd have to think about it. Maybe you're wrong,' he said. He was never given to speculating about things, good or bad, before they happened.

On the next night they went again to dine with the Merediths. Brian had phoned Dee to invite them and said, 'It's ages since we saw you. I hope you're not tired of us.'

Dee had been embarrassed because in fact she and Ben had not been keen to keep up their acquaintance with Brian and Phoebe. 'Of course we're not!' she had said and enthusiastically agreed to go to dinner.

When she told Ben, he had groaned and said, 'I hope we don't have to look at any more films.'

As it turned out, there were no films, the meal was good and so was the wine, a fine bottle of Châteauneuf du Pape. Brian took great advantage of his diplomatic status and was generous in sharing it.

Mellowed by the wine, Ben and Dee relaxed with their host and hostess after dinner on the flat's broad verandah overlooking the sea on which the rising moon cast a broad path of silver like a road leading to eternity.

'This is a beautiful city in spite of all the frustrations of living in it. I'll miss it when we go,' said Brian, sticking out his long legs.

'Surely you're not leaving already? You've not been here

very long,' said Dee in surprise, and added, 'Everybody's leaving. I think Algy'll be off soon too.'

'There's been a few hints from back home, so I might be moved on soon but there's nothing definite. It's interesting that your spook friend is on his way,' Brian said and they all laughed as if he'd made a joke.

'Will you go back to London?' asked Ben.

Phoebe shook her head. 'Probably not. We'd really like to be posted to New York or Washington.'

'Would that be a promotion?' asked Dee.

'You could say that,' agreed Brian in a satisfied tone. 'Our only regret really would be if we had to leave here before we had time to do all the travelling we want.'

'So we're getting in as much as we can in the meantime,' Phoebe added. 'We went up to Poona last Sunday and took the opportunity to drop in on a man who's friendly with people we know back home. I'm glad we did because his bungalow is full of the most amazing antiques. We also met a couple who were staying with him. I believe you know them, Dee. Lorna and Rawley were their names.'

Dee smiled. 'Yes, I know them. Lorna's father owns the Bombay *Tatler* and she edits it for him.' She didn't say anything to the Merediths about what Rawley did for a living, but Brian knew anyway.

'I understand he's a pilot with his own plane,' he said.

'So I believe,' said Dee.

'These adventurous fellows are very glamorous, aren't they?' said Brian in a slightly envious tone and everyone laughed. Glamour was a quality that he markedly lacked.

Dee said nothing because she was not going to be inveigled into a discussion about Rawley's affairs.

'Talking of adventurous fellows,' he went on, 'how's your smuggler friend? He's got company in the Ritz now, hasn't he? Another one was picked up the other day.'

She told them that Ronnie was due to appear again in court any day and this time he was sure to be sentenced. Even Oliver Grace couldn't drag his case out much longer.

Though she'd lost interest in the story it had to be followed to the end.

'He's happier now that he's not on his own any more but I don't think Ronnie and the new man have got much in common,' she told Brian.

'Have you met him?' he asked.

'I've seen him, but I'm not interested in him from a journalistic point of view,' she said.

'But I believe he works for the same syndicate,' said Brian.

'All I know is that his address was given as New York, so it's an American story,' she said, wondering how Brian picked up his information.

'Then your friend with the news agency will be following the story. His agency is American funded,' persisted Brian.

It is, thought Dee, but what she said was, 'If he is working on it, he hasn't said anything to me. But it wouldn't be my business.'

'It might be interesting to find out what the Bombay magistrate does about the American, though,' said Brian. 'He should get off with a lighter sentence than your friend because when he was pulled in he wasn't carrying nearly as much gold. Only ten kilos.'

Driving home from Marine Drive later, she said to Ben, 'I can't make Brian out. Is he what he seems to be or is he something completely different?'

Ben laughed. 'You love mysteries, don't you? If they're not there, you make them up.'

'So what do you think about him?'

'I think he's one of those people who have hobbies. Like the chaps who hang around railways noting down train numbers. His hobby is visiting peculiar places. That's why he's enjoying India so much. He'll go home to London or to New York eventually and bore everybody blind with his tales of the mysterious East.'

Next day Dee took herself off to the city quite early. Algy was in his office, doing nothing very much as usual. 'Did you know the American gold smuggler's coming up in court tomorrow?' she asked.

He raised his eyebrows as high as they would go so that his face looked longer and more lugubrious than ever, leaned forward on his desk and fixed his eyes on her face as he said, 'Listen, I've told you this before. Forget about it. Stay out of it. Go to the court, get the verdict, send a story back if you think it's worth it and then draw a double line underneath the whole business.'

She was taken aback by the intensity of his tone and only stared back at him before asking, 'What do you mean?'

In an instant he was his old casual self again. 'It's not worth writing up. It's a dead story,' he said with a grin. 'Do you want a soft drink? I'll send the boy out for some if you do.'

She shook her head and stood up. 'No thanks. I'm going across the road to see Lorna Wesley.' When she walked down the stairs from his office she was surprised to realise her legs were shaking.

Lorna cheered her up, however, because she was so obviously happy. 'We had a wonderful time in Poona,' she told Dee. 'Rawley's friend Paddy was so kind to us, I could have stayed up there for weeks and weeks. And funnily enough, when we were there, some people who know you arrived: the British Council man and his wife. They're the couple you went to Shivaji's fort with, aren't they?'

Dee nodded. 'Yes, we saw them last night and they told us they'd met you. He's a real oddity.'

'His wife is very knowledgeable about antiques,' said Lorna. 'She and Paddy spent hours looking at the things in his collection. I liked her.'

'Yes, she's OK. It's Brian who confuses me,' said Dee. 'Algy says he's a spy but if he is he's not my idea of one. He's too – *homespun*, somehow.'

Lorna laughed. 'You journalists amuse me. You're always looking for hidden meanings and secrets. You never take anything at face value, do you?'

'Maybe that's what's wrong with us,' agreed Dee reluctantly.

Lorna was once again busy sorting out the contents of her grandfather's trunks and tried to press a painted wall hanging from Nepal on Dee, who admired it greatly but found the strength to firmly refuse the gift. 'You mustn't give things like that away. How do you know they're not very valuable?' she said.

'How can they be? They've been here for years and nobody's shown any interest in them. My father's told me that I can have whatever is in them so they're mine to give away if that's what I want,' said Lorna.

'I think you should show some of those things to an expert – to Phoebe Meredith perhaps, or, better than that, to the man you know in Poona. Next time you and Rawley go up there, take a few of the smaller pieces with you,' was Dee's advice.

Lorna folded up the hanging and said, 'All right, that's what I'll do, and if he says it's worthless, will you accept it then?'

'Certainly, but I don't think it is worthless somehow. Something as stunning as that must have a value,' said Dee, who was dazzled by the intricate, brilliantly coloured painting that covered the large hanging.

'What have you planned for this weekend?' she asked.

Lorna's face fell slightly as she said, 'I thought we might go somewhere in the plane but Rawley's phoned to say he's got an unexpected commission. He's to fly a consignment of something or other to the Gulf tomorrow morning and he won't be back till Sunday because he'll have to wait there for a returning cargo. I miss him so much when he's away and worry all the time in case he has an accident.'

Dee tried to cheer her up by saying, 'I'm sure he's very careful. He doesn't look like the sort who takes risks.'

This reassurance brightened Lorna who said, 'You're right, he's extremely cautious actually, and so's his mechanic. He says that Sher Singh checks his plane carefully before each trip and he trusts him. They've worked together for five years and there's never been one slip-up.'

'Don't worry,' said Dee. 'It seems to me everything's going smoothly for you. The stars are on your side. What's the news about the sale of the magazine?'

'That's going on – three steps forward and two steps back. It's just as well my father's lived his entire life in India or he'd be driven mad with frustration. I think the Advanis will buy in the end though because we are hanging on to our advertisers and this month's circulation's the same as last month's. They'd be silly to start something new when they could buy us out and go on with the same title,' Lorna told her.

'I haven't seen or heard anything about the magnificent Maya, apart from the fact that the marriage negotiations with Dadi are going on. If I hear any more, I'll let you know,' Dee promised.

Before returning home, she rounded off her morning by looking in on Ronnie, who she found sitting in the cocktail bar of the Ritz with Santos. When he saw her approaching, the American got up from his seat and walked away without speaking.

'What's wrong with him?' she asked Ronnie.

'He doesn't like journalists,' was the reply.

'I'm only passing by. It's your hearing tomorrow, isn't it, and his too? Will that be the last one?' she asked.

He looked around as if afraid of eavesdroppers. 'You bet it is,' he said. He was shivering slightly, his eyes were bloodshot and his lips looked dry and cracked. He was obviously under the influence of something, and it wasn't alcohol because on the table in front of him there was only a bottle of Coke and a half-filled glass.

She sat quietly, waiting for him to go on, and as usual he could not bear a silence. He had to fill it with words.

'You won't be seeing me after tomorrow,' he said with a smile.

'You seem to be pleased about that. Aren't you still worried about going to Poona jail?' she asked.

His smile was cunning. 'Not a bit. I'm looking forward to it.'

'That's a quick change-around,' she said.

He leaned across the table. 'Remember what I told you. Ronnie Weston's not so stupid. I knew everything would turn out all right.'

She asked no more questions and a few minutes later got up from the table and went home.

When she was clear of the hotel, Santos returned to sit at the darkened booth. 'I hope you didn't tell that broad anything,' he said.

'Of course not. She's just a woman. She doesn't know what's going on half the time. I told her I was looking forward to passing some time in Poona jail!' Ronnie laughed hysterically but calmed down when he saw Santos glaring at him.

'I wish to God I wasn't lumbered with you,' said the American.

'But you are, aren't you?' Ronnie told him.

'You know what to do tomorrow night, don't you? Take nothing with you except what you're wearing. Leave everything you've got here. At exactly four o'clock in the morning go out into the corridor and break the alarm box beside the escape stairs. In the confusion, get down into the hall and there'll be someone waiting to take you to the boat. Just go with him. He'll have taken care of your policeman and there'll be no trouble,' Santos told him, sitting forward and whispering urgently.

'What about you?' asked Ronnie.

'Don't worry about me. I'll get out the same way as you do but from the back door. We'll meet up on board ship. Now I'm off to have a swim and I don't want to see or hear of you again till then. Keep out of my way.' With an arrogant swing of his shoulders Santos rose from his seat and swaggered out of the bar.

Ronnie watched him go with loathing in his eyes. *You're a hateful bastard, but I'm putting up with you so I can get out of this hellhole*, he thought. Then he and his police minder walked to the street corner, where he managed to buy a small envelope of cocaine. He needed something stronger than cannabis to get him through the next twelve hours.

Twenty-Three

If Ben and Dee thought they were going to spend a quiet evening on their own, they were mistaken, because at half-past six, voices were heard yoo-hooing down the stairs from the car port and Dadi appeared with Maya at his back.

They were both beaming and Ben, who was sitting with his feet on the coffee table reading a crime thriller, jumped up to say, 'I heard about the engagement. Congratulations. So now you're going to be a married man, are you?'

Dadi was giggling like a girl but Maya looked much more inscrutable. It was difficult to tell whether she was really pleased or only reconciled to her fate. Dee, who had been reading a book by Anthony Powell and finding it hard going, was not sad to put it down and went over to Maya. She wondered if she should kiss the girl but decided against it. Instead she took her hand and said, 'I hope you'll be very happy together.'

Babu appeared in the kitchen doorway with his eyebrows raised which meant, *Will I bring out drinks?* and Dee nodded to him. 'Gin and limes please, Babu.' She turned to Maya and said, 'I wish it could be champagne but that's impossible to get here.'

'Actually,' said the girl, 'my brother has a few bottles and he's expecting some more. He buys it by the caseful from the Gulf.'

Dee kept smiling through her irritation, but her mind was whirring along. *I wonder if that's the consignment Rawley's flying in at the weekend*, she thought.

They sat around in the sitting room exchanging news. Dadi

200

was full of the details of the wedding, for Maya's parents were determined to send her off in style and the reception at the Willingdon, Bombay's most exclusive club, was going to cost hundreds of thousands of rupees. Dadi's parents and his younger sister were overwhelmed by the grandeur of it all because, though his father dealt in jewels, they lived a very simple life and never mixed socially with the super-rich.

Now he was dragging them into a different level of society by marrying 'up'. The Bhatias were among Bombay's oldest and richest families, though it was whispered that their funds were running out and there might not be so much left for the next generation, especially because Maya's brother Homi was notorious for extravagance and bad business decisions.

As she listened to Dadi's artless talk, Dee felt sympathy fill her heart, though she had never thought that way about him before. He was a remarkably stupid young man, but well-meaning and kind. Through the years she had known him, she'd become used to his constant complaints about not being able to spend large sums of money as some of his friends did. He was forever complaining about the huge bills he owed for trivial things like imported soap, when Indian-made soap was perfectly good enough for most people.

It never seemed to strike him that his father did not have unlimited money. He had safes full of precious stones, that was true, but they were his stock-in-trade. When Dadi's father died, he would have to share the business with two uncles and three male cousins, and all of them were far better businessmen than he was.

Now he thought he had triumphed by getting married to the cunning girl at his side. Did she think he was very rich? If she did she was in for a disappointment, and what would she do then? With her adroit mind she would run rings round him and make sure he never knew what to expect next, Dee thought cynically.

The couple were talking about where they would live after the wedding. 'My father owns a house on the other side of the road from Breach Candy. It's an old bungalow that's been in the family for years and it's divided into two flats. We're going to have the ground floor and the garden. It needs a lot doing to it but once we're in, I'll organise that. I want to build on a wing and transfer the kitchen into it. Then I'll knock down a wall to make a big drawing room and put en suite bathrooms off all the bedrooms . . .' Maya was saying. As he listened, Dadi's face fell because he was obviously working out how much all the work was going to cost and wondering how he was going to pay for it.

The bronze statuette that Dee had been given by Lorna was perched on a bookshelf behind Ben's head, and when Dadi's eye fell on it he visibly cheered up.

'Where did you get that?' he asked, interrupting Maya's flow of words and pointing with his finger at the dancing figure.

'I was given it as a present,' said Dee.

'Can I see it?' asked Dadi.

It was duly passed over and he handled it with exquisite care and delicacy, making Dee's feelings of sympathy for him grow even stronger.

'This is a very good piece,' he said solemnly. 'It's old and very valuable.'

'Is it?' said Dee, surprised.

'It's exquisite, a collector's piece, and its eyes are made of fine emeralds,' said Dadi. Obviously he was not such a philistine as he appeared because he showed great respect for the figure and talked with authority. Then he crossed the room, placed it back on the shelf, and stood back to admire it from a distance.

'When you leave India,' he said to Dee, 'take that figure with you in your handbag. If the Customs people see it they won't allow you to export it because it's a national treasure.'

'For heaven's sake,' she gasped. 'The person who gave it to me has no idea that it's so valuable. I'll have to give it back.'

'Who gave it to you?' asked Dadi. Maya was sitting

forward in her seat also agog to know and something warned Dee not to tell her that it belonged to Lorna Wesley. 'Just a friend,' she said evasively.

'Well, tell your friend if they have another like that, they own a great asset,' said Dadi solemnly.

Maya and Dadi stayed to dinner and during the meal, Dee managed to bring up the topic of the *Tatler* and the rival magazine.

Maya was rubbing some lettuce round her plate, soaking up the last of the salad dressing as she said casually, 'The Advanis are behind that other one. They asked me if I'd edit it and I might if they ever get it organised but, as I told them, I'm far too tied up for the next six months, what with the wedding and everything. We're going on honeymoon to Ooty for a month. I wanted to go to Kashmir but of course we can't now because of those awful Chinese up on the border.'

Dee and Ben looked at Dadi, whose high spirits were visibly flagging again. *A month in Ooty*, they thought, *that'll set him back a bit!*

When their guests left, Dee sighed and said to her husband, 'I find that girl very tiresome. But at least I can telephone Lorna tomorrow and tell her not to worry about the new magazine. I bet it never gets off the ground. If the Bhatia family were thinking of investing in it, they won't be doing that till they've paid for this wedding, and she'll keep making excuses so she doesn't ever have to show that she knows nothing about editing.'

'Tell Lorna about the dancing girl figure too,' said Ben.

'Yes, I will. Wasn't it amazing that Dadi recognised its quality at once? I'll have to give it back now, of course. When he asked who I got it from, I was praying you wouldn't jump in and tell him. I didn't want Maya to know.'

Ben laughed. 'You needn't have worried. I could tell by the look on your face that you wanted that kept a secret. You closed up like a clam.'

Twenty-Four

W hen the Carmichaels' house was in darkness and everyone inside was asleep a cacophony of alarm bells suddenly rang out on the other side of the Bay and a car went dashing up Churchgate to cut across the Maidan, heading for the airport. If Dee had been able to see the driver, she would have recognised him.

In the Ritz, Ronnie Weston had lain awake and fully dressed for hours, twitching, tossing and turning. He laid his watch on the pillow beside his head and every now and again propped himself on his elbow to check on the time. When four o'clock arrived, he sat bolt upright and slipped his feet to the floor. His hands were shaking as he put on his shoes.

Taking matches out of his pocket, he set fire to an empty cigarette packet, which he tossed, burning brightly, into the middle of his tangled bedcovers. Running his hands through his hair, he quietly opened the bedroom door on to the corridor and saw his night-time police guard sitting slumped and asleep against the wall.

The red alarm box was on the wall about fifteen feet away, so he tiptoed along and smashed the glass with a small hammer that was kept beside it. As the bells began to ring, he turned round and yelled at the top of his voice, 'Fire, fire!'

The guard jerked awake and stood up. Still screaming, *"Fire!"* at a peak of hysteria which he did not have to simulate, Ronnie ran past him to the stairway, thudding on other doors as he went.

The guard turned about confusedly for a little while, still

half asleep. Then he saw flames licking through the nylon sheets on Ronnie's bed and took to his heels as well, leaving his rifle behind him. Two or three guests in nightclothes ran behind him.

One after the other they plunged down flights of stairs till they found themselves in the front hall. A sleepy-looking night porter stared at them from behind the wooden-topped desk. 'Arrey!' he exclaimed and once again Ronnie screamed 'Fire!' before throwing himself into a deep armchair and trying to still his racing heart.

The hotel was not busy and there were only five other guests, but Santos was not among them. From the back premises some servants appeared, hitching up their dhotis as they ran. They all stood around shouting but a hush fell when the imposing figure of Alphonse, the French owner, came down from his penthouse flat on the roof. 'What the hell is going on here?' he demanded.

'Fire!' cried Ronnie in a cracked voice.

'Where?' asked Alphonse.

Ronnie pointed upwards. 'My room,' he said.

Clutching his dressing gown closed, Alphonse took the stairs two at a time and disappeared. Some of his servants followed but Ronnie sat still staring desperately around. He'd been told that someone would meet him. *They should identify themselves. I ought to be out of here.* He looked at his guard, who yawned, showing a pink tongue. Obviously he was not going to be the one who would escort Ronnie away.

Gasping, as if fighting for breath, Ronnie walked to the doorway and threw it open, gulping down fresh air when he went out on to the step. His puzzled-looking guard walked behind him, still keeping him under surveillance. He gazed up and down the road. Apart from a few bodies, asleep on the pavement wrapped in white sheets like cocooned moths, there was not a soul to be seen.

Will I make a run for it? Ronnie wondered.

But where would he run to? He didn't know where the boat was moored.

205

It was only when Alphonse came back down and roared at him that he was an imbecile for smoking in bed that he accepted he'd been left behind. He'd been tricked and Santos had gone without him. He sat down on the steps and burst into tears.

The dash to the airport was accomplished in record time and the two men inside the car spoke little as they sped along for neither of them liked or trusted each other. Enrico Santos was the most composed, remarkably cool, sitting back in his seat with one leg flung over the other. The burning red of his cigarette end made a spot of brilliant light inside the car.

They drove straight on to the tarmac strip and stopped where a small plane was drawn up. There was a barely perceptible lightening in the eastern sky over the distant ghats, but all around them the darkness before dawn was as deep and matt as velvet. The car's headlights, which cut a path through the darkness, were switched off before it reached the tarmac and they crept in slowly, carefully negotiating a way among the slanting shadows that lurked by the sides of the hangars and under the wings of the waiting plane.

Rawley Fitzgerald's taxi drew up at the same time and he saw the car stop as he walked across to the shed where he had to sign in for departure. He was wearing a thick white cricket sweater over his cotton shirt because winter had set in and the temperature was low for Bombay. Two Pathan watchmen, huddled round a brazier at the office door, were wrapped in long shawls against the cold and he hailed them cheerfully. 'Seen Sher Singh?' he asked.

One of the men said, 'He's in the hangar. He came last night to get your plane ready and he slept here.'

There was only one clerk in the office and he yawned widely as he watched Rawley signing the departure sheet. 'You go early today,' he said.

'As soon as possible. Before first light. My cargo's perishable,' said Rawley.

Usually the clerk asked for details of a cargo but today he did not bother, and Rawley, who was ready with a lie, guessed that whoever was arranging his passenger's flight had already taken care of the clerk. A couple of hundred chips would probably be enough to dull his curiosity.

Rawley didn't know the passenger's name or anything about him and it didn't matter to him if the departure was illicit. He was paid to do the flying, not to ask questions except about the destination.

He'd been contracted to ferry his passenger from Santa Cruz to French-controlled Djibouti, a notoriously lax port from which getaways could be arranged to anywhere in the world either by ship or by air. It was reachable in five or six hours with a full tank of petrol and Sher Singh would take care of that because they'd had a conversation about the flight and he trusted his mechanic implicitly.

As he walked back to his plane, he spotted the outlines of two figures waiting beside it, but there was still no sign of the Sikh. Passing the gaping open entrance of the hangar, which seemed to be full of darkness, Rawley gave a whistle to tell Sher Singh that he was ready to leave. The waiting men heard the whistle too and turned to face him. Neither of them smiled.

'Ready to go?' asked Rawley. He didn't know which of them was to be his passenger so the question was aimed at either. The one who answered was mop-haired, young and slim, dressed in a short black jacket that was zipped up to the neck. 'Yeah,' he said.

'Get in then,' said Rawley, walking round to the far side of the plane and hoisting himself up to the door. As he was settling into his seat, he saw the tall outline of overalled and turbaned Sher Singh walking across the stretch of tarmac towards them. Rawley did not switch on his lights because he wanted to slip out as unobtrusively as possible. He wouldn't put them on till he was on the runway, well away from prying eyes.

On his left-hand side the passenger was settling into his

seat too, buckling on the seat belt and fishing in his pocket for a woollen cap which he pulled over his head.

'Ready?' asked Rawley.

'Yeah.' The passenger obviously was not a great conversationalist, which was a pity because good talk always passed a journey pleasantly.

He started the ignition and yelled, 'OK,' out of the half-open window to Sher Singh, who pulled on the propeller blades and jumped back when they began to rotate. With a muffled roar of the engine, Rawley taxied on to the nearest runway and took off without any hesitation, soaring up into a sky that was now showing streaks of the brilliant palette of an Indian dawn. As he headed upwards, wings wavering in an upward drift of air, a chorus of wakening birds in the trees beneath him started singing their hymn of praise to the dawn.

On the ground, the tall figure walked back into the hangar where he stripped off his overalls and unwound the turban from his head. After the waiting car drove away, he pulled the hangar door closed before he ran across to a car parked in the darkness behind the hangar and drove back to the city.

Something was bothering Rawley as he set course due west. He frowned as he checked the instruments. 'Damn,' he said in sudden irritation.

'What's up?' asked the passenger.

'Nothing important. It's just that the instrument panel light isn't working,' said Rawley. *That's not like Sher Singh. He usually checks everything*, he thought.

'Does it matter?' asked the passenger.

'Not really. Don't worry. It'll be daylight by the time I really need to check the instruments for landing,' was Rawley's reply.

'I ain't worried,' said the passenger. 'I reckon you're as keen to save your own neck as I am.'

'What's your name?' Rawley asked, thinking, *If I've got to speak to this man I might as well know what to call him.*

'You don't need to know,' was the terse reply.

'OK, if that's how you want it. I just wondered what I should call you.'

The passenger turned his face towards Rawley. His eyes were very dark, with brilliant whites. He looked malevolent, like a dangerous wild animal. 'I'll settle for *sir*,' he said.

Rawley almost laughed but stopped when he realised that the young whipper-snapper really meant it. 'I don't think I'll be calling you that,' he replied coldly.

'Suit yourself,' was the reply and the passenger leaned back in the seat with his eyes closed.

For two pins, thought Rawley, *I'd turn round and dump you back at Santa Cruz*, but he looked down and they were quite far out over the sea by this time, well past the clusters of inshore fishing boats that were reaping the harvest of seafood soon to be on sale in the fish markets of Bombay. He'd just have to put up with travelling in silence because he was damned if he'd be the next one to start a conversation.

There was still a sense of disquiet haunting him though. What was it? Then he realised. Sher Singh had not made his usual gesture of good luck when he jumped back from the rotating propellor. Normally he'd grin broadly and stick up both fists with the thumbs raised, but today he'd kept his arms down and his head averted. It wasn't like him to sulk or be miserable. What had got into him? Trouble with a woman, probably, Rawley decided. Sher Singh was nearly always in love with some dancing girl or other.

Rawley's mind began to run along on the theme of love as he guided his plane into the vast expanse of dark purple open sky. They were flying away from the rising sun so it was not yet bright but he found it easier to reflect on things in the dark. He thought about Lorna and knew that for the first time in his life he was truly, deeply in love.

He'd never felt like this before. He'd married Rachel when he was little more than a boy, swept along by an adolescent passion that had burned itself out within three months, but he knew that this new love wouldn't do that. It was part of him, it dominated his existence, it gave him purpose.

For the flight he was now undertaking, he was being paid in gold. It had been delivered to his lodgings that night before he left, and lay hidden among his clothes with a love letter to Lorna and photographs of himself with her that he'd had taken on their various outings together. For some reason he couldn't explain, even to himself, he'd been very anxious to snap those pictures, to make a permanent record of their happiness. Maybe one day their descendants would look at the photos with the same sense of longing and nostalgia as he'd looked at Paddy's old pictures of Killygrattan.

He'd left a will too, or at least a handwritten letter for his brother, telling him about the money he'd been carefully banking in the Hong Kong and Shanghai Bank every time he had the chance to make a trip outside India. There was almost enough to start work on the house by now. At the rate he was going it would only take a short time before he was able to sell the plane and head for home.

He was smiling while he thought about himself and Lorna in Ireland. It didn't matter if Rachel wouldn't divorce him; they'd live together and have children just the same.

He'd take Tim and Paulina to Ireland as well. Though she was difficult and temperamental she really cared about Tim and looked after him with complete devotion. Perhaps the house could be divided in half so Paulina could be left to rage about in her own premises.

A tide of scarlet light began to flow across the sky as he flew along. The sun was rising in all its glory and, in front of him, a few cumulus clouds that looked like flying cherubs were sailing serenely across a rose-coloured sky. When there was light enough to read the instrument panel he glanced down and began to check his dials.

At first he thought everything was as it should be – oil pressure, height, speed, and direction. Then his eye fell on the fuel gauge. Its needle was hovering on empty.

He blinked his eyes and looked again. *My God, there's hardly any fuel left in the tank!* It wasn't possible. There had to be a mistake. Perhaps the gauge had stopped registering.

Perhaps that was why the lights had gone out – it had to be a minor electrical fault. Sher Singh always checked and double-checked the fuel tanks. It was the first and last thing he did before a flight.

Check the spare tank, was Rawley's next thought, and he reached over to flick the switch that would turn on the auxiliary supply. That needle also registered nothing. The spare tank was empty too.

He stuck out his wrist and looked at his watch. They'd been flying for an hour and a half and should only have used less than a quarter of the fuel if the tank had been full. They were too far out now to turn back. He'd have to ditch in the sea. Thank God the monsoon was over and the weather was tranquil.

Thoughts jumbled over each other in his head. What had happened? Surely Sher Singh hadn't tried to kill him? It wasn't possible. He couldn't believe it. He didn't want to believe it. No matter how much money was offered, he was sure his old friend would stay faithful.

But who else would have had the opportunity to drain the tank? Tim's trouble had come because he was smuggling guns to the Nagas and Rawley was pretty certain that the Indian secret service had decided to put an end to his activities in the most dramatic way, *pour encourager les autres*, as the French said, because there were other people doing the same thing.

Tim's plane had burst into flames even before it took off. A bomb in the cockpit, it was decided, but the culprit was never discovered. This new way of attempted assassination, sending him off on a long trip with only a fraction of the fuel he needed, was more subtle. Ditching in the sea could be attributed to a breakdown, a miscalculation, or a mid-air accident.

But why get rid of him? He wasn't in the Naga trade. Any guns he ever carried were for the Pathans on the Frontier and they'd always been very friendly to him. The Indian government ignored that trade because it suited them to have the Pathans armed against the Chinese and the

Pakistanis. Pathans didn't like either of them – or anybody else, really.

When he turned his head and looked at his sleeping passenger, inspiration struck. *That's it*, he suddenly thought. *It's not me this is aimed at, it's* you. *Someone wants rid of you. I'm just the unlucky guy who happens to be with you when it happens.*

Deliberately he did not waken his passenger but put the plane into a dive that would do the job for him. Clutching his seat with both hands, the passenger wakened with a start. 'What the hell are you playing at?' he shouted when he was thrown abruptly forward.

'Just a rehearsal,' said Rawley, keeping his eye on the fuel gauge. There was enough left for only about fifteen or so miles, he reckoned. Already the engine was spluttering.

'Rehearsal for what?'

'For ditching.' Rawley was completely calm as he worked out in his mind what he had to do.

'You bastard, you're trying to scare me,' snapped the passenger.

'I won't have to try. We're going to have to ditch.' Rawley was reaching for the radio headphones so he could signal his location to whoever was within contacting distance. When he looked out of the window, however, the vast sea was completely empty and he was many miles from land in every direction.

When he saw Rawley putting the headphones on, Santos snatched them away. 'You're not handing me in,' he shouted.

'Don't be a fool. I've got to radio our situation so they can find us when we ditch,' yelled Rawley, grabbing for the headphones too.

'We're not ditching. You're flying on. You've been paid to do that and I'll make sure you do.' Santos produced a snub-nosed gun from the pocket of his windcheater and pointed it at Rawley. 'Fly on or I'll shoot you,' he said.

Rawley groaned. 'Aw, don't be a halfwit. We're going

down whether you like it or not. The petrol tank's empty. Our only chance is to be picked up before the sharks get us.'

Santos seemed to lose his head completely. 'Going down? Of course we're not going down. You're faking. Get out of that seat and I'll fly this crate myself.' He waved the gun about and Rawley saw that white froth had appeared at the corners of his mouth, making him look like a rabid dog.

He stood up, leaving the controls while the plane bucked in the air. 'OK, take over,' he said.

When Santos stood up too, Rawley threw himself at the other man's legs and they cannoned on to the floor behind the seats. In the mêlée, the gun went off, ripping a hole through the plane's roof. Then there was another shot and suddenly everything went quiet.

In total silence the little red and white plane headed for the sea. Like a toy, it hit the water nose first with a tremendous splash, throwing plumes of white up around itself. Then slowly, very slowly, it sank beneath the surface. In a few minutes it had disappeared, leaving only an ever-widening circle of ripples in the emerald green of the Arabian Gulf.

Twenty-Five

The courtroom at Byculla was only half full and there was no sign of Oliver Grace in the crowd when Ronald Colman Weston was brought up before the magistrate for the last time. His face was chalk white and he seemed to tremble as he stood in the dock. While he was being asked how he wished to plead, Dee Carmichael quietly slipped into a seat among the spectators.

'Guilty,' he said quietly, because he had accepted the inevitability of punishment.

Dee watched him closely. Every visible item of clothing he had on was made of nylon or some other synthetic fabric – suit, shirt, tie and even the handkerchief that flopped out of his top pocket. *Surely someone in his smuggling organisation should have warned him that synthetics are misery to wear in the tropics because you can't sweat through them. At least he'll be more comfortable in prison overalls*, she thought. It was to prison that he was certainly going.

The magistrate did not waste time. 'A year in Poona prison!' he intoned and tapped on the desktop with his gavel for the next felon to be hauled up before him.

Ronnie swayed. He hadn't expected such a long sentence, but when he thought about it later he realised that in fact he'd got off lightly. The five weeks he'd spent in Bombay under house arrest would be deducted from his time and, if he behaved well, he could earn a further remission. He could probably be on the plane home within seven months.

Before he stepped out of the dock, he looked frantically round the courtroom for a familiar face and found Dee. She

214

gave a little wave but she did not intend ever to meet him again if she could help it. From the courtroom she'd go to the cable office and that would be the last of Ronnie Weston as far as she was concerned.

She sat on for a little while to see if the American smuggler was brought up too but there was no sign of him and she left the court when it formally adjourned. It didn't really matter to her what happened to him because he was not her story.

Lord Affleck had made full use of the facilities of the Taj Mahal hotel during the previous day, keeping servants running to the Central Post Office three or four times with telegrams, which he insisted were immediately sent to London.

Answers came back as frequently until the middle of the night. His Lordship sat up very late sipping his gin and, when he was at last forced by weariness to go to bed, he put a sheet of paper over the top of his half-empty glass. On the paper he wrote, 'Do not throw out. This is GIN!' forgetting that none of the bearers, who came in to tidy up his suite the moment he turned his back, could read English. To his wrath, while he was asleep, the last of his precious gin was tipped down the sink in mistake for water.

By early afternoon of Friday he had completed his long-distance business and called for a taxi which took him to Ben Carmichael's company building in the suburb of Worli. Ben was in his office and stood up to greet his guest, who said, 'I've come to say goodbye. I'm flying out tonight, but before I go there's something I want to talk to you about . . .'

At half-past six that night Ben ran down the steps to his house with his heart hammering in excitement. He paused dramatically in the doorway and said, 'Guess who could be the new managing director of McKinley Parks International Ltd!'

Dee, who had spent the afternoon reading, put down *The Diary of a Nobody*, which she always used as a diversion at difficult times, laughed and said, '*You*, of course. I told you he would offer you a job. I've been wondering all day if he'd say anything before he flew home.'

'Well, he did. He offered me the job and told me to think about it. I've to let him know by the end of next week. God, Dee, it's a huge job with tremendous responsibility and the salary's enormous. It's twelve thousand a year!'

She gasped. Average professional salaries ran between two and two and a half thousand. At the moment Ben was earning four thousand and they thought they were very well off indeed. This staggering sum took her breath away.

'But the money's not the most important thing. The job's really challenging. I've to put his engineering company back on its feet. If I take the job I get a car, share options and a mortgage at a low rate. The perks are tremendous – but so's the responsibility.' He was almost incoherent with excitement.

'What do you feel about that?' she asked cautiously, though she did not really need to ask the question.

'I love the idea,' he told her.

A cold little shiver, like a premonition of some sort, crossed her heart. Was this the time to tell Ben that she thought she was pregnant, she wondered? Was that the reason she felt so negative? Why was she not as overcome with delight as he was? Why was she still obsessed by the memory of the magic men who made you see things that weren't there and not see things that were?

'It means we'll have to leave India of course,' she said, thinking, *Perhaps that's what's wrong. I don't want to leave.*

'Yes, we'll have to live in London.' His eyes were shining. She remembered his frequently expressed ambitions to own a house in Cheyne Walk and drive a Rolls Royce. It used to be a joke between them but she realised he saw it as a real possibility now.

'You've made your mind up, haven't you?' she asked. There was no doubt about his answer. She mustn't confuse the issue by talking about new babies. This was the chance he'd worked for and he would be foolish to turn it down. Her own career, such as it was, did not matter. The Pope's

216

visit would probably be the last story she'd ever write as a stringer.

Yet he wanted her agreement. 'Tell me you think it's a good move,' he asked.

She smiled. 'Of course it is. You'll be moving into the big time. It's a tremendous chance for you.' But her inner mind was whispering, *What if he can't do it? What if he's biting off more than he can chew?*

'Then I'll cable him tomorrow and accept,' Ben said.

'Perhaps it would be best to wait a couple of days. Don't look too eager,' she advised. Somehow she wanted to put off the inevitability of what she knew must happen. They would have to leave; she'd have to cope with the packing up in the early months of pregnancy – but it was a tremendous opportunity for him, and for her as his wife. Part of her was elated, and over-awed by the prospect of what he'd been offered, but there was a dark corner full of doubts in her mind that she was unable to articulate or explain.

She knew that, without expecting it, they had arrived at a crossroads in their life. As soon as Ben sent his acceptance, and resigned from his present job, they would start on a new route. She remembered seeing a picture in a storybook she'd loved as a child. It showed a pilgrim in front of a fingerpost pondering which way to go. He stood with his brow furrowed in doubt, but it was obvious that whichever way he chose, his destiny would be changed for ever. The question was, would he choose the right one?

Leaving India would be a wrench because this time there would be no coming back again. Even more, leaving her proxy family of Babu, Prakash, Jadhav and old Alex would make Dee miserable and she knew she'd remember them with affection forever.

These things were not her only worries, however. Her biggest problem was that she was superstitiously afraid of this sudden stroke of good luck. Instinctively she distrusted something that looked so good. It was like fool's gold.

You idiot, she scolded herself. *It's typical of somebody of your Calvinistic heritage to distrust good fortune. That's what makes you always look for the worm in the apple.*

Putting her reservations away, she jumped up and threw her arms round her husband. 'Oh Ben, you've done so well. You deserve this. Nobody deserves it more than you do, and Lord Affleck's a clever man to see what you've got to offer,' she told him.

Sher Singh lived in a chawl near Crawford Market with his mother, his father, two brothers, their wives and an assortment of small children to whom he was an indulgent uncle. He was twenty-eight years old, but when he was ten his entire family had fled from Lahore where Muslim fanatics were slaughtering Hindus and Sikhs in the bloodbath that followed Partition.

Sher Singh had terrifying memories of their escape in a packed train, and of seeing murdered, blood-smeared bodies laying on the platforms of stations through which they passed. His family was luckier than thousands of others, however, because they all ended up safely in Bombay where they had family connections. The fact that they were penniless, after having been rich landowners in the Punjab, did not worry them too much when they reflected on what might have happened.

His elder brothers soon found jobs because they were skilled mechanics. His father and mother opened a small tea-shop and prospered. Sher Singh studied until he was sixteen when he too trained as a mechanic and helped his brothers in the car repair shop they owned by that time. Even then he was fascinated by New York and read everything he could find about it. 'I'll go there one day,' he boasted to his friends.

The change in his life came when Rawley Fitzgerald, passing through Bombay en route for Calcutta, brought an old army motorcycle he'd bought from a friend into the repair shop. It was in bad condition but Sher Singh worked on it till he restored it to peak performance and appearance. When

Rawley returned, the machine roared into life at the first kick on the accelerator. He clapped his hands in delight and said, 'Hop on the back, sardarji. Let's go for a spin.'

The pair of them had set off, the tall Sikh, still in his working overalls and of course his neatly wound turban, clinging on to the back of the Britisher in white shirt and trousers that were soon stained with oil. They roared through traffic-crowded streets to the long straight road that ran past the racecourse, where Rawley opened the throttle and took the bike up to a hundred and twenty miles an hour. Sher Singh had never felt such heady excitement in all his life.

They became fast friends and, after Tim's accident, Rawley moved his operation to Bombay full time and bought a new Piper plane out of Tim's insurance money. Then he hired Sher Singh as his mechanic. They'd been working together for three years.

When Sher Singh did not return home by the afternoon of the day Rawley left for Djibouti, his mother walked up and down their main room wringing her hands and moaning, 'Something bad has happened to my boy. I feel it in my heart. Something evil has hurt him. He went out last night because he was sleeping in the hangar but he said he'd be home today before noon . . . and he hasn't come.'

Her husband and the other brothers ignored her at first but soon her continual plaint agitated them too and as darkness fell the youngest son, Raji, jumped to his feet and said in exasperation, 'Nothing's happened to him. He's often late home. He's probably in the grog shop. I'll go and look for him.'

The mother was swaying to and fro with the end of her sari held up to her face, but she collected herself sufficiently to thank her son as he stormed out.

'I'll beat his head in when I find him,' Raji shouted as he left.

The local grog shop, where home-made liquor was sold, was empty and the owner, who was a friend, said he had not seen Sher Singh for days.

'He's not come home since yesterday and our mother is worried. Where do you think he might be?' asked the brother.

The answer was an eloquent lift of the shoulders and a shake of the head.

'Has he a new woman?' asked Raji. Sher Singh was a bit of a dilettante who liked a sip of grog now and again and was also very partial to pretty, easy-going women, of whom there were many in that section of the city.

The grog shop man shook his head again. 'I do not know,' he said.

There was obviously nothing for it but to get out one of the cars in for repair at the workshop and drive to Santa Cruz. Before he left, Raji went back home to enlist the support of his other brother, Gardari. It would be worse for Sher Singh to be dressed down by two of them than only by one.

They grumbled away to each other as they negotiated the outer suburbs and were soon on the long straight road that fringed the edge of the stinking creek which came as such a horrific shock to visitors from the West when they first landed at Bombay airport.

'His place of work is on the edge of the big airport. I was there with him once. I think the hangar is number twenty-five,' said Raji.

'Yes, I've been there too but it is number twenty-four,' said Gardari, who always argued.

There were only a few people wandering about when they stopped at the security office. The Pathan watchmen sitting round the brazier stared balefully at them, but Raji was polite when he asked if they'd seen his brother Sher Singh.

'So you're Sher Singh's brother!' one of them said. 'He's a good fellow. We like him. He works for the Englishman who flies. He's gone, though. He left early this morning.'

'Sher Singh has left?' asked Raji.

'No, no, the Englishman left. Sher Singh was here all night and saw him off as usual but we haven't seen him since. Perhaps he went away after we left to sleep. We only work during the night, you see.'

The Sikh brothers stood together waiting for more. 'The clerk inside might know,' said one of the Pathans. 'I will ask him.'

When he yelled a question through the office door, however, a negative answer came back. The clerk hadn't seen Sher Singh either. By this time the Pathans had become interested so one of them stood up and said, 'I know which is their hangar. It's number twenty-five. I'll take you there. He might have fallen asleep after working all night.'

In a little procession they walked across the tarmac, led by the Pathan who was shining a flashlight to show them the way. The big door of the hangar was closed but not padlocked, so it was easy to slide open and they squeezed inside, with Raji shouting out his brother's name as they went. The sound of his voice echoed and re-echoed under the high roof but there was no answering shout.

As the Pathan shone his light towards the work and storage area at the back of the hangar, they saw something dark snaking across the concrete floor. Instinctively they froze, exhibiting the native response to what they thought was a snake. It did not move, however, and they approached it cautiously until they were able to see that it was the long strip of cloth that normally formed Sher Singh's blue turban. The brothers were shocked. To take off his turban so carelessly was a terrible thing for a Sikh to do. They hissed in disapproval.

Raji ran forward to pick it up and as he did so, the Pathan's torch lit up the darkest corner of the work area and showed a body stretched out on a bedroll laid on the ground with the head pointing towards the wall. The soles of the bare feet looked very white in the beam of light.

At first they thought that their brother had passed out after drinking – he was only a lad after all – but when Gardari went over to shake his shoulder they realised Sher Singh was dead.

With cries of lamentation, the brothers knelt beside the corpse and tried to turn it over. It was then they saw that he had been strangled. His eyes were bulging horribly and a bright red bandanna was tied tightly round his neck.

All three men drew back in horror. 'Thugs!' they said in unison.

From a telephone in the office, the police were called. They arrived in a squad of jeeps with lights mounted on the roofs. The hangar doors were flung right back for the jeeps to drive inside and train their searchlights on the pathetic body of the dead Sikh whose long, lustrous black hair, as beautiful as any woman's, had escaped from his sacred comb and spread out around him like a shawl.

The police were perfunctory because murder was commonplace in Bombay. 'Where is the man he worked for?' they asked the clerk, who stood, looking shocked, at the fringe of the watching crowd.

'He worked for Fitzgerald sahib who signed in early this morning to fly to Karachi,' he said.

'Karachi?' questioned another of the police officers in disbelief. India and Pakistan were in a state of hostility and Indian planes would find it impossible to land in the enemy capital.

'He is a foreign national. He often goes to Karachi,' explained the clerk.

'When is he coming back?' was the next question.

The clerk shrugged. 'He did not say.'

The policeman closed his notebook. 'Perhaps he killed the Sikh before he left. Perhaps he will not come back,' he said.

Raji protested. 'We know him. They were friends. He would not kill our brother.'

The policeman looked at him with hard eyes. 'We know what happens here. We know about the smuggling and we know about Fitzgerald. He carries guns to the Frontier and brings in alcohol from the Gulf. Perhaps he and your brother were in dispute about the profits.'

Gardari drew himself up to his impressive height. 'Our brother was a mechanic, not a smuggler,' he said.

The police officer was unimpressed. 'But he must have known what Fitzgerald was doing. Perhaps he was threatening to talk.'

The brother shook their heads and Raji said, 'But what about the strangling? It looks as if he was killed by Thugs.'

'There are no Thugs left in India,' said the police officer, but all the men listening to him knew that what he said was not exactly true. Ritual murder in honour of Kali was still practised in out-of-the-way places and the cult was much feared. Seeing their sceptical expressions, the police officer went on, 'Besides, it looks as if your brother was asleep when he was attacked. Strangling would be the most convenient way to get rid of him. He might have cried out if he were stabbed and a gunshot would be heard, especially in the middle of the night. We will have to wait for the return of Fitzgerald before we can do anything more about this case.'

Gardari and Raji looked miserably at each other. They knew what they had to do. When the police left, the brothers very tenderly laid their dead brother on his side and combed out his hair with his sacred comb before tying it into a tight topknot. Then one helped the other to hoist the body on to his shoulder and steadied it while it was carried, with one braceleted arm swinging loose, to their waiting car where it was laid along the back seat and its face covered for the journey back home.

Sher Singh's mother was waiting. A glance at her eldest son's face told her something terrible had happened to her favourite child. Though the Sikh religion forbids weeping at the time of death, which is regarded as the natural end for everyone, she burst into tears and laid her face into her crossed arms on the tabletop.

At dawn next day, after friends and relations had been informed, Sher Singh's body was carried in procession on a wooden pallet to the burning ghat and his corpse was burned.

Gardari read a short extract from their sacred book, the Guru Granth Sahib, and the others chanted:

'So remember the Lord calls, O Nanak,
The day draws nearer for each one of us.'

Sher Singh's ashes were scattered on the sea and the sad crowd of mourners made their way back to his home to begin nine days of mourning.

Every morning, Sher Singh's two brothers looked out of the window and wondered why Rawley Fitzgerald had not come back. As day succeeded day, they began to think that the cynical police officer had been correct and Sher Singh's friend had killed him before running away. If that was true, Raji said to his brother, Fitzgerald had better never come back at all because he in his turn would be killed.

Twenty-Six

I t was not possible for the Carmichaels to tell anyone that they were leaving until Ben had submitted his resignation and had it accepted. He wrote an official letter to his company chairman in London but that would take about seven days to reach him. The time dragged while they waited for a reply.

Feeling aimless, on the Friday following Lord Affleck's offer Dee was driven into town and went to look up Algy. In his office she found only Ernest who seemed hardly able to recognise her at first. For a moment she was afraid that she'd changed in appearance or become invisible.

'I'm Mr Byron's friend. We used to work together,' she reminded him when she saw the look of incomprehension on his face at her request to see Algy.

He seemed to pull himself together. 'Oh, yes, of course. So you are. He's gone, I'm afraid.'

'Gone?' She was astonished. Surely he wouldn't leave without at least telephoning to say goodbye.

Ernest nodded. 'Gone,' he confirmed.

'You mean he's out of the office?' she asked.

'No. He left the country. He flew out three days ago.' Ernest's eyes were a peculiar pale shade of greenish grey that seemed suddenly very sinister to her.

'Where to? Where did he fly to?' she asked, though it was none of her business really.

Ernest shrugged. 'New York, I think. Or perhaps Chicago. I'm not sure.'

The moment Algy left, his assistant must have gone back to doping himself in a big way, she thought, but

225

persisted with her questioning. 'Did he leave a forwarding address?'

'No.'

'But what about his mail?'

'He never got any mail.'

So that was that. In a few weeks' time Ernest would probably have forgotten all about Algy. She gave herself a shake as she found herself wondering if her friend had ever been there in the first place. The whole situation seemed surreal.

She ran down the stairs and across the street to Lorna's building, arriving there so red-faced and puffing that Bubbles laughed when she saw her coming into the outer office. 'Is something chasing you, Mrs Carmichael?' she teased.

'No, no, I've just run up your stairs. Is Lorna in?' asked Dee.

Bubbles' face went grave. 'She is, but I don't think she's seeing anyone. Wait here and I'll tell her you've come.'

She went into Lorna's inner sanctum and quietly closed the door. After a few minutes she came back, still grave, but said, 'Go in. She'll see you.'

Not knowing what to expect, Dee went in and closed the door carefully. Standing with her back against it, she looked across the floor to Lorna's desk in the window. Lorna was sitting in her high chair and her face looked haggard and harrowed. Her fine blonde hair was limp and lifeless and she was wearing no make-up.

'Are you ill, Lorna? Is it the baby?' Dee asked anxiously.

Lorna stared at her in silence for a few minutes and then said, 'It's Rawley. He's disappeared.'

'Oh, my dear, what's happened?' Dee whispered.

'I don't know. He flew out last Friday and was due back on Sunday but today it's Friday again and he's still not come. I've gone to the airport every day but there's no sign of him.'

Dee's mind was darting around, trying to find an explanation that would help her friend. 'Perhaps there's been a problem with his plane. Or maybe it's the weather? He flies to the Frontier, doesn't he? If it's snowing up there he won't be able to fly out. It'll soon be December, after all.'

Lorna shook her head. 'He told the airport clerk he was flying to Karachi but they have been contacted and he never arrived. Nor was he expected, which is worse.'

A terrible feeling of dread seized Dee but she maintained an optimistic look. 'You know what his business was like. He had to keep things secret. He'll be back soon.'

'You don't understand. There's more. His mechanic Sher Singh was found murdered in his hangar the night after he left. He was strangled with a scarf.'

Strangled. *Thugs strangle people*, Dee thought and felt so weak she had to walk across to a bentwood chair against the far wall and sit down. 'I'm sorry,' she said. 'I thought I was going to faint for a moment. I'm pretty sure now that I'm pregnant, you see.'

'So am I,' said Lorna in bleak tones.

'Who found the mechanic?' Dee asked, concentrating on the immediate problem.

'His brothers, on Friday night. They took his body away for cremation. I went to see them and they are very angry because they think Rawley might have murdered their brother. A police officer put the idea into their heads apparently. Every day that Rawley doesn't come back makes it more possible as far as they are concerned.' Lorna was dry-eyed but looked as if she had been weeping recently because her eyes were red and swollen.

'You know that can't be true, though,' encouraged Dee.

'Do I? Half of me thinks so, but then I think perhaps he was getting rid of the only man who knew where he was going. One of the watchmen who guards the hangars at night said that Rawley flew out with a passenger. I can't find out who it was.'

A passenger! Dee thought, and remembered the missing American smuggler. Was he still in the Ritz? She didn't know but she could phone up and find out. *Don't be silly, don't go jumping to conclusions*, she told herself.

'From what I've seen of Rawley I would say that it's highly unlikely that he murdered anybody,' she told Lorna firmly.

Her friend nodded. 'I know. I think the same as you, but you never really know, do you?'

'Yes, you do. You love him, don't you?'

'Yes, I love him and I'm so worried about him, I'm nearly out of my mind and I don't know what to do,' Lorna gasped and then started to cry with shoulder-shaking, dry sobs.

'Can I use your phone?' Dee asked.

Lorna waved her hand in the direction of the squat black instrument. 'Go ahead.'

'Have you a phone book?' Lorna waved her hand again at the bookshelf. Dee found the Ritz number and rang it. When the desk clerk answered, she asked to speak to one of the barmen, Thomas or Raju.

When Thomas's voice came on the line, Dee identified herself and said, 'You remember that English gold smuggler I sometimes came in to see, don't you?'

'Yes,' said Thomas. 'He was taken away to the court.'

'He won't be back because he's gone to Poona jail,' she told him, though he almost certainly knew that already. 'But there was another one staying in the hotel, an American. Is he still with you?'

Thomas was sharply intelligent and loved to gossip. 'That one! The badmash Santos. He ran away the night we had the fire alarm. He's disappeared and the police are furious.'

'You had a fire alarm? When?' asked Dee.

'Last Thursday night or Friday morning. Yes, Friday morning, very early,' Thomas told her.

She hung up the phone and said to Lorna, 'I think Rawley might have been flying an American called Enrico Santos out of Bombay on Friday morning. He disappeared from house arrest in the Ritz that day and he's not been seen since. It's just a guess, of course.'

Lorna said, 'Where would the American want to go?'

'Well, nowhere in India because he's on the run from the law. And you say they didn't land in Karachi. Probably they'd go someplace in the Gulf. Aden? One of the Gulf States? Djibouti?' Dee suggested.

'I'll check every airport,' said Lorna. 'At least it will give me something to do.'

'Rawley has a brother, hasn't he?' Dee asked.

'Yes, he lives in France, near Draguignan. I don't know his address, but Paddy, his friend in Poona, will. He's known them both since they were little boys. I'll send him a telegram.' The arrival of her friend had galvanised Lorna into action. Up till now she'd been sunk in depression, hoping against hope Rawley would turn up.

'Give it to me and I'll hand it into the Central Post Office for you on my way home,' said Dee. She desperately wanted to help but couldn't think of anything practical to do.

Later that day Patrick Bryant received a telegram, which said, 'Rawley has disappeared and I don't know what to do.' Lorna had signed it and given two telephone numbers, one for the office and the other for her home, so he could contact her.

Patrick, who had no phone, walked to the nearby home of his friend, a doctor, and rang the first number. There was no reply there, however, so he tried the second. It was answered by Lorna's mother who seemed unsure whether her daughter was in or out. 'I'll take a message for her,' she volunteered after a period of witless dithering.

'Tell her Paddy is on his way,' said Bryant and hung up. Then he went home to pack and catch the night mail train to Bombay.

It was years since he'd been in the city and the change in it astonished him. It had always been a crowded, throbbing metropolis but now it was much bigger, busier, and more crowded than ever and he reeled when he stepped out of Victoria Station. A crowd of importunate beggars drew back when the white man addressed them in their own language with a flow of invective that even they could not match.

Paddy remembered what Rawley and Lorna had told him about her family magazine and decided to go there first, so he went back into the station to buy a Bombay *Tatler* from the magazine stand to find out the address. A taxi took him to Churchgate Street an hour and a half before work was due to begin. He sat patiently on the office stairs till Bubbles, always the first to arrive, found him.

'Oh, you poor man!' she exclaimed when he told her who he was waiting to see. Impressed by his stately, patrician manner, she installed him in Lorna's office and ran off to make a cup of tea. When she returned with it, he was standing before the biggest case of butterflies with a look of rapture on his face. 'What magnificent specimens!' he exclaimed. 'This must be the best collection of Oriental butterflies in the world.'

Bubbles had never liked the butterflies – they made her skin creep – but she pretended to share his admiration and they were both poring over the case when Lorna came in. The moment she saw Paddy – who she had not expected, because her absent-minded mother had not passed on his message – she burst into tears, which flowed from her as if they were coming from a long-built-up dam.

He held out his arms and she ran into them, clinging to him as she cried. 'Oh Paddy, Paddy, Rawley's vanished and they think he killed his mechanic,' she sobbed.

He let the crying subside before he spoke. 'Sit down, my dear,' he said gently. 'Tell me the whole story.'

She recounted everything, including Dee's theory that Rawley had disappeared while flying out an American gold smuggler. Paddy nodded as she spoke, and then said firmly, 'First of all, Rawley would never murder anybody, especially not his friend. I am absolutely sure of that. I can believe he'd fly out the smuggler though. There were some cargoes he'd never touch – drugs and children being shipped out for prostitution, for example – but guns and smugglers, yes, he'd carry them. When he brought you to Poona, he told me he was almost ready to give up flying and go back to Ireland with Tim because he'd made nearly enough money. He also told me how much in love he was with you, so you mustn't think he's run away and left you. If he's missing I'm sure it's against his will.'

She nodded. 'I *was* afraid he'd left me. I'm having his baby and he didn't know. I never told him. I was keeping the secret till I was sure, but now I am and I can't tell him'

The old man's eyes were full of sympathy as he said in a positive tone, 'Rawley will be delighted. He'll make a wonderful father. I can imagine him in Ireland teaching a child to ride, showing it how to do all the things he and Tim enjoyed when they were small. It's a wonderful free life there.'

'What's happened to him?' Lorna asked brokenly. 'With every day that passes I feel less and less sure that I'll see him again. Yesterday I contacted every airport within flying distance but he hasn't landed at any of them. I reported him missing to the police three days ago but they didn't seem to care very much.'

'Stop worrying,' Paddy told her. 'I've come down to help look for him. First I'm going to the Yacht Club to find myself a room. I've been a member there for over fifty years but I'm sure there's nobody old enough there to remember me now. I'll have to sleep for a bit because I'm an old man but by the afternoon I'll start my investigation.'

Four hours later Inspector Tommy Morrison was in his cubbyhole office at Byculla Police Station when a figure from his past came limping through the door.

'Young Tom,' cried Paddy Bryant. 'You haven't changed a bit!'

Tommy stood up and laughed. 'You were always a glib-tongued, flattering Irish liar, Paddy. What's brought you to Bombay? I haven't seen you for twenty-five years but you haven't changed much either.'

'I've come on serious business. A godson of mine has disappeared and I want you to find out what's happened to him,' said Paddy solemnly.

'Is he Indian?' asked Tommy.

'No, he's Irish, like myself. He's been flying a Piper

231

Cherokee in and out of Santa Cruz for a few years, smuggling guns to the Frontier most of the time, I'm afraid. Last Friday he took off with a mysterious passenger and disappeared completely.'

Tommy clicked his tongue. 'These chaps live dangerously. They nearly always end up dead. Will he have disappeared deliberately?'

'We all end up dead,' Paddy told him. 'But this one wasn't old enough to die and he certainly didn't disappear voluntarily, nor was he reckless. I want to know where he is and what's happened to him. I couldn't think of anyone better to help me than you.'

Their friendship went back to the years before the war when Tommy was a young police officer learning the ropes in a distant part of Bombay State. He'd met Paddy while dealing with a particularly difficult case in which a minor rajah, who was insane, murdered some of his servants. No one could be persuaded to give evidence against him but between them Paddy and Tommy ferreted out the truth and had the killer convicted and shut up for life in a mental asylum.

'Leave it with me,' said Tommy and wrote down all the information about Rawley that Paddy was able to tell him.

Twenty-Seven

Tommy Morrison was tired. He'd been in the police since he was eighteen years old and now he was fifty-three, a widower with two children living abroad, one in America and the other in Australia. When he started his career, to be an Anglo-Indian who looked far more English than Indian, with two English grandfathers and one half-English grandmother, had been a matter of pride, but today he ranked among the pariahs. There was no place for his kind in the new India.

He'd become reconciled to seeing Indians who were junior to him, and not such effective policemen, being promoted over his head. They went on to become chief inspectors and superintendents, but Tommy stayed an inspector and knew that was as far as he was ever going. Most of the other Anglo-Indians who worked with him had left the force long ago. Many had emigrated to Australia, like Tommy's youngest son, or gone to Britain where they found it difficult to integrate, but Tommy proudly stayed on because he loved his work and he loved the country of his birth.

Both of his children continually pleaded with him to go to live with them, but he stubbornly stayed in the Colaba bungalow he'd occupied all his married life. It was near the Anglo-Indian club, near the Afghan Church where he'd always worshipped, near the burial ground where he intended to lie eventually beside his wife who had died far too young.

The request for help from Paddy Bryant was a godsend for Tommy because it galvanised him out of the lethargy that had recently seized him. Because of his old friendship and respect for Bryant, he set about finding out about Rawley

Fitzgerald with the same zeal as he would have used thirty years ago.

First of all he went to the airport to question the clerks and the watchmen. From them he learned about the routine carried out by Rawley and his murdered mechanic. He heard too about their friendship and listened as people who knew them said how ridiculous it was to consider the possibility that Rawley had killed Sher Singh.

He went to Sher Singh's home and questioned the family. The dead man, he discovered, had a substantial amount of money in the bank, far more than a Sikh mechanic of his age would usually amass, so there was no suspicion that Rawley had been cheating him out of his share of the profits of their enterprise.

Sher Singh had been very discreet and had not talked to his brothers about where Rawley flew or who he worked for, so Tommy had to seek information about that elsewhere.

One of the night watchmen told him that Fitzgerald lodged in the home of Philip Gonsalves, one of the air traffic controllers, and Tommy sought him out in the control tower.

Mr Gonsalves said he was genuinely worried about his lodger's disappearance. 'He has been living in my house for three years and is like a son to me and my wife. She goes to church every day now and prays for his safe return,' he said.

'Can I go to talk to her about him?' Tommy asked, because he preferred the soft approach to witnesses rather than the strong-arm bullying tactics adopted by some policemen.

'Oh yes, she will want to help find him. She was so happy when he fell in love with his pretty Lorna. She thought he was going to be really settled at last,' said Gonsalves as he gave Tommy his address.

Mrs Gonsalves was a co-operative, intelligent woman. First of all she showed Tommy her lodger's room, and stood watching to make sure he did not take away anything he shouldn't while he searched it.

She was as astonished as he was when they found the cache of gold tucked under the mattress. It was an ingot as big as a chocolate bar and Tommy knew at once from the look of it that it was part of a smuggled consignment. He weighed the gold in his hands and reckoned it weighed about a kilo, and was worth around 10,000 rupees, the equivalent of six months' wages for Mr Gonsalves.

'This is evidence,' he told Mrs Gonsalves. 'I'll have to book it in but I'll give you a receipt for it, and if he comes back he'll be able to reclaim it.'

She was obviously upset. 'I shouldn't let you take it away,' she said.

'I'm sorry,' he told her, 'but I have to take it. It's probably smuggled gold and it might be possible to match it up with other consignments that have been seized by Customs.'

The last things they found were Rawley's will addressed to Tim and the letter he had left for Lorna. Tommy folded them carefully and put them in his pocket. 'If he doesn't come back I'll make sure these are delivered,' he said.

The suggestion that Rawley had gone for ever made Mrs Gonsalves' eyes fill with tears. 'May God watch over him,' she sobbed.

Tommy's hunch about the gold was correct. Its appearance and markings were found to match exactly the gold taken from the smuggler Enrico Santos who had disappeared from Bombay before coming up for trial.

To assist in his enquiries with Customs, Tommy enlisted the help of a friendly Indian colleague, Chief Inspector Fernandes, who had a particular interest in the smuggling trade and was known to be incorruptible.

Fernandes' approach was tough when he questioned the airport Customs men about Rawley's gold. Immediately he went in on the attack, showing the ingot to them and demanding, 'If you took all the gold off that American, where did this come from?'

'Perhaps another smuggler brought it in,' was the suggestion made by the middle-ranking Customs officer who had been in charge of the case.

'I doubt it.'

After several hours of stiff questioning, the Customs officer admitted that some of the American's gold had been 'distributed' to various people in authority. Some had also been passed on to an Indian contact of Enrico Santos.

Tommy and Fernandes leaned across the table as they questioned their witness. They were both in shirtsleeves and looked fairly cool but he was sweating profusely which told them they had him on the run. 'All we need to know now is the name of the Indian contact,' said Tommy softly.

'And if you don't tell us we'll take you in – and it would be a great pity if you found yourself being beaten up by your cellmates tonight,' warned Fernandes with a cold smile.

'The Advanis,' gasped the terrified man. 'It went to the Advanis. Old man Advani's wife collected it from the airport.'

When they conferred together later Tommy and Fernandes agreed that the involvement of the Advanis in the smuggling business was no surprise. That family had long been suspected of nefarious dealings but because of their friends in high places, they always escaped investigation. Even now there was no guarantee that they could be formally charged with anything.

It was decided that Tommy should pay a call on the Advanis at their family house, which stood in a large garden overlooking Kemp's Corner.

Gopalchand, the father, received the visitor in his salon and, when he heard the nature of the policeman's business, he immediately sent for his sons Raju and Madan who lived with their families in other parts of the huge house.

The brothers scoffed in a jovial way at Tommy's suggestion that they had anything to do with the gold-smuggling trade.

'We are legitimate businessmen,' said Madan with a

smooth smile. 'Why should we mix ourselves up with that business?'

Tommy stood his ground, however. 'I know you are involved and I can prove it,' he said. 'I have witnesses.'

He had one witness – the Customs officer – but he made it sound as if he had many more because he knew he had not yet exhausted the possibilities of finding out information.

The brothers looked at each other and Raju said, 'I think you should be very careful when you accuse us of these things, Inspector.' He stressed Tommy's rank to suggest that people superior to him would countermand anything he tried to do to them.

Tommy took a shot in the dark. 'I doubt if your friends would be able to get you off a charge of murder,' he said.

That changed their attitude. 'Murder! Don't be ridiculous. Who are we meant to have murdered?' asked Gopalchand.

'The pilot Rawley Fitzgerald and also his passenger Enrico Santos,' Tommy told them.

Gopalchand panicked. 'Rubbish! We know Fitzgerald because he flies liquor in for us from the Gulf. I'm prepared to admit that, but what makes you think we would want to kill him?' Their surprise seemed very genuine.

Tommy said, 'Fitzgerald is missing. He has disappeared. It is now ten days since he flew out of Bombay with Santos, as you paid him in gold to do, and neither of them has been seen since. Where did they fly to?'

Raju was the one who cracked. 'We paid him to fly the American to Djibouti. That was Santos's own idea because he knew he could buy himself a passage to Europe from there. He is a very difficult man, very dangerous.'

'Why is he dangerous?' asked Tommy.

'He is violent. He carried a gun. He threatened us. He came to India to fix up more business between his syndicate and us. He was meant to travel as a tourist but he was greedy and, without letting us know, he brought in gold to sell when he was here. It was *unfortunate* that he was picked up at the airport and we had to go to a great deal of trouble to arrange for him to be granted bail and stay with the other smuggler in the Ritz.' The way he stressed 'unfortunate' suggested that Santos's arrest could have been arranged.

'The other smuggler, the Englishman, was he working for Santos?' asked Tommy, who remembered how Dee Carmichael had come in to Byculla Police Station to interview the man from London.

Gopalchand made a face that showed his distaste. 'Santos is important but there are others above him. Weston was only a decoy. London meant him to be picked up to divert attention from more important carriers but when he made such a fuss about going to prison, we were afraid that he'd talk too much, so we paid for him to be pacified.'

Tommy shook his head and said sarcastically, 'Oh, the complications! But that doesn't help us find out what's happened to Rawley Fitzgerald. It seems to me that it might also be convenient for you – and perhaps for the people in London – if Santos disappeared.'

'I can assure you that we know nothing about where he is or what happened to him. On his instructions we arranged for him to be ferried to Djibouti and we have not seen either him or the pilot since,' said old Mr Advani.

'Have you contacted the people in London to find out if he got back there?' asked Tommy.

The Advanis shook their heads in unison. 'Because of the trouble with Santos we have severed our connection. We are no longer involved with gold smugglers,' said the old man grandly.

With her wet hair clinging to her face, Lorna leaned over the washbasin in her bathroom. Every morning for a week she'd been sick as soon as she wakened, and she knew now without a shadow of doubt that she was pregnant. She staggered as she walked back to bed to lie down. Then she lay flat on her back, staring up at the ceiling in utter hopelessness.

I'm pregnant. Soon it will show. Rawley has disappeared and I might never see him again. I do not know what to do.

The thoughts ran through her head over and over again as if they were printed on ticker tape.

It would almost be better, she decided, if she knew for certain that Rawley had run away from her. Then she could make up her mind. She turned on her side and looked at the calendar that hung beside her bed. She'd been marking off the days of his absence and, as she did every morning, she counted them. *One, two, three, four, five, six, seven, eight, nine, ten, eleven, twelve, thirteen.* Today would be the fourteenth. He'd been away for two weeks. She had to act soon if she was going to act at all.

Suddenly she decided what she had to do. She stood under the shower, washed her hair, made up her face and dressed carefully. Without consuming any breakfast apart from a cup of strong black coffee, she left the bungalow. Walking swiftly, she headed for the cluster of trees near her home where she knew Hussein and Jehangir took up their station every morning, waiting for her to appear.

'Take me to my doctor in Chor Bazaar,' she said shortly as she lay back against the prickly seat.

Hussein said nothing but looked at her sharply over his shoulder as if he knew what was going on.

The doctor's consulting room was in the Mohammedan part of the bazaar, in a narrow street lined on both sides with deep monsoon drains. Ramshackle wooden houses leaned towards each other across the roadway, and from their shuttered overhead verandahs, silent, faceless women in black burkas watched the traffic passing to and fro beneath them.

Lorna stalked into one of the buildings and disappeared up a narrow stairway. The doctor lived on the first floor and he was sitting in his room waiting for customers. Though the street outside was filthy, his clothes were immaculately white and his head was swathed in a tightly wound white turban.

When he saw her, he lifted both hands in a gesture of greeting which she copied. Then he gestured at a deep white cushion on the floor and she sat down on it. He had sharp, slanting eyes like a cat's. They stared at each other for a

239

few minutes before she said in Hindi, 'I think I am carrying a child.'

He nodded and said, 'Yes.'

'You can tell?' she asked.

'Yes.'

'How?'

'By your eyes.'

'So it's definite?' she wanted to know.

He nodded.

There was another pause and then he said, 'You want this child?'

She looked over his shoulder at a patch of blue sky showing above the roof of the house on the other side of the road. 'Part of me does, but it is not practicable now.'

'You want me to help you?' he asked and she nodded. Her hands were so tightly clenched; she could feel her fingernails cutting into the pads of her palms.

'How far on are you?' he asked.

'Almost two months,' she told him.

'That should not be too difficult. I will send a woman to you. She will massage your belly and within a day you will lose the child. Are you sure you do not want it?'

She nodded silently. 'Will it hurt?' she asked.

'No,' was the reply.

'Is it certain?'

'Almost certain. If it does not work you can take a special medicine, but this way is easier,' was his reply.

'How much will I pay the woman?' Lorna asked.

'Fifty rupees,' he said. *Fifty rupees!* she thought. *So little for something so important. So little for my baby's life.*

'When will the woman come?' she asked bleakly.

'She will be at your house this afternoon at four o'clock. Then you must go to bed and stay there till it happens,' said the doctor.

When she left Chor Bazaar she went to the office but did no work. Her eye was continually on the clock and at half-past three she stood up, grabbed her handbag and rode home in the gharry. All the time there were tears prickling behind her eyelids but she could not weep.

At four o'clock she was waiting on her verandah when a woman came sidling into the garden. She was small, thin and poor-looking, dressed in a cheap cotton sari of the sort that beggar women wore. When she saw Lorna she approached with her head bent and whispered in Hindi, 'You are the lady?'

Lorna stood up and gestured with her hand so the woman would follow her into the bedroom. They stood in the middle of the floor looking at each other. 'You know what you have to do?' Lorna asked.

'Yes, I know.'

'You have done it before?'

'Many times.'

'All right. Tell me what to do now.' There was a note of desperate acceptance in Lorna's voice.

The woman gestured at the bed. 'Lie down please.'

'Do I undress?'

'Not necessary. Just lie down. Pull up your dress. Be comfortable.'

Lorna stretched herself on the bed with her golden head propped up by lace-edged pillows and the woman produced a small bottle of oil out of a knot of cloth at her waist. Her arms were thin and sinewy and she had long-fingered hands. There were no golden bangles round her wrists, only thin, cheap ones of coloured shellac. Round her neck hung some sort of amulet from a necklace of leather like a bootlace.

'Close your eyes,' she said and Lorna felt the hands land very lightly on her naked abdomen. The first movements were very soft and light, hardly touches at all. Then, suddenly, they became stronger.

At that moment a knock came to the door and the woman stopped. The voice of Lorna's father's bearer could be heard saying urgently, 'Missy sahib, missy sahib, there are two men to see you. Please come. They say it is important.'

Lorna sat bolt upright. 'Who is it?' she shouted.

241

'Bryant sahib and a policeman. They say please come,' said the bearer urgently.

She jumped off the bed and ran to the door. 'Bring them to the verandah,' she told him. Her heart was hammering and she had forgotten all about the masseuse who stood by the bed watching. When Lorna remembered about her she just said, 'Wait,' and ran out of the room.

She was standing by the verandah rail with her hands gripping it tightly when Paddy and Tommy Morrison walked through from the main house. Paddy's face was grave and he did not smile as he said, 'Lorna, my dear, I'm afraid we have very bad news. I'm so sorry to have to tell you that poor Rawley is dead.'

A low moan came from her but all she said was, 'How do you know?'

'News has just come in that a Japanese tanker spotted the wreckage of a plane in the middle of the ocean about ten days ago. They hauled it aboard and found the remains of two bodies inside. They buried them at sea. We'd put out a general alert and when they heard about it, they contacted Bombay. The plane was definitely Rawley's. Its number was still legible.'

The old Irishman walked across to her and put both arms round her, holding her tightly. 'I am so very sorry. I loved him too,' he told her.

She leaned her head against his shoulder and he felt her hot tears through his shirt. 'It's a miracle you came just now. I nearly did something awful,' she said in a choked voice.

He thought she meant she'd been contemplating suicide. 'He wouldn't want that,' he told her. Then he looked across at Tommy and said, 'My friend Inspector Morrison has something for you, Lorna. He had to search Rawley's room when he disappeared and he found a letter for you. He's brought it now. And there's another letter and some gold for Tim. I'll send that on to him.'

The two men sat on either side of her when she took the letter. 'Don't read it now,' said Paddy.

'But I want to. I must,' she said and tore the envelope open. They tried to leave but she would not let them go so they sat silent and embarrassed while she read. When she finished, she put her hands over her face and wept.

Seeing her so overcome, they crept away, but before he went Paddy whispered, 'I'll come back and see you tomorrow.'

An hour later, when Lorna went back to her bedroom, she was surprised to find the masseuse still squatting in a corner. Hurriedly she fished fifty rupees from her handbag and gave them to the woman who protested, 'But it is not finished!'

'I don't want you now. I'm keeping the baby. You haven't hurt it, have you?'

The woman shook her head. 'It is not finished,' she said, not understanding and still trying to hand back the money.

Lorna waved it away. 'Go, go,' she cried and hustled her out of the house.

Twenty-Eight

Bubbles Bulabhai phoned Dee and said, 'I thought you would want to know what's happened to Lorna. Her lovely man Rawley's been killed in a plane crash. She's terribly sad. Perhaps you could come to see her.'

'Oh, that's awful. Of course I'll come. Where is she?' asked Dee.

'She's here, in the office.' Bubbles was whispering as if she was afraid of being overheard. 'She says she doesn't want to stay at home. Come today if you can.'

Dee went straight away and found Lorna in her office, rummaging about among her papers like someone totally distraught.

'I am so sorry,' said Dee and tried to put her arms round the other girl.

Lorna shook her off. 'Don't be sorry for me. I don't want people to be sorry for me,' she said angrily.

'I can't help being sorry. Poor Rawley. Poor you. It's terrible,' said Dee. She did not want to have to ask what happened, but Lorna was eager to tell her.

'Paddy came to see me and said the plane wreckage was picked up by a Japanese tanker. They only hauled it out of the sea to find out its number and identification and buried the bodies at sea. Is the right word "buried" when they've just been thrown into the water? It was Rawley's plane though. There's no doubt about that,' said Lorna. Two bright red spots were burning in her cheeks and she looked like someone suffering from fever.

'Bodies?' Dee queried.

'There were two of them. You were right about him having a passenger and it probably was that other gold smuggler you told me about. Inspector Morrison thinks so anyway,' Lorna told her.

'Did the plane crash?' Dee asked.

Lorna snapped, 'It must have, because it was wrecked – and now it's at the bottom of the sea so they'll never know exactly what happened. Anyway, Rawley's dead.' Her voice broke and she began to cry.

'Oh God, Lorna, don't fight it. Cry. Let it out. He was a lovely man and you're right to be broken-hearted,' said Dee.

'He left me such a wonderful letter,' said Lorna. 'The police found it among his things. When I read it I can hear his voice talking to me, saying the most wonderful things.'

Dee said nothing because there was nothing she could say and words would be little consolation for her friend. Lorna was walking up and down the room distractedly but suddenly turned round and blurted out, 'I nearly did the most terrible thing. I nearly got rid of his baby. In fact I'm not absolutely sure I haven't hurt it. I hope to God I haven't. I must have it. It's all I've got left of him!'

Dee grabbed hold of her and said sharply, 'Stop this at once. You're coming home with me and I'm going to give you a very stiff drink. I don't care if you say you never drink hard liquor, you're going to have some now. Come on. My car's outside. Don't argue.'

Surprisingly Lorna did as she was told and sat white-faced and silent while Jadhav whisked them through the city streets to Walkeshwar Road. In Dee's sitting room, with the curtains closed against the glare outside, they drank ice-cold gin and lime and Dee listened while Lorna told her about consulting the masseuse. 'She'd started to work on me really hard when Paddy and Inspector Morrison arrived, but I made her stop,' she said, twisting her hands together as she talked.

'Did anything happen?' asked Dee.

'No.'

'Then I don't think anything will if it hasn't by now. She probably didn't have time to really start on you.'

Lorna groaned. 'I hope not. I hope it's all right. I must have this baby.'

'What about your parents? Have you told them?' Dee asked.

Lorna shook her head. 'I've told Paddy, but not my father or mother. My father's too busy arranging the sale of the magazine. You were right when you said the Bhatia thing wouldn't come off. The Advanis have come back with an offer, not as much as my father wants but at least it's something. They say they're diversifying their interests and have decided they want to invest in publishing after all. He can talk about nothing else.'

'What did your friend Paddy say about the baby?' Dee wanted to know.

'He thinks I'm right to have it. He says Rawley would love a baby and so would his brother Tim, who can't have any himself because of his accident apparently.'

Dee shook her head doubtfully. 'But it's you who has to have it and bring it up without a father. You'll not be able to give it Rawley's name.'

Lorna swept those objections aside. 'I'll manage. Though the money from the sale of the magazine isn't as much as my father wanted, I'll get something, and my father's insisted I keep those two trunks full of the things I showed you. Perhaps they will be worth money after all.'

'Will you stay here?' asked Dee.

'No. I'll go back to Europe. I might go to Switzerland. There's a man there who wants to marry me.' Lorna had a vague, half-formed notion that she'd look up her old suitor, perhaps even marry him. It would be a cynical thing to do, she knew, but she'd tell him the truth first and if he accepted her and the baby, at least they could be a family. And he was rich. That would help a lot.

'I haven't told anyone else yet, but Ben and I are definitely

246

going home soon. He's been offered a big job in England,' Dee told Lorna.

'That's good,' was the reply, but Lorna was not really interested – and who could blame her, thought Dee.

Suddenly she remembered about the dancing girl figurine and said, 'I've something to tell you about your treasures. Ben's friend Dadi – the one who's going to be lumbered with Maya as a wife – is a jeweller and he says that the eyes of that statue you gave me are real emeralds. It's very valuable apparently. I insist that you take it back. Especially now.'

Lorna looked up. 'Is he sure about that?'

'He's certain, and he knows what he's talking about.'

'That's interesting because I've looked at all the other figures now and several of them have green eyes too. Bigger eyes than the one I gave you. Keep it. You don't give back presents, you know. It's very bad manners,' said Lorna firmly.

'You're being stupid. Dadi says the figure is so good I mightn't be allowed to export it,' Dee told her.

Lorna made a disparaging noise. 'Smuggle it out. Everybody else seems to be smuggling things, why not you? I'm going to let Paddy have a look at my box of treasures before he goes back to Poona. He'll know what I should do with them.'

'That's a good idea,' agreed Dee. 'If they're really as valuable as Dadi says, perhaps you'll not have to worry about money.'

Later in the afternoon, when they had eaten lunch and Lorna was calmer, Dee told Jadhav to drive her friend home, which he did with unusual courtesy because he respected the yellow-haired white woman for her fluency in his native Marathi.

After they left, Dee sat thinking about Rawley and his untimely death. Lorna had said that Inspector Morrison had turned up with Paddy Bryant to tell her about the discovery of the plane wreckage. What connection did Tommy have with this business?

On impulse she lifted the phone and rang him up.

When he heard her voice, he said, 'Hello, Dee. I was intending to call in and speak to you about that smuggler fellow you knew.'

'In connection with Rawley Fitzgerald's death by any chance?' she asked.

'Yes, it's a sad business,' he said.

'Do you think it was an accident?' she asked.

'What else could it be?' he replied.

'I don't know. It's just so strange. His mechanic was found strangled, wasn't he? Why was he killed?' said Dee.

'I'll call in at your place and we'll talk about it tomorrow. Will half-past ten be convenient?' he said.

When Tommy came she gave him coffee and told him all she knew about Ronnie Weston and Enrico Santos.

'When I heard that Rawley'd flown out with a passenger I guessed that it was Santos because he vanished from the Ritz that night. Yet Algy kept telling me that he wasn't important,' she told Tommy.

'Who's Algy?' Tommy asked.

She told him about her old friend, the news agency and Ernest who took drugs. 'And Algy's disappeared too. He went the day after Rawley. Never said a word about it. Just went. Brian Meredith, the British Council man, says that Algy was a spy. You don't think he's been eliminated too, do you?' she said.

'Not unless *he* was Rawley's mystery passenger – but according to the Advani family, it was Santos right enough. They fixed up the flight and paid for it,' Tommy told her.

'The Advanis? They're buying Lorna's father's magazine. She told me yesterday that the sale's almost finalised now,' she said.

Tommy grinned ruefully as he said, 'Really? They must be going legitimate.' Then he became solemn again and asked, '*Who* said your friend Algy was a spy?'

She told him, 'Brian Meredith, the British Council representative in Bombay. The joke is that on the same day he said Algy was a spy, Algy told me that Brian was one too. They were like a couple of kids, calling each other names.'

Tommy frowned. 'They could both be spies, I suppose. I don't know Meredith though. What connection has he with all this?'

'None really. He runs the British Council office and reading room in Marine Drive. Ben and I went to Shivaji's fort with him and his wife and he scared me to bits when we were there. He's fascinated by Shivaji and the Thugs who he says still worship in the temple at the fort . . .' Her voice trailed away and as she looked at Tommy she knew he was thinking the same thing as she was. Sher Singh had been strangled in traditional Thug style.

'I'm not suggesting anything,' she said hurriedly.

'Of course not,' said Tommy smoothly.

Twenty-Nine

The Wesley family was having a conference over the tea table. Jack had sent the bearer over to his daughter's apartment with a special request that she take tea with him and her mother.

'I have something to tell you. After all their dithering, the Advanis have made a definite offer for the *Tatler*,' said Jack, looking over the tray of teacups and saucers at his wife and daughter. In spite of his distraction about business, it struck him that Lorna was not looking well. Her cheeks were sunken and there were dark purplish half-circles under her eyes. She was unusually silent, contributing little to the discussion.

'That's good,' said Ella. 'Is it a satisfactory offer?'

'Not particularly, but there's nobody else interested so I think we've no option but to accept it,' he told her.

Lorna lifted her head and asked, 'How much will they pay?'

'Nine hundred and fifty thousand rupees. I wanted two and a half million but there's no chance of getting that from them or anyone else,' said Jack.

A low sigh of disappointment came from Ella, but Lorna said nothing. *The Fates are working against us at every turn*, she thought.

Trying to cheer them up, Jack added, 'At least I got them to add to their original offer. They started off at eight hundred thousand but they expected me to bargain, of course.'

'It's not a lot of difference. You can't have bargained very hard,' said his wife, whose lips had taken on a petulant droop.

Jack turned to look at Lorna. 'There's not much to share between us, I'm afraid, my dear.'

She said up straight in her chair and said, 'I don't want any of it. You and Mother must have it all.'

'I won't do that. You'll have your share. I promised you that when you came back. I was going to give you fifty thousand rupees, the butterflies and the contents of the cabin trunks in the office,' said her father.

Her mother protested, 'And what will we live on? Eight hundred thousand rupees won't keep us going for the rest of our lives. It's only about fifty thousand pounds and you'll have to pay bribe money to get it out of India. How much are you thinking of giving to Lorna now?'

'I've told you I don't want any money. Just my fare and enough to keep me till I get a job,' Lorna protested again.

Her father looked fondly at her as he said, 'I might have found you a job already. The Bhatia girl who was going to edit the *Tatler* for the Advanis has backed out and Mr Advani asked me if you would like to continue as editor. He's prepared to pay you a good salary and write your appointment into the sale contract.'

Lorna gave a strange little gasp and said, 'No, oh, no. I'm sorry. There is absolutely no way that I want to stay on here. He'll have to find someone else for that job.'

Her mother looked surprised. 'But I thought you loved India! You're always going on about how superior everything Indian is compared to European things – their medicine, their food, their clothes. All my friends are astonished at the way you behave, just like a native, talking native languages and riding about everywhere in that gharry!'

Lorna glared at her. 'The sooner I can leave this place, the better I'll feel. I'd go today if I could,' she snapped. Then she stood up and pushed back her chair. 'Sell the magazine. Do what you like and don't think about me. Neither of you have ever done much of that anyway. I'll manage on my own.'

As she stormed from the room, Jack and Ella stared at each other in total amazement.

Elisabeth McNeill

'What did she mean by saying that we never think of her? We love her!' said Ella in a quavering voice, and as far as she was capable of loving, it was true.

The sound of running feet on the gravel path outside was heard and Jack walked over to look out of the window, just in time to see his daughter speeding towards the gate of their compound.

There was no sign of Hussein and Jehangir on the road so she was forced to flag down a black and yellow taxi to take her to the Yacht Club, an old building next door to the Taj and overlooking the Gateway of India. Lorna averted her eyes from the huge stone gateway as she dismounted from the taxi because she had not been back there since sailing in the harbour with Rawley.

Paddy was in an apartment at the front of the first floor and saw her emerging from the taxi, so when she went into the club, he was coming down the stairs. Without speaking he put an arm round her shoulders and took her up to his sitting room, telling a servant to bring them tea as he went.

When he had her seated and calmer, he poured the tea and put a generous slug of brandy into each cup from a battered silver hip flask. 'There's nothing like brandy to soften pain a little,' he said, handing a cup to her.

She sipped at it and felt warmth flow through her. It seemed that everyone was pressing spirits on her these days. She hoped she didn't start liking them too much.

'What will I do, Paddy?' she asked after she told him about the magazine sale.

'What do you want to do?' He answered her question with another question.

'I want to have the baby, but I worry about not being able to look after it,' she whispered.

'In what way?' he asked.

'Financially. My father's sold the magazine but it hasn't brought in enough to look after three of us, far less four. I've been thinking about going to Switzerland and marrying a man

252

I know there. He's very rich and I know he'd marry me,' she told him.

He shook his head gravely. 'That doesn't sound a very good or honest thing to do.'

'I don't think I can afford morality right now,' she said bitterly.

'How much money will you need?' he asked.

She shook her head. 'I've no idea. More than I have, in any case. I want to have the baby in Europe and that'll be expensive.'

'Have you thought of selling something? Those butterflies in your office are very valuable, and I don't imagine they'll be included in the sale to the Advanis,' he told her.

'Are they valuable? I've never liked them but one of the reasons I came to see you tonight was to ask your advice about some other things I own. My father's given me the butterflies and the contents of two cabin trunks full of bits and pieces that my great-grandfather collected. Dee Carmichael tells me that they could be valuable. Will you come with me and look at them now?'

He consulted his watch. 'Dinner's at eight thirty and I don't want to miss it. At my age, food is one of the last pleasures left. Where are the things you want to show to me?'

'In my office, not far away. I have the key in my pocket; let's go now, please,' she said, standing up.

He sighed and smiled. 'All right,' he said.

The watchman who looked after the office block salaamed respectfully when she walked into the entrance at the bottom of the stairs where his bedroll was already spread out. She told him that she was going to her office for half an hour and that he could lock up again when she left.

Paddy followed her up the stairs and paused for a moment before the glass cases of butterflies which shone like jewels in the harsh light of the overhead bulbs. With a sigh he said, 'They're magnificent. Very rare, very fine.'

Over his shoulder she said, 'Wait till you see what's in here, though.' She gestured to tell him to follow her into the cupboard that held the cabin trunks. When she threw back the lid of the first one and started bringing out figures and carved heads, he gasped in utter amazement.

'My dear girl,' he exclaimed, 'that's a Gandhara head you've got in your hands. Have you any idea what it's worth?'

'Not a clue, but I think it's lovely,' she said cradling the noble stone head in her cupped hands.

Paddy dropped to his knees by the trunk and reverently began to lift out piece after piece. There were images of Hindu gods, dancing girls, kneeling bulls, stone heads with slanting, knowing eyes and sensual lips. He gasped in astonishment when he found the two Chinese pottery horses.

'Where did these come from?' he asked.

Lorna told him, 'Apparently my grandfather and his father travelled all over the place looking for butterflies and picked up these other things on their travels.'

One by one Paddy laid the pieces on the floor beside him as he watched Lorna open the second trunk, which was full of embroidered and jewel-encrusted textiles. She held out what looked like a large, stiff bedcover studded with gems. 'Look at this,' she said.

'It's a coat for an elephant,' he told her, 'and those stones are rubies and sapphires.'

He was frowning when the time came to repack the treasures. 'You're sure that you have legitimate ownership title to all this?' he asked.

She nodded. 'Oh yes, it isn't loot. And it's mine. My father has given it to me because he can't give me as much money as he'd hoped. My great-grandfather bought every single item and he's listed them all, with their prices and the date he bought them, in a book I found in the second trunk. Do you think they have a commercial value?'

'Very much so, but I'm wondering if the government of India would let you export them if they knew what you've got here,' he told her. Then he thought for a bit and said, 'You don't like the butterflies much though, do you?'

She agreed with a shake of the head. 'They make me feel creepy. I much prefer these other things. Besides, I'll have to leave the butterflies here because transporting them will be far too complicated. They're so delicate.'

'You could donate the collection to a museum,' Paddy told her. 'I know a man who's high up in the Indian Museum Service. He'd look after the butterflies well, and he'd love to have them because they are a remarkably fine collection. Some are no longer in existence. I think you might do a sort of trade-in. You give my friend the butterflies and he'll get you an export licence for your cabin trunks.'

She was watching him carefully. 'And what will I do with the things in the trunks when I get them to Europe?' she asked.

'A relative of mine has a son who works for Sotheby's in Bond Street. I'll contact him and ask his advice. We'll have to take some photographs of the more unusual pieces so he can tell what we're talking about, though,' he said.

'So you really think they're saleable?' she asked with a note of hope returning to her voice.

'They're more than saleable. Collectors all over the world will be fighting to buy them,' he assured her.

Thirty

Ben Carmichael's resignation was accepted with bad grace and he was told that he would have to serve out three months' notice. A check-up with the woman doctor who delivered her first daughter confirmed Dee's suspicion that she was pregnant and, in order to have a holiday before she faced an ayah-less life, it was decided that she would sail home with the children in two months' time. Ben would follow a month later by air.

The sad business began of saying goodbye to the servants in the house and to the friends they would probably never see again. Tears were often shed but not everything was gloomy. Party followed party and for a time Dee put the tragedy of Rawley Fitzgerald and Lorna to the back of her mind, though she never fully forgot. The memory hung over her like an ever-present cloud. She saw Lorna once or twice but her friend was growing distant as she too set about cutting her ties with India.

The magazine changed hands and the Advanis honoured their agreement with Jack Wesley, paying the purchase money in full. Before he went back to Poona, Paddy was as good as his word in making sure the bulk of Lorna's treasures was safely shipped out by freighter. The butterflies were formally gifted to the Natural History section of Bombay Museum in the name of Edmund Wilberforce Wesley, and rapturously received by the curator.

Bubbles Bulabhai was appointed editor of the Bombay *Tatler* and quickly began to make a great success of the job. Six weeks after Rawley's death, in the anticlimactic days that always follow Christmas, Lorna booked an air passage to Geneva.

When she announced her departure to her parents, she told them that she was pregnant and that she was going to Switzerland to meet up with François Picard, an old friend who wanted to marry her.

Ella was thunderstruck. 'But he can't be the father of your baby,' she said.

'He isn't,' agreed Lorna. 'It's Rawley Fitzgerald's baby – and he's dead, as you know. But I've told François about it and he still says he wants to marry me. It's me that's not sure.'

'Is he able to look after you?' asked Jack cautiously.

'More than able. He's a millionaire,' Lorna told them and her mother brightened up visibly. 'That's all right then,' she said.

Dee and Ben went to see Lorna off at the airport, but their farewells were restrained. From the viewing gallery Dee watched her friend's still slender figure walking alone towards the plane and was harrowed by its tragic gallantry.

She compared that view with her other recent airport memory, of seeing the Pope's tall, ascetic figure emerging from his plane a month before. Where Lorna stirred her heart with affection and pity, he had chilled her because of his glacial indifference to the hysterical worship of the crowds of Christians who had gathered to see him.

The Papal visit was Dee's last assignment as a stringer and, while she was busy following in the hysterical press contingent, she received a letter from Ronnie Weston. He sounded very cheerful and wrote to ask her to send him a recipe for *pâté maison* because he'd been put in charge of the Class A kitchen and wanted to upgrade the menus. He also wondered if she knew how to cook onion soup – 'the kind with cheese in it'. She wrote back with recipes and told him they were leaving but gave no forwarding address. She never heard from him again.

In the chaotic cavalcade that followed the Pope, Dee looked

for Ernest Nilsen in every gathering but he was never there. Wondering if he'd heard from Algy, she went to the office of WWN but found it deserted. The desks were thick with dust and a coil of yellowing ticker-tape paper snaked across the floor. There was no one about apart from the tea boy who spoke no English and rolled his eyes with terrified incomprehension when she asked him questions.

During the Carmichaels' last week in Bombay, Brian Meredith phoned to invite them to a farewell dinner. It was not a success because all the time she was in the Marine Drive flat, Dee could not clear her mind of the memory of Brian's fascination with treachery and ritual killing. Had he anything to do with the murder of Rawley's mechanic? she wondered.

Brian himself was as innocently hearty and brash as ever, pouring claret with a generous hand and laughing at his own jokes.

'We're sorry that you're going,' he said to his guests. 'But Phoebe and I are on our way as well. The news came over yesterday.'

'Is your new posting to Washington?' asked Dee, remembering that was what they wanted.

Phoebe shook her head. 'Oh no, it's much more interesting than that. We're thrilled with it.'

'Where are you going that'll be more interesting than Washington?' asked Dee, who longed to visit America.

Phoebe looked at Brian and they both smiled. 'Guess!' he said.

Dee hated pointless guessing games. 'I couldn't possibly,' she said.

'It's Ulan Bator!' said Brian as if he was announcing, *Utopia!*

'Ulan Bator? Where's that?' asked Ben.

'It's the capital of Outer Mongolia,' Brian told him.

Ben almost choked on his wine. 'You poor—'

Phoebe interrupted. 'Oh no, we're very pleased. We're going to look at every site associated with Genghis Khan.'

258

Another ruthless killer, thought Dee.

On their way home the guests talked about Brian's posting and Ben said, 'I think Brian must have blotted his copybook pretty badly if he's been posted to Outer Mongolia.' Then they both burst into laughter.

One of the last visitors to the house in Walkeshwar Road was Tommy Morrison, who brought Ben a group photograph of the police rugby team as a farewell present.

Dee asked him what had happened about the killing of Sher Singh and the tragic crash of Rawley's plane. 'Is the investigation still going on?' she wanted to know.

'I'm afraid that we haven't been able to find out much. The only people who could really help us were the two in the plane,' Tommy told her.

'I keep wondering who would want to kill the mechanic at the same time as Rawley and his passenger crashed,' said Dee.

'Of course, it's always possible that the plane might have come down on its way back to Bombay and not on its way out,' said Tommy.

'But there were two bodies in it, weren't there?' queried Dee.

The policeman nodded. 'That pins it down a bit, but we don't know anything definite. The mechanic could have been killed because of a woman, or a gambling debt. He had quite a few girlfriends and he gambled a lot too. It might just be a coincidence that he died at the same time as his boss.'

'The weather wasn't bad when the plane crashed, was it?' Ben asked.

'No,' said Tommy. 'It was very good. And there are no reports of a collision with another plane or anything like that. It was probably a mechanical failure, and that's what makes me think the mechanic was put out of the way: it was so that the plane could be nobbled. I'll never prove it, though.'

'Who'd do that?' Dee asked.

Tommy frowned as he said, 'I investigated every lead and I think the real target was Santos. I went to see Meredith, that friend of yours in the British Council, and he told me that he'd been watching your other friend, the news agency man, for some time. He thinks he had something to do with it. According to him your friend Byron works for the CIA.'

Dee gasped, 'The CIA! That's crazy.' But as the thought sunk in she realised that it wasn't really impossible. The CIA was exactly the sort of organisation that would appeal to Algy, who lived more in imagination than in reality. 'But why would the CIA want to kill Rawley?' she asked.

'He was just unlucky to be around when they were killing Santos, who definitely had underworld connections in America and who was rocking the boat a bit. The CIA specialises in backing disruptive elements and then getting rid of them when they become too difficult. We knew someone was working for them in Bombay but we suspected that Burmese chap, Nilsen. He was questioned about the night the Sikh died and had a watertight alibi, provided by his boss Byron. Byron's turned up in New York and I got someone there to question him, but his statement backed up Nilsen's completely. They provide alibis for each other – such good alibis that I smell a rat,' said Tommy.

Dee frowned. 'But what about Brian? He might have been involved too.'

'I suppose he might. He certainly was watching everything that went on, but his wife's provided his alibi and it's watertight as well. Officially it's been decided that Fitzgerald and his mechanic fell out and he either murdered him or had him murdered. He was friendly with Pathans and they'll kill someone for a friend as a favour,' said Tommy.

Dee looked angry as she burst out, 'That's very unfair! I'm sure Rawley never killed anyone and he's being used as a convenient scapegoat. But I'm not so sure about the others. I went into the WWN office the other day looking for Ernest, but he wasn't there. Has he disappeared too?'

'We told him to get out of the city. He's gone to Calcutta,' Tommy told her.

Ben looked at his wife with disapproval as he said, 'It's a

good thing that you're getting out of all that snooping around among those unsavoury characters.'

She sat silent for a few moments, not really listening to him. Then she said, 'If I wrote a story about this I'd say Brian Meredith was the chief suspect. He's pretty weird. Why should he tell you all that about Algy anyway?'

Tommy shrugged. 'Because he's the British agent in Bombay. There's always one. Sometimes they work for the High Commission and sometimes not, but we find out about them eventually.'

'Why should he be watching Algy, though?' Dee wanted to know.

'Professional rivalry, I guess. They pretend to be friendly towards the Americans but they seem to spend more time spying on them than on anyone else,' Tommy told her.

'Listen, Dee,' insisted Ben, sitting forward, 'I really think it's time you forgot all about this stuff. You stumbled into the situation and I reckon you're lucky not to have got farther drawn in than you were. Three people have died and no one's ever going to find out who did it or why. Forget it now.'

'Yes,' agreed Tommy. 'I think that's the wisest thing to do. I'm afraid that this is one case that's always going to have a question mark hanging over it.'

Thirty-One

A doorman in dark green livery opened the door of Sotheby's Bond Street salerooms to a tall young woman with well-cut blonde hair. She was trying to push her way through while burdened with several carrier bags bearing the logo of the White House, which was only a short distance up the street.

'Good morning, madam,' he said.

'I have an appointment with your Oriental Antiquities expert,' she told him.

'Allow me to help you with your parcels,' he said politely, taking the bags from her. When she handed them over it was possible to see that she was pregnant. The carriers, which were full of baby clothes, had hidden her bulge.

One of the vigilant girls on the reception desk came bustling over, saying, 'Are you Mrs Wesley? Mr Pryce told me you were coming this morning. I'll ring him and tell him you're here.'

'I'm *Miss* Wesley,' said Lorna with dignity, looking around for a chair. 'And I'm pregnant, so is it possible for me to sit down, do you think?'

Without blinking an eyelid, the doorman produced a chair into which Lorna subsided with a deep sigh. It was April, the sun was glinting on the pavement outside and London was looking springlike and beautiful with white, yellow and purple crocuses spangling the grass beneath the trees of the Royal parks.

She closed her eyes with a sigh, but opened them again almost immediately because she heard a discreet cough to alert her to the fact that a man was looking down at her.

'Lorna Wesley?' he asked, neatly avoiding having to say 'Miss' or 'Mrs'.

'Yes,' she said.

'I'm Dominic Pryce, the Orientals chappie,' he told her and grinned disarmingly. He was tall, angular and mousy-brown-haired, looking as she imagined Paddy must have done when he was young. His dark, pin-striped suit was immaculate and hung on him as only a Savile Row suit can.

'Hello,' she said and struggled to rise to her feet. Solicitously he put a hand on her elbow and guided her to a glass-panelled door. 'Come up to my office. I've got a lot of things to tell you,' he said.

In his chaotic office, where half-unpacked boxes surrounded a lovely partner's desk and one of her Chinese horses perched on an upturned packing case, he produced a comfortable seat for her and asked, 'Care for a glass of champagne?'

She blinked, laughed and said, 'If it's properly chilled.'

'Of course,' he said solemnly, and opened a small fridge behind the desk.

The champagne was a very good brand which set bubbles tingling in Lorna's nose and filled her with a delicious feeling of bonhomie such as she had not felt for months. She raised her flute to him and he solemnly toasted her back, his brown eyes scrutinising her carefully.

'My great-uncle Paddy tells me that you have proof of ownership of the things you've sent to us,' he said carefully.

'Oh yes. My father gave them to me and I've a letter saying so. The things belonged to my grandfather and great grandfather, and they were such careful men that they listed everything they ever bought, along with the dates and the prices,' she laughed.

'That's good. Perfect provenance. We have to be careful,' he said.

A slight look of worry crossed her face as she said, 'I hope you're not going to tell me that you can't sell them or that it's just junk.'

He laughed. 'Not at all. There's not a bad piece among them. Your ancestors were very astute buyers. You should be proud of them.' As he spoke he pointed his glass towards the Chinese horse and said, 'Ming! Very valuable.'

She stared silently at him and he stared back with a bland smile till she eventually had to break the impasse by saying, 'Well – tell me. Will you sell them?'

He laughed, leaned over and refilled her glass. 'Not only will we sell them but we'll give them a sale all to themselves. We're thinking of calling it the Wilberforce Wesley Collection. It'll be advertised in America as well as in this country and we're confident that there will be huge international interest.'

Lorna leaned back, feeling faint. Then she said, 'Thank heavens! I really need money, you see, especially right now.' In an involuntary gesture she patted the bulge beneath her navy smock. As if to back her up, she felt the baby inside give a great kick of delight.

'There's no Mr Wesley?' asked Dominic Pryce.

'He's dead, I'm afraid. I'm a – widow,' said Lorna. It was easier than going into all the details.

'How sad,' he replied. 'But I'm delighted to be able to tell you that you're going to be a very rich widow.'

Oh, to hell with discretion, she thought. 'How rich?' she asked.

'At a conservative estimate I would say that the entire collection is likely to fetch around one and a half million—'

She interrupted him sharply. 'Rupees?'

'Pounds,' he went on smoothly.

She stuck out her empty glass. 'Is there any champagne left in that bottle?' she asked.

He refilled it and said very solemnly, 'Of course we, as auctioneers, will take our percentage. That's usually ten per cent but, for such large collections, we often do a special deal. We also charge you for the cost of the catalogues and things like that, but it won't be crippling. We're planning to hold the sale at the start of the autumn season if it's all right with you.'

She did a rapid little calculation in her head. The baby was due at the end of June and the money she'd got from her father was not going to last much longer. 'Can't it happen sooner?' she asked.

He shook his head. 'We need to advertise it well and that takes time. We don't want to run the risk of missing the really big buyers.' As if he could read her mind, however, he went on, 'But if you need money, we'd be happy to let you have some on account.'

She frowned. 'Wouldn't that be a bit of a risk for you?'

'Not a bit. I assure you that unless you want us to advance you a couple of million, our investment will be quite safe,' he said.

She looked at him with appreciation. *What a smooth operator*, she thought.

'What relation are you to Paddy?' she asked.

'He's my mother's uncle,' he told her.

'Have you ever met him?'

'He used to come and take me out of school for the day at weekends sometimes if he was home on leave, but I haven't seen him for a long time. He keeps in touch with my mother though. They're very fond of each other. My family have close links with Ireland and I dream about going back there to live one day myself,' he confessed.

'I'm very fond of Paddy too,' she said. 'He was wonderful to me when Rawley died.'

Dominic Pryce nodded. 'He wrote to me about that,' he said. *So he probably knows I'm not a widow*, she thought, *but he didn't blink an eye. How tactful.*

She stood up. Her head was reeling after the champagne on an empty stomach and she could not get to grips with the realisation that she was on the verge of being very rich indeed. *Thank heavens for Great-Grandpapa*, she thought.

'There was a painting of my great-grandfather hanging in

my office in Bombay. I wish I'd brought it with me when I left,' she said, feeling grateful to the stiff old man for the first time.

'Is it still there?' he asked.

'As far as I know,' she said.

'Then I'll write and ask them to send it on. We can use it in the catalogue,' he enthused.

Lorna laughed. 'I'll give you my successor's name. I'm sure she'll be glad to get rid of it. He's a very gloomy-looking old boy.'

Before she left she wrote Bubbles' name and the *Tatler*'s address on a piece of paper for Dominic Pryce and, in return, accepted a cheque for thirty thousand pounds – on account.

When she was out on the pavement again, London was looking even more wonderful, as if it had been brushed with gold. She wished she could put her parcels down and do a war dance, but what she did instead was wave at a passing taxi and tell him to take her to the Ritz.

Later that afternoon, after more champagne, a delicious lunch and a visit to the bank, she went to Victoria Station and boarded a train for Paris.

Three days later she arrived by train at St Maxime on the Mediterranean coast of France. Summoning up a taxi, she said, 'Drive me to Draguignan.'

Thirty-Two

Tim Fitzgerald lay sunning himself in a canvas chair on the flagged terrace of his little house near Draguignan. Nearby a group of men were playing *boules* and shouting at each other.

Suddenly he felt a hand on his arm and his lover Paulina's voice hissed urgently, 'A woman has come.'

He sat up, blinked his sightless eyes and asked her, 'What woman?'

'A woman with yellow hair – *enceinte.*'

'A pregnant woman with blonde hair? Who is it?'

'She says she is Rawley's woman,' said Paulina.

'My God! Bring her out,' he said sharply, smoothing down his rumpled shirt and saying, 'How do I look? Am I neat and tidy?'

'You are beautiful,' she said, fondly stroking his cheek before going off and, in a very different tone of voice, saying to Lorna, 'This way. He is out here.'

Lorna was very tired from her journey and could only waddle as she progressed across the terrace towards the man in the chair. From the side he looked so like Rawley that she felt the desire to weep almost overwhelm her. He had the same broad-shouldered build; the same proud head set on a strong neck; the same beaked, Wellingtonian nose. Then he turned to face her and she saw that his face was ravaged by scars, red and livid puckerings of skin that disfigured him completely.

'Oh!' she gasped.

'I'm sorry if I shocked you. Didn't you expect me to

267

look like this?' he asked. His voice and accent were like Rawley's too.

'Rawley said you'd had an accident,' she said softly, sitting down on another chair beside him.

'So I did. And so did he. We've been an unlucky pair,' he said.

Instinctively she put out a hand and took one of his. 'I'm so glad to meet you at last. Rawley talked about you a lot,' she said.

He put up his other hand and gently felt her face. 'You're Lorna. Rawley said you were lovely. He's right, too. I can sense it.'

Tears choked her voice as she asked, 'Did he write to you about me?'

'Yes, several times, but most of all he wrote about you in his last letter. His will, really. I've just managed to get it through probate. He said if anything happened to him, he hoped we would be able to meet. When the letter was sent on by Paddy I tried to contact you, but they said you'd left Bombay.'

'I left soon after he was killed. I couldn't stay there any longer,' she told him.

'I wrote to your parents and they said you'd gone to Switzerland to get married,' he said.

She clicked her tongue. 'They *hoped*! I said I was going to see a man who wanted to marry me but in the end I couldn't go through with it. My mother was disappointed because he's very rich. She wouldn't have cared if he was Bluebeard provided he had plenty of money.'

'So you didn't marry him? But Paulina said you're pregnant. Is it his baby?' he asked.

'It's Rawley's baby. That's what I've come to see you about,' she said.

Tim drew back as if she'd struck him. 'Rawley's baby? Are you sure?'

'I'm positive. I was going to tell him just before he flew out for the last time but I wanted to be certain, so I planned to tell him when he got back. I think the baby was conceived in Goa. We were so incredibly happy there,' she whispered.

'He wrote to me about taking you to Goa,' Tim said.

'It's his baby,' Lorna said again, 'and I want it to have his name. But we weren't married and I can't register it as his, so I thought I'd ask you to adopt it so it can be called Fitzgerald. You don't have any children of your own, do you?'

He nodded but didn't answer that question. After a short silence he called out, 'Paulina! Come here, Paulina.'

She was a big woman, quite a bit older than him, heavily built and very dark but elegant, with menacing eyes like a Mafia matriarch. She did not look at Lorna.

'Do you want to have more children, Paulina?' Tim asked her.

'Are you mad? I have two sons already as you well know and they are now men. I have no wish to bear more children,' she snapped.

'Would you mind if I had a baby?' Tim asked.

Paulina's glittering eyes shot over to Lorna. 'You are really mad,' she said. She pretended to be about to walk away but it was obvious she was intrigued. Coming back and pointing at Lorna's belly, she asked, 'Is that the child you are going to have?'

In rapid Spanish Tim explained to her what Lorna had suggested, and Lorna, who could follow a little of what was being said, added, 'But I don't want you to keep it. I'll keep it myself.'

Tim looked at her and asked, 'Why should I adopt a child that I cannot keep? I doubt if that would be legal.'

Lorna panicked. 'But I'm not giving my baby up. It's all I have left of Rawley.'

'Then we must think about your suggestion. It's not a thing one rushes into,' said Tim. In a different tone of voice he added, 'It's fortunate you arrived today because tomorrow Paulina and I leave for Ireland. Rawley left money to restore our old house, Killygrattan. Probate's just come through and we're going over to see what can be done with the funds available.'

Lorna clasped her hands together, 'Oh, please can I come too? I might be able to help, you see.'

'Help?' Tim laughed, but not unkindly. 'What can you do to help rebuild a house in your condition?'

'I'm sure I'll be able to do something,' she said confidently.

Paulina drove them across France in Tim's battered old Volvo. They took their time and spent nearly two weeks on the journey, stopping at small hotels and auberges where Tim was greeted as a friend. If Lorna tried to pay their bills, her travelling companions were most insulted so every expense was shared. Eventually they reached St Malo and boarded a ferry for Cork.

Once on board Tim was in a state of marked agitation because he had not been home for many years. When the misty blue outline of Ireland appeared on the horizon early in the morning, he stood on deck, sniffing the air and saying, 'I can smell it. I'm home. I can smell Ireland.'

Killygrattan was about ten miles from Cork and as they drew nearer to it, his excitement increased.

'I wonder who's still alive,' he said, leaning forward in his seat. 'Have we reached the peat bog yet, Paulina? Is there a donkey in the field over there? Old Gilly always kept his donkey there.' There was a donkey and when they told him so, he sat back with tears trickling down his scarred cheeks.

He soon recovered and began to give sharp directions. 'Turn left at the crossroads. Go on half a mile and you'll see a high wall. After another hundred yards, you come on the main gate. Go through it and up the drive then we're there.'

They were all silent when the car turned in at the gate and carefully negotiated a deeply potholed drive fringed with ancient trees. Finally it drew to a stop in front of a derelict-looking house. Paulina and Lorna, who had become *almost* friendly during the journey, looked at each other in alarm. *Is this it?* Lorna wondered, but said nothing.

Tim was the one who spoke first. 'Has it still got a roof?' he asked.

Lorna got out of the back of the car, stretched her arms and legs, looked up and said, 'Yes, it has a roof but there's a lot of weeds and grass growing out of it.'

He laughed, 'Weeds and grass always grew out of it. Has it still got a door?'

She looked to the top of the short flight of steps in the middle of the pillared façade. 'It has a door with a big knocker but the paint's very blistered.'

'Give the knocker a rap, then,' said Tim, getting out too, 'and let's see what happens.'

What happened took a long time but eventually the door creaked open and an old man with tousled white hair and a very red face stared out of it. 'Who are you to come knocking on the Fitzgerald door without a by-your-leave?' he asked Lorna angrily.

Tim stepped away from the side of the car and said loudly, 'Who better to knock on the door than a Fitzgerald, Barney?'

The old man almost knocked Lorna over when he went rushing down the steps. 'May the saints preserve us! It's yourself, Master Tim. Oh my heavens, what's happened to your face? Have you been fighting again?' he shouted, clasping Tim round the waist and hugging him tight at the same time as pulling him towards the house.

'Hey, don't pull me over. I'm blind and I can't see where I'm going,' Tim shouted back.

'Aw well, I've seen you blind drunk often enough so that's nothing new,' said the old man and led Tim into the house, leaving the women to follow.

Inside there was such desolation that for a moment Lorna was glad Tim could not see it. A once fine plaster ceiling was badly cracked and parts of it had fallen on to the floor where it lay in forlorn heaps. Long green mildew stains ran down the walls. There were several rails missing from the elegantly curved banisters on the stairs. Some pigeons roosting on a marble mantlepiece flapped about in alarm when the visitors stepped inside. The old man shooed them out of the open door and said, 'The devils. They come in all the time. Even the cats is scared of them!'

He ushered them through a door that was still covered with tattered green baize and along a long, damp-smelling passage to a huge kitchen where a bright fire burned in an iron range and unpolished copper cooking pots hung along a rail above it. A woman in a long skirt and a black shawl was sitting on a wooden chair before the fire, and a bare-legged girl with bright red hair was wiping eggs and putting them in a shallow bowl.

'Master Tim's come home!' the old man announced and the women looked up with expressions of astonishment. Then the older of the two ran over to Tim and took his hands, crying out, 'Holy Mother of God, we heard about poor Rawley, but what's happened to you?'

'Is it you, Mary? I had an accident,' he said bleakly.

'And blind too!' she cried, bursting into tears. No one paid the least attention to Paulina and Lorna who stood in the doorway registering the unkempt state of the kitchen. Paulina's expression of disapproval changed to horror when a trio of clucking hens came walking out of an open cupboard and crossed the kitchen floor in a leisurely way, excreting as they went.

With great cries and flurries of apparent efficiency, the residents of the house, caretaker Barney, his wife Mary and their granddaughter Sally, brewed tea and ran about preparing the bedrooms.

'Is it possible to stay here?' Lorna whispered to Tim, forgetting that he was in a state of blissful ignorance because of his lack of sight. He replied, 'Of course. Where else would we go?'

Within an hour, a smoky fire of peat and wood was lit in the drawing room but did little to dispel the miasma of damp that filled it. The ghostly shapes of shrouded furniture were piled up in a far corner. Sally was sent upstairs to light fires in the bedrooms and when Lorna was shown to her room later she could hardly see across it for swirling smoke. 'It'll clear soon,' said Sally, waving her arms about. 'It's because crows roost in the chimney pots. When the fire catches their nests, they get out fast enough.'

They ate in the kitchen and the food was surprisingly good – home-baked bread, roasted chicken and a delicious egg custard. Their glasses were filled with a liquid that looked like cold tea but it burned Lorna's throat so much when she tasted it that she coughed and spluttered, which made Tim laugh and say to Barney, 'Making potheen again, are you?'

The old man beamed. 'The still's in the bathroom but Sally'll heat water for you to have hip baths if you need to wash.'

Paulina leaned forward to ask, 'There is only one bathroom? In this huge house?'

'That's one more than lots of other houses round about have,' Tim told her.

They slept deeply from sheer exhaustion, oblivious to the fact that the sheets were damp and that mice scrabbled across the floor all night. The next morning was beautiful and a kindly sun beamed down while the two women led Tim around his property, telling him everything they saw and pulling no punches in the process.

Words almost failed them when they ventured into a Victorian extension wing at the back of the house that had once held a ballroom, a music room, a conservatory, and elegant bedrooms. Dry rot had taken such a hold that it was impossible to walk across the floors for fear of them collapsing.

The best preserved part of Killygrattan house turned out to be the stable which a local farmer used for housing his hunters in the winter. Three boxes and five stalls stood inside a long stone building with a harness room at the far end and a good dry hay loft running along the upper storey. There was a pleasant smell of hay and linseed oil and no undernote of damp, so Lorna said, 'We'd be better sleeping here than in the big house.'

'I agree,' said Paulina. 'Tonight we make beds in the hay. That is, if we have to stay.'

'Of course we stay,' said Tim. Having come home at last, he had no intention of ever leaving again.

Within a week they had worked out what to do. The Victorian wing would have to be demolished because it was beyond saving, and the old Georgian house would be restored bit by bit. Word was put out to summon local tradesmen.

'I'd forgotten what Ireland's like. I don't think this job will ever be finished,' said Tim sadly, after days of consulting an army of builders and labourers from the surrounding district.

'Why? There seems to be plenty of workers eager to start on the job,' Lorna said, leaning her elbows on the table beside him.

He sighed. 'Because in spite of all Rawley's saving we simply haven't enough money. The state of the place is worse than I thought. The farm was sold off by our father and there's nothing left to bring in any money except a couple of grass fields that are let out and they only bring in a pittance. It'll be possible to fix up a part of the house for Paulina and me to live in but that's it, I'm afraid.'

'Have you been thinking about the suggestion I made to you about giving my baby your name?' she asked.

He groaned. 'I doubt if that would be any great advantage to it now.'

'But I want it to have Rawley's name,' she said firmly.

'But you'll not be able to stay on here, will you? How could you bring up a child in a house that's half falling down? You'll go away and forget about us eventually,' he said.

'I won't. I'm absolutely certain about that. Please say you'll adopt my child.'

She was agitated and felt the baby heaving around inside her as she spoke.

'Lorna,' he said softly, 'I can only just afford to look after Paulina and myself. I can't afford a baby.'

'I'm not asking you to afford it. I'll pay. Listen, Tim, I'm not exactly poor now but I'm going to be very rich soon,' she told him.

'This house has lived on expectations for too long and look what's happened to it,' he said sadly.

'I'm not talking pie in the sky,' said Lorna and told him about the Wilberforce Wesley Collection sale.

He listened attentively but she could sense that he thought she was exaggerating. 'Even if your things make big prices, there's no reason why you should waste any of it on this white elephant,' he said at last.

She stamped her foot in exasperation. 'Why do you think I went all the way to Draguignan to see you? For Rawley's sake I want to spend money on this house. He dreamed about it, and even though he's dead I want to help make his dream come true. Let me pay my share and in return you can give my child your name and leave the house to him or her in your will so there'll be another Fitzgerald living at Killygrattan.'

That was the clinching argument. When Tim began to come round, Lorna drove to Cork and bought champagne. That night they sealed their agreement with a toast to Rawley and a handshake.

Builders, tractors, and a demolition team – who blew up the unwanted wing with explosives and almost brought the whole building down because they were too generous with the dynamite – moved in. In the middle of the chaos Paulina urged Lorna to go back to London to have her baby. 'I do not trust these people,' she hissed, eyeing the workmen.

Lorna laughed. 'There must be a maternity hospital round here someplace. I'll go into town and sign up with a doctor. I'd like the baby to be born in Ireland, you see.'

Paulina gave an expressive sigh. She had grown fond of Lorna and was genuinely worried about her. 'You are mad like my Tim,' she said.

*   *   *

June was a beautiful month and Lorna spent most of her time outdoors. The hedgerows around Killygrattan were bright with scarlet and purple fuchsias and luxuriant honeysuckle scented the air while she grew more and more enormous. When she was beginning to worry in case she would always be pregnant, on a night when the moon was full she woke up with peculiar pains in her belly.

Paulina heard her cry out, for they had divided the hayloft into makeshift rooms and were still sleeping there. She came padding through on bare feet and took in the situation at a glance. Lorna's waters had broken and she was lying in soaked sheets.

'I have to go to the hospital,' Lorna said.

Paulina shook her head. 'You're staying here. It's too far.' The hospital was ten miles away and the journey took quite a long time because it was reached by a narrow, twisting lane that ran between high grass banks.

There was no working telephone at Killygrattan that night because the overhead wire had been cut by a careless digger driver, so Paulina woke Mary and between them they delivered Rawley Fitzgerald's son.

He was a fine boy, dark-haired and noisy, shouting with joy at being born. When Paulina took the baby to Tim, he burst into tears.

'Who does he look like?' he asked.

'Exactly like your brother,' was the reply.

'Then I hope she calls him Rawley Fitzgerald,' said Tim. She did.

Thirty-Three

In the second week of October, the Wilberforce Wesley Collection went up for auction. Lorna did not attend the sale because she could not bring herself to leave her son. Instead she tried phoning Sothebys the day after the sale to ask if it had gone well.

'Oh yes, it went well,' said a cool girl over the crackling line. 'I expect Mr Pryce will be in touch with you soon, Mrs Wesley.' She sounded so distant that Lorna could not summon up the courage to be so vulgar as to ask exactly how much money she had made. Nor did she know that she could ask for the prices of items that had been illustrated in the glossy catalogue.

For several days she examined each morning's post with her heart beating fast, but there was no communication from Sothebys. She said nothing to Tim about her fears but lay awake at night worrying in case Dominic Pryce had cheated her, or was so disappointed at the poor showing of her sale that he couldn't bring himself to break the bad news.

Instead of any letter for her, the mail brought in bills, and daily her money was dwindling. *My God*, she thought, *what if I run out of funds? What if I've persuaded Tim to spend money that he wouldn't have spent without me urging him on?*

It had been a brilliant summer and the benison of the sun enhanced the joy of her son. The agonising grief she'd felt after Rawley died was lessening. One day, she thought, her heart might heal. She knew she'd never forget him but she was beginning to realise that life went on and that she and little Rawley should look towards the future.

This sense of optimism was increased by the wonderful transformation that was being brought about at Killygrattan. Day by day, week by week, month by month, dereliction and decay were driven back and the house began to re-emerge in its Georgian elegance.

On a late October afternoon, when the Indian summer was at its height, Lorna heard Paulina calling her name while she was playing on the cropped grass of the paddock with her son, who kicked and gurgled on a spread-out blanket.

'Lorna, Lorna,' called Paulina, who, by this time, had completely taken the girl to her fierce heart. 'You have a visitor.'

I wonder who it is, thought Lorna. Lifting the baby up from his blanket, she walked towards the house.

A tall figure was standing on the half-constructed terrace outside the drawing-room window and her heart gave a funny little jump when she saw it. The figure waved and she waved back.

'It's Dominic Pryce,' she told the baby. Her heart was still thudding and she felt her face burning with a nervous rash as she walked along. *I must look awful*, she thought. But what a good-looking man he was, elegant as ever in his country clothes.

He smiled at her and, pointing at the baby, asked, 'What did you have?'

'A boy,' she told him.

'Well done. Have you put him down for Eton?'

She laughed. 'Of course not!'

'Why not? You can afford it,' he said with a grin.

Obviously delighted at being the bearer of good news, he produced a slip of paper from the breast pocket of his jacket and held it out to her. She stared at it. 'What's this?' she asked.

'It's a cheque. For you,' he told her.

She swallowed and words stuck in her throat. He was almost jumping up and down in his excitement as he asked, 'Don't you want to know how much?'

278

She walked towards the French windows that opened into the drawing room. 'I have to sit down,' she said.

He followed, still grinning. 'All right, I'll tell you. Congratulations. Your share of the profits is one and a half million.'

There was a plank saw bench standing in the middle of the floor and she sank on to it with the baby clutched close to her heart. 'How much?' she whispered, in shock.

He told her again and she said, 'Is that all mine? Have you taken your share and the money you lent me?'

'Oh yes; Sothebys have done well too. You should have been there. The bidding was frantic. I was so excited I thought I was going to have a coronary!' He was hopping about like a little boy, beaming all over his face.

She was having trouble taking it in. *What does one and a half million look like in figures?* she thought and slowly opened the cheque so she could see. 'Oh, heavens!' she gasped when she looked at the elegantly penned figures. Then she stood up, gave a wail and threw herself at Pryce's chest, baby and all. He grabbed them both and held them tightly in his long arms. While he and Lorna stood hanging on to each other and laughing in delight, a wonderful thing happened.

They fell in love.

Epilogue

Dee's son Hugo was born a week before young Rawley, by Caesarean section in St Mary's Hospital, Manchester.

It rained every day of the two weeks she spent in hospital. The view from her private room was over a derelict part of the city and a sluggish, disused canal. When she slowly began to recover from the birth, she stared out at the dreary scene and wept, racked with longing for Bombay.

Over the following months her misery deepened and settled into a depression which she hid from Ben, who was riding high. His new job was as magnificent as it had seemed, and the only drawback was that his head office was in Manchester and not London as they had hoped. The *Financial Times* ran an article, with a photograph of him looking very solemn, because he was Britain's youngest managing director of a public limited company.

The Carmichaels bought an imposing house, with an acre of landscaped grounds and a tennis court, in a Derbyshire village about twenty-five miles from the city.

Dee hated it.

She hated it because the climate was so harsh that it snowed in June and it was impossible to grow fruit trees in her garden; she hated it because she was lonely. Ben went off every morning by half-past seven and it was nearly always late when he returned. The little girls ran wild, free of Mary's restraining hand, and Dee made no friends. The neighbours were unfriendly because they could not understand how such a young couple could afford to buy the biggest house in the village. Rumours went around that the Carmichaels had links with organised crime.

Not only did Dee miss her many Bombay friends, she missed her journalistic work. She was too harassed trying to run the vast house with the help of a churlish and thieving charlady to turn her hand to anything else.

Most of all she missed her Walkeshwar Road household – Babu, Prakash, Jadhav, Alex and Mary – not because of the many things they did so cheerfully and efficiently for her but because of their constant companionship. They had been part of her family and she loved them. For a very long time she dreamt that she was back with them and woke in the morning to a terrible sense of loss.

She was still shakily recovering from Hugo's birth when she read an article in *The Times* about Sotheby's auction of the Wilberforce Wesley Collection. It was illustrated with a photograph of a bronze dancing girl like the one Lorna had given her. The caption beneath the photo said that it had fetched £8,000 in the sale.

Lorna! thought Dee. *What's happened to Lorna?* Obviously the collection was hers and so, wherever she was, she'd be a rich woman now. *I hope she's happy. Oh, how I hope she's happy*, Dee thought. It would be lovely to meet her again.

A telephone call to Sotheby's met with no success. The Wilberforce Wesley Collection was only listed as 'property of a lady' who had requested no publicity and so it was quite out of the question for the saleroom to provide Dee with any information about her.

Attempts to contact Lorna's parents were equally fruitless. Jack and Ella had gone to Portugal and no one, not even Bubbles, could provide Dee with their address.

Finally she wrote to Tommy Morrison and asked if he knew how to get in touch with Paddy.

A few weeks later the reply came back saying that the old man had died in March at the age of eighty-one. Tommy had attended his funeral in Poona and he'd been burned

281

on a funeral pyre like a devout Hindu, as was his wish. His companion Ajit had sold the bungalow and gone back to his native village.

With all leads exhausted, Dee gave up the search for Lorna but the knowledge that the sale of the Wilberforce Wesley Collection had made Lorna a rich woman helped her fight off despair. *No matter how bleak things look*, she told herself, *there's often something good waiting for you in the future.*

Fifteen years later, waiting in Heathrow Airport to fly to Dublin on a journalistic assignment, Dee watched a boisterous family who were boarding the same plane. There were three boys, a father and a mother, all happily arguing among themselves. The oldest boy seemed to be the same age as Dee's Hugo and he reminded her of someone, though she could not recall who. The other boys were identical, flaxen-haired twins, aged about eight, and they were excitedly running wild.

The father, tall and elegant in well-cut tweeds, absorbed himself in the *Sporting Life*, oblivious to his sons' sur-reptitious punches at each other; the mother, plump and comfortable-looking, was dressed in country-matron clothes with a Hermes scarf knotted round her neck and magnificent diamond rings on her fingers. They were travelling first class and when they rose to take their seats, the most unruly of the twins tripped over Dee's briefcase. His mother smiled in apology and Dee smiled back. They did not recognise each other.